A Father Among Gods:

Chapter One

The Hearth and the Sword

Morning came slowly over the fjord, gray before silver, as though the light had to bargain with the mountains before it could touch the water. Winter still clung to the air. Frost lay in thin seams along the fence posts and in the hollows of the yard, though spring had already begun its quieter work beneath the thawing earth. Down by the shore, the ground smelled of salt, wet peat, and old smoke.

Eirik Halvardsson stood where the grass gave way to stone, one boot sunk in mud darkened by the night. A split length of timber rested against his thigh while he shaved its edge clean with a knife, cutting away the soft places where rot had begun its patient claim. The work was plain. It needed doing. That was reason enough to be at it before the rest of the house had fully stirred.

Beyond him, the fjord breathed under the waking sky.

It was never truly still. Even in fair weather it moved with its own old mind—dark, heavy, and patient. Small ripples caught the pale light and broke it into shifting silver. Farther out, the water deepened to iron-gray, and the mountains lay across it in long, fractured reflections.

The fjord ran long and crooked. **Ash Fjord, men called the southern stretch where the trading ships anchored—a full day's row from the village, where the mountains pinched the water tight and the wind came sharp from the open sea.**

Eirik let his gaze rest there a moment.

It was habit more than thought. Men who lived by water learned to read it the way other men read weather or fields. He watched for sails, for turns in the wind, for anything that did not belong. This morning there was only distance, a lifting band of mist, and the pale promise of a clear day that might yet sour before noon.

Behind him, the house had begun to wake. A beam creaked. Clay touched wood. Someone crossed the floor with a step careful enough to be Sigrid. He could picture Astrid within without turning to look: sleeves bound back, hair gathered away from her face, steady in the hearthlight while the children still belonged more to sleep than to sense.

The thought almost softened his mouth.

Instead, he set the point of the post into the earth with his boot and reached for the mallet.

The fence had not come kindly through the winter. One rail had split clean through, another bowed where the frost had heaved it, and two posts leaned enough to shame a lazy man. The goats would find weakness soon enough. Leif would likely help them by leaving a gate half-latched and then swear himself innocent before anyone had thought to accuse him.

Eirik raised the mallet and struck.

Wood answered wood. The sound carried over the shore in a rhythm older than speech.

He worked in silence for a time, driving the post deeper, testing the rail, setting the join. The morning held together around him in the way he trusted most. There was peace in useful labor. Not joy, perhaps, but something steadier than joy and less likely to vanish when the day turned hard.

Then came footsteps over the stiff ground above the shore—light, quick, and innocent of patience.

“Father.”

Eirik did not turn at once. He set the peg between rail and post, held it steady, and answered, "You're awake early."

Leif came down the slope with his tunic half fastened and one boot tied badly enough that it would not survive the hour. He had grown again over winter. His limbs had lengthened faster than his judgment had settled into them, and there was still something coltish in the way he moved, as if his body had outrun its own sense. His hair had not been tamed. His expression suggested he saw no reason it should be.

"I heard you working," the boy said.

"That is not the same as waking early."

"It is if I am awake now."

Eirik glanced at him, dry-eyed. "A sharp answer turns dull quickly when used too often."

Leif grinned, untroubled.

He stopped beside his father and looked out over the water with the solemnity of someone doing his best to resemble a man. At moments, the effort nearly held.

"Is it calm enough to row?" he asked.

"For whom?"

"For anyone."

"For sensible men, perhaps. Not for you."

Leif made a face. "I row well."

"You row loudly."

"I do not."

"You splash like a seal the gods are trying to drown."

Leif opened his mouth to deny it, then failed to find a shape of words that would defeat the image.

Eirik handed him the rail. "Hold this."

Leif obeyed. For several breaths, he even held it well.

Eirik fitted the rail into place and drove the peg through. "Better."

Leif glanced from the shore to the water, then to his father's hands. "Arn says a boy should know how to kill before he's old enough to marry. Preferably before winter. He says both punish fools."

A rough breath passed through Eirik's nose. "That sounds like Arn."

Leif brightened. "So you agree?"

"No."

The answer came so flat and clean that Leif blinked.

Eirik tested the rail and found it sound. "Arn says many things because he enjoys hearing them in the air. Sometimes they grow wiser by accident."

Leif frowned. "He says the gods laugh at men who wait too long to become useful."

"The gods laugh at many things," Eirik said. "That does not make them right in all of them."

Leif fell quiet, and in that quiet Eirik heard the true question before the boy spoke it. Boys circled the matters that frightened them, then touched them all at once. Men often did the same, only with more pride and less grace.

At last Leif said, "Then when should a boy learn?"

"A boy learns all the time."

"You know what I mean."

"I do."

Eirik set the mallet down and rested both hands on the fence rail. Farther out, gulls had begun to cry over the water. Somewhere above the yard, a door opened and shut again.

Leif waited. His jaw had taken on that stubborn set that came to him from both parents and would likely be the making of him one day and the misery of him on many others.

"When should I learn to kill?" he asked more quietly.

The question settled between them like a stone laid upon a grave.

Eirik looked toward the fjord before he answered, as though the water might lend his words a truer shape.

"Later than boys want," he said at last, "and earlier than fathers would choose."

Leif groaned. "That is not an answer."

"It is the truest one."

"Everyone says things like that when they do not wish to answer."

"Then listen harder."

Leif folded his arms. It was a poor imitation of defiance, but a determined one.

Eirik let the silence stand. He had learned, with sons as with storms, that rushing to fill a quiet often spoiled whatever truth might rise out of it.

"There is a difference," he said at last, "between learning to fight and wanting to kill. The first may keep you alive. The second rots something in a man."

Leif said nothing.

"A blade is a tool before it is glory," Eirik went on. "Remember that first, and you may live long enough to understand the rest."

"But you kill men."

"When I must."

"How do you know when you must?"

Eirik's face changed, though not into anger. Something older moved there.

"When failing to do it would cost more than the life before me."

Leif took that in with a seriousness that made him look younger, not older. "That still feels like no answer."

"It will grow clearer when you have the weight to bear it."

Leif scowled at the fence. "That means you do not trust me with it."

"No," Eirik said. "It means the answer is heavier than you are."

The boy muttered under his breath.

"What was that?"

"I said Arn would just tell me."

"Arn would tell you quickly," Eirik said. "That is not the same as telling you well."

That won the smallest unwilling twitch at the corner of Leif's mouth.

Eirik took up the mallet again and drove the last peg home. "A warrior is not made by the first life he takes."

Leif waited.

"He is made," Eirik said, "by what he serves before and after."

The boy lifted his eyes.

"Any fool can swing steel. Any frightened man can stab if fear corners him. That is not the measure. The measure is whether your strength serves only your hunger, or whether it can be mastered by something better."

Leif looked unconvinced, but he was listening. That mattered more.

Eirik straightened to his full height. "Hear me plainly, Leif Eiriksson. Strength is not only what you can break. A warrior must know how to be a son without burdening his father, a brother without smothering his sister, and a man without making his hunger everyone else's cost."

Leif blinked. "That sounds worse than sword practice."

"It usually is."

The boy laughed then, quick and helpless, though he still looked cheated by the lack of blood in the lesson.

Eirik rested the mallet on his shoulder and looked out over the fjord. The water had darkened beneath the strengthening light. A longboat rocked at its mooring. **Ash Fjord stretched southward, where the trading anchorage lay a hard row from the village—close enough for commerce, far enough that news from those waters arrived slower than the ravens.**

He watched the boat lift and settle.

Leif followed his gaze. "Are you thinking about the traders?"

"I am thinking distance makes men careless."

Leif frowned. "Do you think something is coming?"

Eirik kept his eyes on the water. "Something is always coming."

Leif did not like that answer. Good. Some truths were only of use if they lodged in a man and troubled his sleep.

From the house, Sigrid's voice came sharp and clear over the yard.

"Leif! If you've escaped morning work again, Mother says you can carry twice the water."

Leif shut his eyes in wounded outrage. "She sees everything."

"She misses very little."

"That is worse."

"It is better," Eirik said, "unless you mean to be foolish."

Leif narrowed his eyes. "You say that as if I already am."

"You were born halfway to it."

Leif barked a laugh despite himself and turned toward the house. Then he stopped and looked back.

"Father?"

"Yes?"

"When will I hold a real sword?"

Eirik met his gaze without softening. "When you can carry a full bucket without washing your boots in the process."

Leif looked scandalized. "That has nothing to do with swords."

"It has everything to do with them."

The boy trudged uphill muttering darkly about injustice, honor, and the cruelty of old men.

Eirik watched him go until the house swallowed him.

Then the hint of a smile left his face.

He stood alone again with the fence, the tools, and the long reach of water before him.

The village had fully stirred now. Smoke rose in thin blue threads from the turf roofs. Nets hung drying on poles. Somewhere a dog barked and was answered. A woman called to another across the lane. Life moved in its ordinary circles—mending, carrying, cooking, feeding stock, checking lines—and there was something holy in that ordinariness, though no priest would have called it so.

Eirik bent to gather the tools.

He heard Astrid before he saw her—not because she made noise, but because her quiet had a shape he knew. Unlike Leif, she never arrived by force. She simply came, and the place about her seemed to settle into better order.

By the time he straightened, she was already near, carrying a wooden cup with steam lifting from it into the cold.

"You left before the porridge was ready," she said.

"I hoped to avoid correction before sunrise."

"You failed."

She handed him the cup. Her tone stayed level, but that faint dry amusement remained in her eyes, never wasted and therefore always sharp.

He drank. Bitter herbs and hot water—enough to wake a man whether he desired it or not. "Was it Sigrid or you?"

"She noticed first. I agreed more elegantly."

He drank again and glanced toward the house. "Leif found me."

"He heard you before the gulls."

"That sounds like him."

Astrid let her gaze travel over the repaired rail. "He asked you something heavy."

Eirik looked at her. "He told you?"

"No." She shifted the cup in her hands. "His shoulders told me. Yours did as well."

A breath that almost counted as laughter left him. Men crossed seas, buried friends, and stood in shield walls. None of it taught them how to hide much from a woman who watched with patience and spoke only when she had cause.

"He asked when a boy should learn to kill."

Astrid was quiet a moment. Steam drifted between them in pale threads.

"And what did you say?"

"That he asked too early."

"That is an old father's answer."

"It remains useful."

"It also remains incomplete."

Eirik looked back toward the fjord. "He is hungry for manhood."

"He is hungry for everything. That is his age."

"He thinks steel is the same as worth."

Astrid followed his gaze. "Then he is a son of this world. Boys are taught the loud lesson first."

"And what teaches the better one?"

She turned her head and looked at him, calm as still water. "Usually pain. Sometimes fathers. The fortunate get both in tolerable measure."

Eirik drank and said nothing.

Astrid stepped nearer the fence and laid her fingers along the rail he had just set, testing its firmness rather than merely seeing it. "This will hold."

"So will the next ten things that break."

"Good," she said. "Then mend them before they grow proud."

There was that quiet edge in her voice, easy as breath and keen as a blade not yet drawn.

He studied her a moment. Astrid did not fear silence, and she did not spend words for company's sake. It was one of the reasons peace felt truer when she was near.

Inside the house, Sigrid called again, this time with the weary patience of an elder sister already overburdened by her brother's continued existence.

"Mother, Leif says the buckets are a test of warriorhood."

Astrid closed her eyes for half a breath. "Then may the gods grant him a heroic spill."

Eirik's mouth moved before he could stop it.

She looked out over the water again. "You are far away this morning."

The truth of it landed harder because she spoke it so simply.

He could have turned aside from it. Blamed the season, the traders, the work, the weather. But there was little use in hiding the shape of his thoughts from her. She would see the shadow even if he denied the thing that cast it.

"The water feels watchful," he said.

Astrid was still.

"Not wrong," she said at last. "Watchful."

He turned slightly toward her. "You feel it too."

"I felt it when the fire drew sideways at dawn, though there was no draft in the room."

Another woman might have said it with fear, or with the need to be reassured. Astrid offered it as plainly as one might speak of frost.

Eirik set the cup on the fence rail. “Men can make omens of anything if they hunger for them badly enough.”

“Yes,” she said. “And men can call a thing ordinary because they hunger for peace.”

He held her gaze. No superstition in her face. No fear either. Only attention.

From the lower path came the scrape of boots on stone.

Both of them turned.

Arn came up from the waterline with a coil of rope over one shoulder, moving with the loose balance of a man who trusted swiftness more than caution and had survived long enough to make the choice seem wise. His twin bearded axes hung at his hips. He carried no shield because he thought shields slowed the hand and taught a man to lean too hard on safety.

He lifted a hand when he saw them. “Good. You are both awake. I dislike speaking to empty houses. They never answer properly.”

Astrid’s expression did not shift. “You have not improved your company enough to make walls regret that.”

Arn grinned. “Then I am fortunate you came outside.”

He reached them and gave Eirik a short nod. “I came from the lower cove. A boat passed far out before dawn. Too far to mark well in the dark, but it was not one of ours.”

Eirik’s attention narrowed. “Heading where?”

“South first. Then east enough that I disliked it.”

“That is not a direction.”

“It is when a man has instincts worth keeping.”

Astrid folded her arms. “And do your instincts often arrive with useful detail?”

“Often enough to be irritating afterward.”

Eirik looked back toward the fjord, though the water showed nothing now but distance and morning light. “One boat?”

“One that I saw,” Arn said.

The silence that followed was deliberate.

Arn tipped his chin toward the southern water. “Could be traders leaving early. Could be fools. Could be worse. I thought you would rather hear it while the day still had the decency to pretend to be ordinary.”

Eirik gave a single nod. That was why Arn remained what he was to him: reckless, sharp-tongued, half too pleased with danger, and still one of the few men whose instincts Eirik trusted when explanation had not yet caught up.

Leif burst out of the house carrying two buckets, with Sigrid behind him wearing the face of a girl long practiced in disappointment.

“Arn!” Leif called. “Father says carrying water is sword practice.”

Arn looked at the buckets with grave attention. “He is correct. Many men fail at the dull things long before they fail at the glorious ones.”

Leif stared. “That does not make sense.”

“It will later,” Arn said. “My best wisdom always arrives before its manners.”

Sigrid’s eyes moved from face to face and settled at once on the part of the morning no one had yet named aloud. “What happened?”

“Nothing yet,” Astrid said.

Sigrid disliked that answer on sight. "That sounds like the beginning of something."

"It often is," Eirik said.

Leif set the buckets down harder than needed. "Is there going to be a fight?"

"No," Astrid said.

"Yes," Arn said at the same time.

Astrid turned her head toward him, calm as judgment.

Arn raised one hand. "Eventually. There is always eventually."

Eirik ignored them both and looked at Leif. "There is work. Do that first."

The boy bristled, but whatever protest rose in him died under his father's gaze. He seized the buckets again and stomped uphill. Sigrid followed, carrying more patience than any child should have been forced to learn so young.

Arn watched them go. "He has a warrior's stride."

"He has a boy's impatience."

"They often walk together."

Astrid looked at Arn. "And in you?"

"In me they fought for mastery," Arn said, "and both lost."

That drew the faintest breath of laughter from her. Arn looked pleased enough with himself to count the morning improved.

Then Eirik said, "If there was a boat, I want eyes on the southern water by noon."

Arn's face shifted—not grim, exactly, but intent in a way humor could not quite conceal. "I can take two men and the ridge path."

"Take three."

"Three men slow the clever one."

"Take three."

Arn rolled one shoulder in surrender. "Then I will choose men who know how to breathe quietly."

Astrid looked at Eirik. "And you?"

"I'll finish here. Then speak with Sten."

Arn gave a short laugh. "The jarl will say you worry too much, then begin worrying in a louder voice."

"That is among his better qualities."

Arn's grin flashed once, then faded as he looked again over the water.

When he spoke next, the humor had gone from his voice before the words themselves.

"The fjord feels thin today," he said.

Neither Eirik nor Astrid answered at once.

Thin.

Not empty. Not dangerous. Something stranger than either. As though the skin of the world had worn fine in the night, and what lay beyond it had leaned a little nearer.

Arn shifted the rope on his shoulder. "Maybe it is nothing."

"Maybe," Eirik said.

Arn gave him a look that said he believed that no more than Eirik did. Then he turned and went back down the path without another word.

The wind rose lightly from the south.

It touched the fence posts, stirred the grass, and carried the taste of salt farther inland than before. Eirik stood with the tools at his feet and watched the long bend of the fjord, where Ash Fjord lay beyond sight, where traders anchored, where tidings lingered on the water before they reached men's ears.

Behind him, the village still held its ordinary shape—smoke, chores, children, wood, cups warming cold hands.

Yet beneath it, quieter than fear and older than reason, ran the sense that something unseen had turned its gaze their way.

Not a warning.

Not yet.

Only the feeling that the day had been noticed.

Chapter Two

The Call to Raid

Snow had fallen in the night and laid a thin white hush over the village.

It silvered the turf roofs, filled the seams of the fences, and softened the ruts in the paths between the houses. Smoke rose from the roof vents and drifted low in the cold air, carrying peat, pine, fish oil, and damp wool. Down by the fjord, mooring ropes creaked against weathered posts, and the hulls of the drawn-up boats knocked softly together like men speaking low in the dark. From the smithy came the ring of hammer on iron, steady and far-reaching.

Eirik Halvardsson stood in the yard with an axe in one hand and a split log waiting upright on the block before him.

He had stood there long enough for frost to gather at the edge of his beard.

The log waited. The work waited. But his thoughts had gone where they had gone through the night—back to the messenger's voice at the door, back to the few plain words that had changed the shape of the coming days.

Jarl Sten had called for men.

Eirik knew what such a call meant. It was never only vengeance. It was answer. It was whether blood spilled under a jarl's protection would be repaid, or whether men along the coast would begin to wonder if Sten's reach had grown short. Eirik understood that well enough. He had lived too long among such men not to know how quickly silence could be taken for weakness.

That was what made the weight of it worse. There was no confusion in him.

Only reluctance.

The door opened behind him.

Astrid stepped out with a basket against one hip, the morning cold catching in the pale strands that had slipped loose from her braid. She stood a moment beneath the roof's edge and looked over the yard in the way she always did, seeing three things at once and naming only one.

"The wood fears you," she said. "It has not yet dared split itself."

Eirik looked back at the waiting log. "I gave it time to choose a better nature."

"Then it is stubborn." She shifted the basket slightly. "You may be kin to it."

A small smile touched his mouth and was gone.

She studied him with that same calm, measuring gaze. Astrid did not ask needless questions. She let a man carry his silence until he was ready to set it down.

"The horn will sound before noon," she said.

He nodded once.

From inside the house came a crash, followed by Leif's quick voice and Sigrid's calmer one.

"I nearly had it," Leif said.

"That is what people say just before things break," Sigrid replied.

Astrid tipped her head slightly toward the doorway. "Your son is at war with a stool."

"He should choose a weaker enemy."

"He tried. The weaker enemies moved first."

She went back inside, and Eirik stood another moment in the cold. Then he lifted the axe and split the waiting log in one clean stroke. The crack rang sharp through the yard.

It did not clear his thoughts, but work rarely made them worse.

Inside, the long room held warmth like cupped hands. The central hearth glowed red and gold. Steam rose from the pot over the fire. The smell of barley broth, drying herbs, leather, wool, and smoke wrapped around him with such familiar comfort that for a moment his chest tightened.

Leif was halfway under the bench, one arm stretched beneath it, while Sigrid stood beside him with both hands clasped behind her back, as if she had no intention of joining whatever foolishness he was in.

"I can reach it," Leif said, his voice muffled.

"You said that before you knocked over the stool."

"I only brushed it."

"With your whole leg."

Leif backed out and pushed himself upright in one quick movement. At ten winters old, he seemed made mostly of momentum. His brown hair stuck out in every direction, his cheeks were red from the draft at the floor, and his eyes were bright with the kind of energy that often arrived before thought. He moved fast, spoke fast, and most days seemed to believe the world would wait for him to catch it.

Sigrid, two years younger, stood almost perfectly still by comparison. Her braid was neat, her face composed, and her gaze had already taken in her brother, the stool, the spoon beneath the bench, and their father all at once. Where Leif flung himself at the day, Sigrid met it like a narrow bridge—carefully, steadily, and with an eye for loose planks.

Leif saw Eirik and straightened at once. "Father, is it true?"

Eirik unfastened his cloak. "That depends on what truth has found its way here."

"Bjorn's brother said traders were killed south of Skarvik," Leif said quickly. "He said one ship was burned and Sten is calling men, and maybe two ships will go, maybe three, and if it was southerners then—"

"If it came from Bjorn's brother," Sigrid said, "half of it was likely born during breakfast."

Leif barely glanced at her. "But some of it could still be true."

Astrid stood at the hearth, stirring the pot. "A bent arrow may still strike something. That does not make it well made."

Leif looked from his mother to his father. “So is it true?”

Eirik took the bowl Astrid handed him and warmed his hands on the wood before he answered. “There will be a council. After that, we will know what men mean to do.”

Leif frowned at once. He always disliked waiting when action seemed near enough to touch. “But if traders were killed, then of course men will go.”

“Of course?” Sigrid asked.

Leif turned toward her. “Yes, of course. You cannot let men burn ships in our waters.”

Sigrid did not blink. “No one said you could. Only that men who run first sometimes find they were chasing the wrong thing.”

Leif opened his mouth, shut it, then opened it again. “You say things like you are fifty winters old.”

“And you say things like you are already dead in a saga.”

Astrid’s mouth twitched faintly.

Even Eirik had to hide a smile in his bowl.

Leif caught it anyway. “I only mean someone has to do something.”

The words came out hot and quick, but Eirik heard what sat beneath them. It was not only excitement. It was admiration, longing, that boyish hunger to stand near importance and be shaped by it.

“I know,” Eirik said.

Leif quieted.

Then Sigrid asked, clear and direct, “Will you go?”

Leif looked at his father so quickly he nearly struck the stool again.

Eirik held his daughter’s gaze. “I may.”

Leif's face lit before he could stop it. Pride moved through him so openly it hurt to see. He was trying to master it, trying to stand straighter and look older, but he was still a boy who saw ships and swords and distant shores before he saw the spaces left behind by them.

Sigrid noticed it too.

"You should not smile like that," she said.

Leif flushed. "I'm not smiling."

"You are."

"I'm not glad he would leave. I only—" He stopped, struggled, then finished more quietly, "I only know why he would."

That stilled the room for a breath.

Eirik looked at his son a moment longer than he meant to.

Astrid broke the silence first. "If you are done wrestling furniture, Leif, bring in the wood by the door."

"I was not wrestling it."

"The stool would tell another tale."

"It would lie."

"Then it is fortunate for you that wood has no tongue."

Leif snorted and went to the door.

The morning passed into work.

The village beyond the walls was already shifting beneath the news. Men moved with more purpose than the day alone required. Voices carried farther in the cold. Down near the boat sheds, someone had dragged out barrels of pitch. Even the dogs seemed more alert, as if they understood that human tension meant something coming.

Eirik went about the chores because they needed doing. He checked the goat pen, fetched water, and helped Astrid move a sack of dried grain farther from the draft near the wall. Leif followed him from task to task at first, asking questions faster than most men could answer them.

"If Sten sends a scout boat first, would it be the light one with the patched sail or Hakon's old hull?"

"Whichever rows straighter," Eirik said.

"But Hakon's old hull rides lower, and if men want speed—"

"If men want speed, they should put you in the water and let you talk at the wind."

Leif laughed and continued anyway.

"If you go south, would you take the boar-crested helmet or the plain one? I think the boar one makes you look—"

"Like a man wearing too much iron on his head."

"It makes you look like a man worth following."

Eirik glanced at him sidelong. "And the plain one?"

"Like a man worth listening to."

Eirik smiled at that. "That was better."

Leif looked pleased enough to split with it.

But when Eirik handed him the practice shield and told him to tighten the loose strap properly, the change came over the boy at once. The quick speech quieted. The restless motion settled into care. He knelt by the bench, tested the leather with his thumb, and began again from the first knot.

Sigrid passed by carrying a bundle of dried herbs to Astrid. She paused only long enough to inspect his work.

"That side will twist."

Leif did not snap back this time. He looked, frowned, and retied it. "Not now."

Sigrid nodded once and went on.

There was affection between them, real and deep, but it came wrapped in friction. Leif watched for dangers he could see—a barking dog, a slick stone, a boy bigger than Sigrid near the well. Sigrid watched for the ones he missed—loose straps, open latches, sharp words, forgotten tasks. He tried to protect her by stepping between. She protected him just as often by steering him before he put a foot wrong.

Near midday, Eirik found them in the yard with Leif holding the shield on his arm and Sigrid standing before him with a stick.

"You need to strike from the side," Leif was saying. "So I can block it properly."

"If I do that, you will stumble into the woodpile."

"I won't."

"You will."

"I need to practice."

Sigrid tapped the rim of the shield once, testing his grip. "Then keep your elbow down."

Leif blinked. "That's what Father says."

"Yes," she said. "And he is still right."

Eirik stood in the doorway and watched a moment before speaking. Leif's stance had improved. Not good, not yet, but better. His shoulders were less stiff. His feet were set more honestly beneath him. The shield no longer swung like a door on a poor hinge.

Sigrid saw Eirik first. "He was about to bruise himself."

"I was not."

"You were."

Eirik came down into the yard. "Show me."

Leif squared himself at once. All boyish excitement drained into concentration. Eirik took the stick from Sigrid and gave one light strike to the shield rim. Leif held. Another, harder. Leif shifted but kept his feet. On the third, he overcorrected and stumbled half a step backward.

Sigrid said nothing.

She did not need to.

Leif's face tightened with frustration.

Eirik lowered the stick. "Again."

Leif reset at once.

This time he held all three strikes better. His breath came quicker by the end, but his eyes had narrowed into real focus.

"That's better," Eirik said.

Leif let out his breath slowly. "I fixed the strap."

"I saw."

Sigrid lifted her chin slightly. "After I told him where it would fail."

Leif glanced toward her. "Yes. And now it doesn't."

Eirik looked from one child to the other and saw the shape of them plain as carved wood. Motion and stillness. Fire and stone. Each correcting the other just enough to keep balance.

Then the council horn sounded.

Its low call rolled across the village and over the fjord. Men stepped from houses. Women paused in doorways. The sound gathered the whole settlement toward one thought.

Leif straightened so fast the shield nearly slipped from his arm. "That is it."

"That is the horn," Sigrid said.

"It means the same thing."

"No. One is a sound. The other is your excitement pretending to be wisdom."

Leif pulled the shield off and set it carefully against the wall this time. "Can I come as far as the longhouse?"

"No," Eirik said.

Leif's disappointment showed at once. "I would only stand outside."

"You would stand outside until someone said something you liked. Then you would edge closer and think no one saw."

"That is not true."

Sigrid looked at him. "It is exactly true."

Leif opened his mouth to argue, then saw Eirik's expression and stopped. The effort of swallowing his first answer showed plainly on his face.

"All right," he said at last. "Then I'll fix the other strap too."

Astrid, who had been slicing bread at the table, said, "Conquer one shield before you conquer the sea."

Leif grinned despite himself. "I can do both."

"In that case," Astrid said, "do the shield first. The sea will not flee before supper."

As Eirik turned to go, Leif stepped after him. "Father."

Eirik looked back.

Leif stood very straight, trying once again to seem older than his winters. “Watch the men who talk too much before sailing. They row badly.”

For a heartbeat Eirik only looked at him. Then he heard Hakon Varseye in the words—some remembered lesson caught and kept in the boy’s quick mind.

“That is good advice,” Eirik said.

Leif tried not to beam and failed halfway.

Eirik left the house and went toward the longhouse.

The village had changed in the short space of an hour. Men clustered in twos and threes, blades at their belts though no cutting needed doing. The air felt tighter, every sound carrying farther. Smoke lay low between the houses. The dark fjord beyond the shore looked hard as forged metal.

The longhouse stood broad and dark at the center of the settlement, its carved doorposts crusted with frost. Inside, heat and smoke met him at once. Fire ran along the central hearth. Shields and antlers hung between the carved beams. Wet wool steamed. Ale was already being poured. Younger men stood too straight. Older men sat as if they had seen too many councils to waste effort on posture.

Jarl Sten sat near the far end, broad-shouldered and stern, the gray in his beard bright in the firelight. Around him were his sons, sworn men, and the village elders. Across the room stood Hakon Varseye, lean and weathered, with his one good eye as sharp as ever.

Bjorn Ketilsson spotted Eirik at once.

“There he is,” Bjorn called. “I thought perhaps his wife had hidden his boots.”

Eirik pulled off one glove. "If she had, I would still be in better company."

Laughter moved through the hall. Bjorn grinned.

"You'll need more than wit where we're going," Bjorn said.

"That is well enough," Eirik replied. "I left mine at home with the children."

That drew harder laughter. Bjorn took it well enough.

When the hall had filled and the muttering quieted, Jarl Sten rose.

"You know why you are called."

His voice carried easily.

"Three nights past, two trading ships under my protection were taken south of Skarvik—where the coast bends beyond Ash Fjord and the anchorage lies more open to passing keels. Goods stolen. Men slain. One ship burned."

A dark murmur passed through the room.

"This was no storm," Sten went on. "And no starving fisherman. Men did this to see whether my protection means anything beyond my own hearth."

Bjorn spat into the rushes. Orm, young and broad through the chest, leaned forward eagerly.

"I will not have it said," Sten said, "that traders under my word can be butchered without answer. Nor will I have every jackal on this coast think winter has made us soft."

That word did its work. Eirik felt it pass through the room. Soft. Men would rather be called cruel than that.

Orm rose first. "Give us two ships and we'll bring back heads."

Several younger men struck the benches in approval.

Hakon spoke from across the hearth. "Best make sure the heads belong to the right men first."

That drew a few hard laughs. Orm sat again, displeased.

Sten raised one hand. "We answer this. But we answer it with purpose. We find who did it. If they are southerners testing our reach, we break them. If they are raiders from farther shores, we teach them what these waters cost."

That won nods from most of the hall. Then came the talk of ships, numbers, rope, stores, scouts, weather, and rowers.

Eirik listened.

He heard the eagerness beneath the words. He heard the pressure too. No man wanted to be absent when blood called for answer. Honor was one part of it. Pride another. Fear of seeming smaller than the man beside you was a third, though few would have named it.

It was Bjorn, of course, who turned the room toward him.

"We have strong arms enough," Bjorn said, with studied carelessness, "if every man remembers his place."

His eyes slid to Eirik.

Sten noticed. "Eirik Halvardsson," he said. "You have heard much and said little."

Eirik stepped from the carved post where he stood. "There is no shortage of speaking here."

A brief ripple of laughter moved through the room.

Sten's mouth twitched. "Then be useful with yours."

Eirik nodded. "We should not sail blind because our blood is warm. Send a light boat first. Learn whether the men who did this are still near or already scattered."

Bjorn scoffed. "By the time a scout boat returns, the killers will be drinking our ale on some other shore."

Eirik looked toward him. "Then we should be grateful you are not rowing after them. You would stop to describe yourself first."

That drew laughter, even from Hakon. Bjorn's grin thinned, but he did not press it.

Orm stood again. "You speak as though caution were courage."

Eirik answered without haste. "No. I speak as though dead men row poorly."

That quieted some of the younger men.

Sten struck the floor once with his staff. "Enough. He is right not to go blind. You are right not to go slow." His gaze moved across the hall. "A scout boat leaves before dusk. Two ships prepare. If word returns with good sign, we sail at first good light after."

That settled it well enough.

Men began offering themselves aloud. Bjorn did so at once, broad and eager. Orm followed. Hakon grumbled that someone had to keep fools from mistaking noise for bravery. More names followed after.

Then Sten looked to Eirik.

"Will you take a place on my ship?"

The room watched.

Eirik felt the weight of their eyes. Not because he feared battle. Battle itself was often simpler than the hours before it. Once steel met steel, waste fell away. A man did what he must, no more and no less.

What weighed on him was leaving.

He saw his house in his mind: Astrid by the hearth, saying little and seeing much. Leif trying to stand like a man already called to sea. Sigrid noticing what others missed and holding it close. He thought of how a house changed shape when one body was gone from it. He thought of children learning to step around absence as though it had always belonged there.

Then he thought of the burned ship, the dead traders, the slow danger of letting such a blow go unanswered.

Kindness, he thought, was not weakness. Family was not weakness. But both needed guarding, or hard men would gladly teach the world otherwise.

When he spoke, it was with quiet certainty.

"If you sail, I sail."

Approval moved through the hall in nods, fists against benches, and the grim satisfaction of men hearing the answer they expected. Sten gave one short nod.

"Good."

The council went on after that, but the heart of it had been decided. The rest was rope, dried meat, blades, sailcloth, rowers, and all the plain hard labor that follows any choice once men agree to pay its cost.

When Eirik had heard enough to know his place was fixed on Sten's ship, he left before the hall's heat thickened into boasting.

Outside, dusk had already begun to gather. Fine snow drifted sideways on the wind. Men were carrying pitch toward the boat sheds. The dark water moved under the gray sky like iron breathing.

By the time Eirik reached home, the village felt smaller somehow.

Astrid was in the yard mending the latch on the goat pen. She crouched with one gloved hand steadying the wood and the other fitting the pin back into place. She looked up only when he was close enough to read.

"Well," she said.

"Two ships," he answered. "A scout boat first. If it returns with sign enough, we sail after."

Astrid tested the latch once and rose. "So the eager men got their ships, and the careful men got their scout. That should satisfy everyone until they remember they are kin."

Eirik smiled faintly. "Nearly."

Her eyes moved over his face. "And you?"

"I gave Sten my place."

She nodded once. No surprise. No wasted display. "Then the path is a path."

He looked at her. "You said that before."

"Yes. It was true then as well."

Inside, the children were waiting near the hearth.

Leif was on his feet before the door was fully shut. "Well?"

Sigrid stayed seated, but her eyes were just as fixed on him.

Eirik pulled off his gloves. "A scout boat goes first. If it returns with word enough, I go with Sten's ship."

Leif drew in breath. Pride and worry crossed his face so quickly they nearly became one expression. "I knew you would."

Sigrid looked at him. "That does not mean you should say it like a victory."

Leif's jaw tightened. "I didn't."

"You did."

"I meant I knew he would do what was right."

Sigrid was quiet for a moment. "That is different."

Leif glanced toward his father, then toward the shield leaning by the wall. "I know it is."

Astrid set bread on the table. "Sit down, all of you. Serious talk always sounds wiser when people are chewing."

Leif sat. Sigrid sat straighter. Eirik took his place by the fire.

The meal passed beneath the news rather than away from it. Leif asked quick questions about scouts, winter rowing, and how long it took to tar a hull before a cold-weather sail. Sigrid asked fewer, but hers cut closer.

"If the men who did it are gone by the time you reach them, what then?"

Eirik looked across the fire at her. "Then we do not kill shadows to feel strong."

Leif frowned as he turned that over. "But if you find their shore, and you know they were there—"

"Knowing they were there is not the same as knowing who they are," Eirik said.

Leif started to answer quickly, then stopped. He looked down at his hands and nodded once. "All right."

When the bowls were empty, Leif rose at once and fetched the practice shield.

"I fixed the strap," he said. "And the other one too."

Sigrid added, "After I told him where it would fail."

Leif ignored that. "Will you test it?"

Eirik stood and took the shield. "In the morning."

Leif tried to hide his disappointment and failed.

"In the morning," Eirik repeated, "when your arms are not tired and your head is steadier."

Leif opened his mouth, thought better of it, and nodded. "Then I'll be ready."

"You had better be," Sigrid said. "If he bruises you in front of me after all that work, I will be embarrassed for the family."

Leif gave her a wounded look. "You are harsh."

"I am accurate."

Astrid said, "Both of you have inherited too much from both of us. Sit down."

Later, when the children had gone to their bedding and the house had quieted, Eirik stepped outside.

The night had cleared. Stars shone cold above the fjord. Snow lay pale over the village. The drawn-up boats were black against the shore. Somewhere a horse stamped in its shelter. Otherwise the world was still.

Astrid came out a moment later and stood beside him with only a shawl over her shoulders.

"You'll freeze," he said.

"Not before you. I have less to prove."

A faint smile touched him and passed.

For a while they stood in silence, facing the black water.

At last Eirik said, "I will go with Sten's ship when it sails."

Astrid's hand found his. Her fingers tightened once. "I know."

"I needed to say it."

"Yes." She looked out over the fjord. "Spoken things stop pretending they are mist."

He let the cold fill his lungs. "Leif nearly smiled when I told them."

"He is young."

"He sees the bright edge first."

Astrid nodded. "And Sigrid sees the shadow under it."

Eirik thought of them together in the firelight. Leif always moving, always trying to stand ahead of his years. Sigrid steadying what he knocked loose without asking thanks for it. Chaos and control. Warmth and caution. Both dear to him in such different ways that loving them felt almost like carrying two separate aches.

"He'll learn," Eirik said quietly.

"Yes," Astrid replied. "If he keeps listening after he begins speaking."

He breathed out what might almost have been a laugh. Then he grew quiet again.

"I do not want him thinking this is glory."

"Then come back," Astrid said, "and teach him what it costs."

"And Sigrid?"

Astrid's mouth curved faintly. "Sigrid already knows cost. She counts it before most people see the debt."

That was true enough to sting.

Eirik looked toward the dark line of the shore. "I hate leaving."

Astrid did not answer at once. When she did, her voice was calm as ever.

"I know."

Nothing more. Nothing less. It was enough.

He turned that simple answer over in himself and felt, as he often did after speaking with her, that even hard truths sat more steadily for having passed through her voice.

When they went back inside, he paused by the children's bedding.

Leif slept on his back, one arm flung wide, as if even in dreams he were reaching for something beyond the walls of the house. Sigrid lay turned inward, blankets tucked close, one hand beneath her cheek. Even sleeping, they looked as they lived—one open to the world, the other measuring it.

Astrid stopped beside him.

"There is your answer," she said quietly.

He glanced at her. "To what?"

"To why this matters."

He looked at the children again.

Not honor alone. Not pride. Not the talk of men in halls. This. A warm house. A brother and sister learning each other's shapes. Bread on the table. A latch mended. A shield strap tied well enough to hold. The small human things that made a life.

He took down his shield and set it within reach of the bed.

At dawn there would be ropes to tar, blades to sharpen, food to pack, and the plain hard work of turning choice into action. But for now there was only the glow of the hearth, the warmth of the house, Astrid's steady nearness, and the knowledge that going did not lessen love.

It made it heavier.

And as he lay down at last, listening to the fire settle and the breathing of those he loved, Eirik thought that perhaps this was the truest burden of any raid—not the battle, not the danger, not even the blood.

It was knowing exactly what waited at home, and choosing to leave it guarded by hope alone until a man could return.

At dawn, he rose and fastened his cloak. Astrid stepped near and adjusted the fold of it at his shoulder.

"Listen for the thing beneath the thing," she said.

He gave her a faint look. "Speak that more plainly."

Her eyes lifted to his. "Hear what men want hidden."

He nodded once.

Chapter Three

The Battle of Ash Fjord

Morning came to Ash Fjord in layers of gray.

Mist lay low over the water, thick enough to soften the far shore and turn ships into dark shapes without edges. The tide moved in slow breaths against the stones. Ash trees clung to the steep ground above the narrow beach, their bare branches black against the pale sky, and the cliffs on either side held the fjord like a pair of closed hands.

Eirik stood near the waterline with his shield strapped on and his spear grounded beside his boot. He watched the opposite shore through the shifting veil and listened to the sounds behind him: leather pulled tight, iron rings settling over wool, a whetstone passing once along a blade and then stopping because there was no more use sharpening what would soon be blooded.

Thirty-two men.

Enough, if they held.

Not enough, if pride got into them.

Footsteps came over the stones.

Arn stepped up beside him, carrying an axe in each hand as casually as another man might carry kindling. Both were bearded axes, narrow and wickedly shaped, their edges freshly honed. He wore mail over dark wool and nothing on his left arm but old scars and a leather wrap at the wrist.

Eirik looked once at the empty place where a shield should have been. “Still refusing to learn.”

Arn rolled one shoulder. “Still refusing to slow down.”

“One day someone will notice you have no shield.”

“One day you will notice I have two axes.” He tilted one in each hand as if that settled the matter. “That is twice the advice and half the hesitation.”

Eirik gave him a flat look.

Arn grinned. "Besides, Tyr has one hand and Thor prefers hammers. I have already compromised with both."

A few men nearby laughed quietly. Arn always did that before a fight. He walked near tension and prodded it until it either broke or turned useful.

He was restless even while standing still. Weight shifting. Eyes moving. Axes changing angle by finger-widths. He never looked settled, yet Eirik had seen him sleep in a storm and wake at the exact moment danger crossed the threshold. Arn trusted motion the way other men trusted walls.

Across the water, the enemy gathered among the rocks and brush above their beached ships.

Hrolf Ketilsson had brought forty men south, perhaps more if one counted the boys too young to grow proper beards and too foolish to fear what they did not yet understand. He had already stripped two coastal settlements of food and livestock. Ash Fjord was the next narrow place between hunger and easy taking.

Not today.

Eirik looked along his line.

Some men were veterans. Some were steady farmers who knew how to stand in mud and pain without talking about either. A few were young enough that they still looked surprised by the weight of mail on their shoulders. He knew every face. That always made command heavier. Men were easier to spend when they were not known.

"Listen."

The murmur died.

"We hold the shore. Let them climb the stones and lose breath before they meet us. Shields together. Spears first. No one breaks line for glory. No one chases a wounded man into foolish ground. If one falls, the man beside him closes the space."

He let the men keep their eyes on him.

"We are not here to make songs. We are here to send them away from our homes."

Arn twirled one axe once and caught it again. "You hear that? No songs. If any of you die dramatically, do it in silence."

A few men smiled despite themselves.

Eirik did not.

Arn glanced sideways. "What? It is good advice. Dead men are often too loud."

Then Eirik saw movement above the line, on the slope near the birch scrub.

Astrid stood there with a spear in hand and a dark cloak over her mail. She did not stand like someone waiting helplessly behind the fighters. She stood as though she had chosen the better place from which to see the shape of things. Beside her were Leif and Sigrid.

Leif could barely contain himself. Even from this distance Eirik could see the boy leaning into the coming clash, eager and bright and untested. Sigrid stood very still, her eyes moving more than her head, noticing things other people missed because she never wasted attention on the obvious. Astrid, between them, said nothing. She rarely needed to.

Sigrid lifted a hand and pointed toward the eastern ridge.

Eirik followed the gesture.

Two shapes among the stones. Men trying to circle the flank before the main push.

He nodded once and motioned Hakon and Bjorn's eldest son over. "East ridge. Quietly. Drive them off. Do not chase."

They went at once.

Arn watched them go. "Your daughter sees ghosts before they choose bodies."

"She sees what matters."

"That is worse for the rest of us."

A horn sounded from across the fjord.

Low. Rough. Close enough to feel in the chest.

The enemy began to move.

They came down over the rocks in a broken front, boots slipping on wet stone, shields raised, spears angled. They had numbers, noise, and downhill certainty. None of those mattered as much as they believed.

"Hold."

His men crouched behind shields. Spears leveled through the gaps.

Arrows came first, badly judged in the mist. One skipped from a shield rim. Another struck the stones near Eirik's foot and shivered there.

The enemy closed.

"Hold."

A big man in a wolfskin cap broke ahead of the others, yelling as if his own voice could make him immortal. He splashed through the shallows, axe lifted high.

"Now."

Spears drove forward.

The wolf-capped man jerked, stumbled, and went down hard before he ever reached the wall. The men behind him piled into confusion. One fell over him. Another tried to step around and exposed his side.

The line met them.

Eirik moved with it, not ahead of it.

He thrust at the thigh of the first man over the stones, dragged the spear free before it stuck, turned his shield into a sword blow, and struck with the boss hard enough to send teeth and blood into the mist. Arn was suddenly beside him, then gone, then there again, weaving through the front rank with terrifying ease.

He fought exactly as he lived: as if stillness were a kind of death.

No shield burdened him. He slipped between men, ducked under spear shafts, and cut in flashing, brutal arcs with both axes. One blade hooked behind a shield rim and ripped it aside. The other bit into the exposed shoulder beneath it. He pivoted before the body had finished falling, one axe low, one high, moving like a man listening to music no one else could hear.

A sword came for his ribs.

Arn twisted away from it by what looked like nothing more than instinct, laughed in the man's face, and buried an axe in his thigh.

"Tyr likes your left side open. Thor likes mine busy."

Then he was moving again.

Eirik hated how effective it was.

An enemy spear snapped past the front line and caught old Ketil beneath the arm where his mail had shifted. The old man cried out and sagged. Eirik hooked him backward with the edge of his shield and stepped into the gap himself before panic could widen it.

"Breathe," he snapped at the younger man beside him, who had started swinging too wide.

The man swallowed and steadied.

That was how battles were lost as often as by steel. Not in grand failures. In one frightened breath, one open space, one bad step that turned a line into pieces.

The fighting thickened.

Iron rang on iron. Boots slid on wet stones mixed now with blood. Men grunted, cursed, gasped. The fjord threw the sounds back strangely, so that somewhere behind the real clash came thinner echoes, like old battles waking in the cliffs.

Hrolf's men pressed hard at the center, then tested the west slope where the footing narrowed between cliff and shore.

Astrid saw it before Eirik fully did.

Her voice cut down from above, calm and sharp. "Leif."

The boy moved instantly.

Eirik's gut tightened.

Then he saw where Leif ran: not toward the blades, but toward the stacked poles, stones, and old net weights left above the west path. Sigrid was already there, bracing herself against a wedge-stone. She struck it loose with a hooked staff while Leif hauled on the rope Astrid had pulled free from the pile.

The whole mass gave way.

Poles, rocks, and weights crashed down the narrow slope in a violent clatter. Three men trying to flank the line looked up too late. One was knocked flat. Another leapt backward and slipped into the shallows. The third turned and abandoned the attempt entirely.

Leif threw both fists into the air in triumph.

Sigrid said something to him that Eirik could not hear, but the boy's expression soured at once.

Astrid reclaimed her spear and resumed watching the battle as if children collapsing a hillside onto armed men were a reasonable part of morning work.

Arn saw it too and barked out a laugh while splitting a man's guard with crossed axes. "Your family is rude."

"They prepare."

"Same thing, if done well."

The clash surged again.

A broad-shouldered raider broke through the first push at the center, swinging a long axe in circles wide enough to drive men back from him. One of Eirik's younger spearmen caught his foot between stones and could not withdraw in time.

Eirik stepped in low. Not strength against strength. Never, if there was a better choice.

The long axe swept over him. He rammed the edge of his shield into the raider's knee, felt it buckle, then rose with his sword already free, cutting across the forearm and taking the weapon from the man's grip. The raider dropped to one knee, dazed, bleeding, open.

Eirik had the line for the throat.

He checked the strike.

Instead he hit the man with the flat of the blade across the temple. The raider pitched sideways onto the stones and lay still, but breathing.

Arn glanced over at exactly the wrong moment to remain silent. "You struck him like a wife-beater at winter feast."

"He is done."

"He is alive."

"For now."

Arn buried one axe in another attacker's collarbone and wrenched it free with a wet sound. "That is exactly the sort of answer that gets revisited later."

Eirik did not waste breath arguing.

Through the press of bodies he finally saw Hrolf.

The man moved differently from the others. Less noise. Less fury. More intent. He wore bright ring-mail under a wolf-fur cloak dark with spray, and black paint ran from brow into beard. He was not roaring men forward. He was measuring where resolve thinned.

He found the center and drove toward it with two seasoned fighters at his shoulders.

"There," said Arn, and something in his voice sharpened. "The loud one pretending not to be."

Hrolf hit the shield wall hard, using his men well. One opened space with a spear feint, the other crowded with shield pressure, and Hrolf's sword struck short and efficient behind both. A man on Eirik's left screamed and dropped his blade. Another nearly lost his footing.

Eirik stepped forward.

Arn moved with him, not because he had been told but because he had already decided.

"You take the black stripe. I take the mistakes around him."

"That assumes he brought any."

Arn smiled without humor. "All men bring mistakes. Some only wear better mail."

The two friends entered the same danger from different angles.

Eirik met Hrolf shield to shield with a crash that shuddered up both arms. Hrolf's eyes were pale and cold, not wild. The man's first cut came low and direct, testing. Eirik turned it away, answered with a thrust, and found steel waiting for him. Good. Better than good.

To the right, Arn was already among Hrolf's companions.

He moved like a break in weather. One axe hooked behind a shield and yanked it outward. The other flashed across exposed knuckles. When one of Hrolf's veterans lunged, Arn flowed inside the thrust, shoulder turning, torso bending like a reed in wind. His axe bit once into the man's ribs and again into the back of the thigh before the veteran understood he had already lost.

Arn kicked the body away and ducked under a second sword cut.

"Too slow. And you came here with only one plan. Thor dislikes that."

Hrolf drove at Eirik with hard, disciplined force. He fought like a man who knew battle was labor before it was glory. Short cuts. Shield punches. Constant pressure. Eirik gave ground only where the footing demanded it and took it back the moment he could. No wasted motion. No anger. Every strike had purpose.

"You are Eirik," Hrolf said between blows.

"I am."

"I expected a berserker."

"You were told a child's version."

Hrolf's mouth bent once. "I prefer men who finish things."

Eirik caught a cut on the shield rim and returned one that scraped sparks from Hrolf's mail. "Then you should have stayed north."

Hrolf feinted high, then punched forward with the shield. Eirik absorbed it and pivoted, but the angle let one of Hrolf's men come in from the side.

Before Eirik could turn, Arn's first axe caught that man in the upper arm. The second struck the side of his neck. Arn yanked both free in one smooth, terrible motion and shoved the body backward into another attacker.

"You are welcome."

"I had him."

Arn grinned. "No. You were about to become a lesson."

They moved apart again without another word. They had fought together too long to need one.

The battle narrowed around Hrolf.

Men on both sides began to feel where its center truly was. That strange current took hold, the one that comes in hard fighting when everyone senses that one small knot of violence is deciding the rest.

Hrolf saw an opening and struck low.

His blade scraped Eirik's mail skirt and bit into leather at the hip. Pain flashed hot and mean. Hrolf came in at once to finish it.

Eirik stepped back.

His heel found a slick stone that should have taken his balance.

It did not.

For one impossible instant, the rock beneath him felt fixed, certain, as if the earth itself had chosen not to let him fall. The mist shifted sideways, against the wind. Up near the standing stones above the shore, something seemed to move at the very edge of sight: tall, gray, and not quite shaped like any living man.

No voice spoke.

No light blazed.

But the hair on Eirik's neck rose beneath his helm.

Hrolf's sword came for the opening he thought he had made.

Eirik turned with perfect timing, as though his body had remembered something his mind had not. Hrolf's blade slid past his side. Eirik caught the sword arm with his shield, stepped in, and drove his own blade beneath Hrolf's collarbone where the mail had shifted with the lunge.

Not a killing depth.

A stopping one.

Hrolf gasped and dropped to one knee in the surf-wash, blood running dark through the rings of his mail.

Around them, the clash faltered.

Arn ended it first on his side. He planted one axe in the stones, held the other ready, and barked at the nearest enemy, "That is the sound of losing. Learn it quickly."

No one seemed eager to test whether he meant to continue.

Eirik put the edge of his sword at Hrolf's throat.

"Do it," Hrolf said, voice tight with pain.

The men nearest them waited.

The fjord itself seemed to wait.

"Do it," Hrolf said louder. "Or be called weak by men who know better."

Arn looked at Eirik with a face that revealed nothing and everything. He would not interfere. But neither would he pretend agreement if mercy came.

Eirik raised his voice.

"Take your wounded. Take your dead if you can carry them. Leave this fjord and do not come south again."

Silence moved through both sides.

Hrolf stared at him as if the words were harder to understand than the wound.

Arn shut his eyes once, briefly, as though speaking to a god about patience.

"You spare me?" Hrolf asked.

"I spare the men who would die proving what I have already proven."

Hrolf's expression twisted. "Mercy from a man in mail."

"Call it a warning."

For a long moment, no one moved.

Then one of Hrolf's men lowered his shield.

Another bent to lift a wounded companion.

The shape of the battle broke apart.

Not into panic. Into decision.

Men gathered their injured. A few dragged the dead. One of them hauled away the great red-bearded raider Eirik had spared earlier, still unconscious and very much alive.

Arn watched that with narrowed eyes.

Hrolf rose slowly, one hand pressed to his wound. He was pale now, but standing.

"This will follow you."

"Yes."

"They will call you soft."

"Some will."

"And if I return?"

Arn answered before Eirik could. "Then I stop being polite."

Hrolf looked at him. "You have not been polite."

Arn shrugged with one blood-slick axe in hand. "You should see me at feasts."

A few of Eirik's men laughed despite the tension. Even one of Hrolf's looked briefly uncertain whether he had missed a joke or a threat.

Hrolf turned his eyes back to Eirik. "Next time I will not trust your honor."

"Then do not come back expecting it."

Hrolf held the look a heartbeat longer, then turned and made for the boats.

The enemy withdrew in ragged silence, carrying what they could. No song. No curses cast over the water. Only oars, boots, and the dull labor of surviving defeat.

Eirik lowered his sword at last.

His arm felt suddenly heavy.

Arn stepped near, breathing hard, both axes still in hand. Blood streaked one side of his face. His eyes were bright in the way they always were after battle, as if some wild inward fire had not yet decided to settle.

"You should have killed him."

"Yes."

"That is not agreement."

"No."

Arn snorted. "Good. I was worried the head wound had worsened."

Eirik looked at him. "You were not hit."

"Not on the outside."

That was exactly the sort of thing Arn said that sounded foolish until later, when it proved true in some unpleasant way.

Men began tending the wounded. Eirik moved to them at once, kneeling beside old Ketil, binding one man's arm, directing another to tear cloth for a tourniquet. Battle left no room for glory after it ended. Only work.

Arn crouched by a fallen spear, cleaned one axe on a dead man's cloak, then the other. "You know he will speak of this."

"I know."

"He will tell the north you wounded him and let him live."

"Yes."

"That breeds one of two things. Gratitude or revenge."

"Men like Hrolf are not built for gratitude."

Arn gave him a sharp glance. "Then why?"

Eirik tied off the bandage, sat back on his heels, and looked toward the receding ships.

"Because I have seen too many Norse die proving whose pride was taller. Because his men were already breaking. Because killing him there would not have protected anyone more than ending the fight did."

Arn listened without interrupting, which for him was a form of respect.

At last he said, "You always speak as if the best choice should also be the clean one."

Eirik stood. "And you always speak as if blood makes truth simpler."

Arn rose too, sliding the axes through the loops at his belt. "It does not. It only removes some options."

Then his gaze lifted past Eirik toward the standing stones above the shore.

His expression changed.

Not fear. Not surprise. Recognition, perhaps, though of what Eirik could not have said.

"You felt that," Eirik said quietly.

Arn's jaw shifted once. "I felt something."

"What?"

Arn looked back toward the empty mist above the stones. "Like a hand on the back of the neck. Not pushing. Only reminding."

Eirik said nothing.

Arn rested one palm briefly on the head of one axe. A private gesture. Almost a prayer. "Tyr teaches that a hand given is not always a hand lost. Thor teaches that thunder arrives before some men hear it. I do not know which of them watched you there." He glanced sideways. "Maybe neither. Maybe something older, and less interested in names."

Up the slope, Astrid was already coming down with Leif and Sigrid.

Leif came first, full of wind and pride and ten questions fighting each other for escape. "Did you see the stones? We dropped the whole pile. I pulled the rope. Sigrid did the wedge, but I pulled most of it."

“You nearly pulled yourself over the edge,” Sigrid said.

“I leaned heroically.”

“You slipped.”

“I did not slip.”

Astrid spoke without raising her voice. “You slipped with conviction.”

Leif opened his mouth to protest, then thought better of arguing with a statement that had already won.

Eirik almost smiled.

Astrid stopped near him and let her eyes take in the cut at his hip, the blood on his mail, the ships moving away.

“That could have gone worse.”

Arn laughed. “There is the comfort every man seeks after battle.”

She looked at him. “You are alive. Let us not waste the occasion with softness.”

“See?” Arn said to Eirik. “This is why I like her. She speaks like a riddle and lands like an axe.”

Astrid’s expression did not change. “And yet I still carry a shield.”

Arn touched his chest as if wounded beyond healing. “Cruel.”

Leif looked from one adult to another, then back to the water. “Why did you let Hrolf leave? You beat him.”

Eirik put a hand on the boy’s shoulder.

“Winning is not always killing.”

Leif frowned. “It should be, if the man comes to kill you.”

Sigrid spoke before Eirik could answer. “Not if killing him makes the next fight larger.”

Leif looked at her, irritated by the possibility that she was right.

Astrid adjusted the spear in her hand. “Mercy is not softness when it is chosen from strength.”

Arn folded his arms. “True. It is simply dangerous in a slower way.”

There it was. Not insult. Not mockery. Honest challenge.

Eirik looked at him. “And yet you stayed your axes.”

Arn met the look squarely. “Because I follow you in battle. Not because I agree with every turn in the road afterward.”

The answer was sharp, but not disloyal. That was Arn’s way. He was one of the few men Eirik trusted to speak against him without stepping away.

Sigrid glanced toward the standing stones above the shore. “Something was there.”

Leif straightened at once. “I did not see anything.”

“You do not look where quiet things happen,” she said.

“That is because quiet things rarely need me.”

“They often need you not to interfere.”

Arn barked a laugh.

Astrid’s eyes remained on the ridge. “The air changed.”

Eirik followed her gaze.

The mist was thinning now. The stones stood bare. The ash trees above them stirred with the faintest wind. Nothing visible remained.

Yet the feeling lingered.

Not finished.

Chapter Four

The Veil Thins

Two days after the battle at Ash Fjord, the sun went down slowly, as though reluctant to leave the fjord to night.

Its last light lay red across the water and caught the wet black stones below the village. Smoke drifted low from the houses, touched with gold at the edges. Men were still out in the lanes and yards, though the work of the day had thinned. A few lingered near the fires with ale in hand, their voices louder than the hour required. Relief had not yet fully left them. Some still wore it like armor.

Above the village, hidden among scrub pine and stone, Hrolf watched.

He had wrapped a dark cloak over his shoulders and kept low behind the rise, with six men scattered near him among the rocks. They had come before sunset and lain still long enough to learn the shape of the place. They had watched women carry water. They had seen which doors opened most often, which men walked unarmed, which homes held children, where the boats were drawn up, and where the lanes narrowed between the longhouses.

They had watched Eirik's house the longest.

Hrolf's face was drawn hard by pain and old fury. The wound Eirik had left him was healing badly. One side of his jaw was swollen. He moved stiffly when he shifted his weight. But his eyes were clear, and all the more dangerous for it. Shame had done its work in him. So had hatred.

Below, he saw Eirik cross his yard carrying a bucket, Astrid step out to meet him, and the children near the fence line. He saw the rhythm of them. He saw what mattered.

Then he smiled, and the smile was thin as a knife blade.

“First the house,” he murmured.

The men near him nodded.

The light drained lower.

In the yard below, Leif had made a spear from a willow shaft and was testing its balance with a seriousness that made him look older at first glance and very much his age at second. He had wrapped leather at the grip himself and shaved the shaft until it ran almost straight.

Almost.

“It bends left,” Sigrid said from the step.

Leif turned it in his hand. “It does not.”

“It does.”

He squinted along the shaft. “Only a little.”

“That is still bending.”

He looked toward Eirik, who was setting the bucket by the wall. “Father?”

Eirik came over and took the spear. He ran one hand along the shaft, turned it once, then handed it back. “Your sister is right.”

Leif tried not to look disappointed and failed. “I can fix it.”

“Yes.”

“It’s still better than the last one.”

“That one tried to become a fishing pole halfway through.”

Sigrid’s mouth moved faintly. “It had more ambition than skill.”

Leif gave her a look. “You say that as if you could do better.”

“I would do slower,” she replied. “Which is often the same thing.”

Astrid came from the doorway with a folded cloth over one arm. “If the two of you are done wounding one another with wisdom, bring in the split wood before dark.”

Leif moved at once, because he was always moving at once. He caught up three logs in his arms, nearly lost one, caught it against his hip, and hurried toward the door. Sigrid watched him go, then stooped and picked up the single piece he had missed by the chopping block.

“You see?” she said.

Leif, already halfway up the step, twisted around. “I was coming back for that.”

“No,” Sigrid said. “You were going to forget it, and later say you were coming back.”

Astrid took the wood from Leif’s arms before he dropped it on her feet. “Both of you are correct in the most tiring way.”

Eirik stood a moment with one hand on the fence post and watched them.

This, he thought, was the thing men fought for and spoke around badly. Not only land. Not only honor. This yard. This bickering. This warm house breathing smoke into the falling dusk. His son’s quick temper. His daughter’s cool eyes. Astrid’s voice in the doorway, dry and calm as ever, making order sound like wit.

Something pricked at him then.

Not thought. Not sound. A shift.

He turned and looked toward the rise above the village.

Nothing moved there that he could name. Pine. Stone. Long grass darkening in the lowering light. Yet the skin between his shoulders tightened.

Astrid saw him go still.

“What is it?”

Eirik kept his eyes on the hill. “I’m not sure.”

Leif looked up at once. “What?”

Sigrid followed her father’s gaze. She said nothing, but her face sharpened.

A raven lifted suddenly from the ridge and crossed the reddened sky alone.

Then another.

Then three more at once, breaking from the scrub as if disturbed.

Eirik’s hand went to his belt knife.

The first shout came from the next lane over.

Not a warning. Not yet. Only a cry, cut short.

Then feet pounded on hard ground.

Eirik did not wait for a second sound.

“Inside.”

Leif froze only a heartbeat before moving. Sigrid was already at the door. Astrid dropped the cloth where she stood and stepped toward the children, but the attack had been timed well. Too well.

A man came over the side fence like a wolf over a sheep wall, one boot on the rail, axe already lifting. Another crashed through the gate an instant later, shoulder-first, splintering the latch bar. Behind them, out in the lane, more voices rose—alarm now, and steel striking steel.

The raiders had come through the village all at once.

The man on the fence landed badly, one knee slipping in the frost, and Eirik was on him before he regained his balance. Eirik drove the bucket into his face with enough force to burst the man's nose and half-spin him, then slammed him down with the edge of his forearm across the throat. The raider hit the ground choking. Eirik tore the axe from his grip and buried it in his chest in one brutal downward stroke.

No wasted motion. No roar. No flourish.

The second man came through the broken gate with a sword in hand and a curse in his mouth. Astrid met him before he reached the children. She had no shield, only the long hearth knife she had snatched from inside, but she moved with perfect economy. She turned his first cut with the knife's back, stepped in, and drove her shoulder into him hard enough to break his footing on the churned ground. The sword slashed her sleeve but did not bite skin. She cut him across the forearm. He grunted and came again.

"Leif! Bar the door!"

Leif grabbed Sigrid's wrist and pulled her toward the threshold. She pulled back just enough to seize the dropped wood hook by the step with her free hand.

"Inside!"

"I am trying!"

They stumbled through the doorway together.

The man Astrid was fighting lunged past her toward them, seeing children where he had failed to find easy blood before. Astrid slashed his cheek open, but he kept coming.

Then another figure stepped through the broken gate.

Hrolf.

Even wounded, Eirik knew him at once. The same hard brow. The same thick shoulders. The same face Eirik had left breathing on the black shore of Ash Fjord. But now one side of that face was scar-drawn and swollen, and what lived in his eyes was not battle fury.

It was colder than that.

Chosen.

For a single beat, the yard narrowed to just the two of them.

Hrolf saw recognition land and smiled around it.

"You should have finished it."

Then the whole yard broke apart at once.

The man lunging toward the doorway raised his blade high for Leif.

Leif, in the blind instant between training and terror, did the only thing his body knew.

He thrust.

His practice sword had a rounded tip and dulled edges, meant for bruises and correction, not blood. But the raider was already off balance from Astrid's strike, already falling forward, and Sigrid—quick as thought—swung the wood hook hard into the back of his knee.

The man buckled.

Leif's thrust, meant for the chest or belly, drove upward instead.

The blunted wooden blade struck under the jaw, jammed deep beside the throat, and tore through the soft place there with a wet choking crack.

The raider stopped.

His eyes went wide with disbelief before all expression left them.

Blood came hot and sudden over Leif's hands.

The boy made a sound Eirik had never heard from him—not a shout, not a sob, but something caught halfway between.

Sigrid seized Leif's arm and dragged him backward through the doorway as the dying man collapsed across the threshold.

It happened in less than a breath.

Yet Eirik saw all of it.

His son's hands red.

His daughter's face gone white and set.

The body jerking once in the dirt.

The door frame of his own house splashed dark.

And Hrolf still standing in his yard.

Something in Eirik changed then.

Not loudly. Not wildly. It did not burst. It locked.

He had spared a Norseman on the shore because he would not take joy in killing a beaten man of his own blood and tongue. He had left Hrolf one last chance to meet the gods on some straighter road than this.

And Hrolf had brought steel to his children.

Mercy curdled into cold iron inside him.

Hrolf saw it too late.

Eirik came at him with the fallen axe in one hand and the dead raider's short sword in the other. Hrolf barely got his own blade up in time. The first clash rang so hard it jarred Hrolf's wounded arm. Eirik did not press with rage. Rage wasted strength. He struck with killing purpose now, each blow placed to end, not argue.

Hrolf gave ground at once.

Astrid was still moving. She kicked the dead man clear of the threshold and slammed the door half-shut with one hand. "Bolt it!" she shouted to the children.

Inside, Leif had gone shock-still, staring at his hands. Sigrid snatched the bar free from its pegs and shoved it into place across the inside hooks. Then she caught Leif by the shoulders.

"Look at me."

He did, barely.

"Look at me."

His eyes found hers.

"Breathe."

He sucked in air once, ragged and thin.

"Again."

Behind them, another cry rose in the lane, then the crash of wood breaking somewhere near Bjorn's yard.

Outside, Astrid turned to help Eirik—but a third raider came around the side wall, having climbed through the herb bed, and forced her back into the fight. He was younger than the others, half panicked already by how quickly the attack had gone wrong. That made him dangerous. He slashed too wide. Astrid retreated one step, then another, drawing him away from the door, and when he overreached she cut his wrist and drove the heel of her palm under his chin. He staggered. She took his knife from his own belt and opened his throat with it before he hit the ground.

In the yard, Eirik broke Hrolf's guard with two savage cuts and a shoulder strike. Hrolf stumbled into the fence. The short sword went spinning from his hand.

"You spared me," Hrolf spat, blood on his teeth.

"Yes."

Hrolf lunged for the dropped blade.

Eirik drove the axe through his upper arm and into the fence rail, pinning him there.

Hrolf screamed.

The sound was swallowed by the wider noise spreading through the village—men shouting, women calling children in, the first ringing answers of armed resistance. Too late for some. Not too late for all.

Eirik stepped in close enough that Hrolf had to see his face clearly.

"You came to my home."

Hrolf tried to wrench free and could not. His eyes flashed with pain and hate and the first crack of fear.

"I should have killed you on the shore."

This time there was no hesitation.

He drew the short sword once across Hrolf's throat, clean and hard.

The raider captain sagged against the fence, pinned and spilling his life into Eirik's yard.

Eirik did not watch him die.

He turned at once toward the lane beyond the broken gate.

"Astrid."

She stood over the body of the younger man, breath coming fast but steady, one sleeve cut and darkened at the edge. Her eyes flicked toward the door, then to the lane, then back to Eirik. She knew him well enough to see at once what had settled over him.

"The children are barred in."

"Keep them there."

"And you?"

He looked toward the shouting. Toward the firelight jerking between houses. Toward the rest of the raiders spilling their revenge into men who had gone soft with ale and relief.

"I finish it."

Astrid caught his forearm as he passed. For one heartbeat only. Not to stop him. To steady the road between them.

"Come back."

Eirik looked at her, at the blood on her sleeve, at the iron calm in her eyes despite the terror he knew lay under it.

Then he was gone into the lane.

The village had become a tangle of running figures, torchlight, confusion, and sudden death.

A farmer from the lower sheds lay facedown near the path with a wood axe still in his hand, his back opened by something sharper than farm work had ever asked him to face. Two more men were wrestling one raider near the well, drunk enough that all three moved badly. One of them took a knife in the belly before Eirik reached them. Eirik split the raider's skull with the axe and hauled the wounded man clear before he fell too.

Another attacker came out of the smoke near Runa's house with a torch and seax, trying to set the thatch alight where the straw was driest. Eirik threw the short sword and caught him between neck and collar. The man dropped without a sound.

Someone shouted Eirik's name from farther uphill.

He knew the voice.

Arn.

Eirik ran toward it.

The lanes blurred around him—shadow, fire, fence, faces, blood. He no longer looked for mercy, surrender, or names. The first raider he found near the goat pens died with Eirik's knife under his ribs. The second turned too slowly and lost his head to Arn's twin axes before Eirik even reached him. Arn stood over the body, breathing hard, one cheek streaked dark, grinning like a man half mad with battle and still too alive to fear it.

"You finally stopped being generous."

Eirik did not answer.

Arn's grin faded as he read his face. "Ah."

A child was crying from inside one of the longhouses. A woman dragged him away from the door just as sparks flew from the roof where a dropped torch had caught dry grass and old pitch.

"They came like rats," Arn said, wheeling toward the noise uphill. "Small teeth. Bad timing."

Eirik stepped over the dead and kept moving.

Three raiders had come for the boats.

That much he understood the moment he saw the glow near the sheds. If they could not punish the village fully at the hearth, they would leave it crippled at the shore. One hull was already smoking where pitch had taken fire along the seam.

Bjorn Ketilsson was there, finally armed and finally sober enough to matter, bellowing as if he could frighten flame itself. Hakon stood with him, one eye narrowed against the smoke, spear planted in the chest of a man who still kicked weakly in the sand.

"Two more went that way!" Bjorn shouted, pointing toward the lower rocks.

Eirik did not break stride.

The path to the shore dipped between dark stones and rough grass. The sea below the boat sheds breathed in and out against the black rock, slow and hard. Smoke drifted sideways on the wind. Somewhere overhead, ravens cried once, then fell silent.

He saw the last two raiders near the tide line.

One was trying to push off a small skiff they must have hidden among the rocks. The other turned at Eirik's approach with spear in hand. The man charged, desperate and clumsy. Eirik stepped inside the thrust, caught the shaft under one arm, broke it at the middle, and drove the jagged end back through the man's throat.

The other raider panicked and shoved the skiff harder toward the water.

Eirik leaped the rocks after him.

The man wheeled with a knife and slashed wild. The blade cut Eirik across the side below the ribs, a hot tearing line through wool and flesh. He felt it, registered it, and killed the man anyway—one hard strike with the axe behind the ear that sent him crumpling half into the surf.

Then the rock under Eirik's lead foot shifted.

It was slick with weed and blood. Or perhaps only weed. Later he could not be sure.

His boot slid.

His wounded side seized.

The world lurched.

He went down hard against the rocks at the edge of the tide, the axe flying from his hand. Something cracked low in his body. His head struck stone. Cold black water surged over him, dragging him sideways into the narrow cut between two boulders where the sea pounded and sucked like a living throat.

For a moment he was all force and impact. Stone. Water. Blood. Weight.

Then time changed.

Sound did not vanish. It dulled. It moved far away, as if the world had been lowered beneath the surface of a deep lake. The shouts from shore stretched thin and strange. The crash of water became enormous and slow. His own breath was no longer breath, only ache.

He tried to rise and could not.

The sky above him was a narrow torn strip between the black edges of rock. The last red of sunset had faded into a color that was not yet night and no longer day. Water washed over his legs and dragged at him, and every small thing became impossibly clear.

A bead of blood clinging to the edge of his knuckle.

The frayed thread at the cuff of his tunic where Astrid had meant to mend it.

The rough grain in the rock by his cheek.

The way frost still clung in white needles to one patch of shadowed stone above him.

He heard someone calling his name.

Once.

Twice.

Then from very far away.

He thought it might be Arn. Then Sten. Then no one human at all.

The world felt thin.

That was the first true thought of it. Not broken. Not gone. Thin, like scraped hide held up to winter light with something pressing from the other side.

Water filled his ear and withdrew. The strip of sky narrowed further, though he knew the rock had not moved. Or perhaps it had. It became hard to tell what was happening and what only seemed to be happening because he was no longer fully anchored to himself.

He should have been dying.

He knew that with a strange calm. A man knew when his body had crossed from pain into the place beyond pain, where cold and distance replaced the honest signals of flesh. He had seen it in others. He felt it now in himself.

He tried once more to move and found that his arms answered too late, as though they belonged to another man farther down a long hall.

Then the sea breathed.

Not wave. Not current. Breathed.

In and out beneath him.

The strip of sky changed. Not in color. In depth. It seemed suddenly farther away than sky should be, as if the space between him and it had opened like a path.

Something stood there.

Or someone.

He could not tell.

Not a clear figure. Never that. Only a suggestion where none should have been. Height. Stillness. A presence shaped almost like people were shaped, but wrong for flesh. One form became three, or perhaps had always been three. One seemed cloaked. One seemed winged. One seemed only shadow gathered with intention.

Ravens perched above them all, too still.

He tried to focus and could not.

The cold receded strangely. So did fear. He felt, for one impossible heartbeat, not as though he were being taken, but weighed. Held at the edge of some choice that was not his to make.

No voice spoke.

No god named itself.

Yet the pause itself was wrong.

Wyrd did not hesitate. Men were born into its weaving, lived in it, and were cut from it when their thread ended. Clean. Final. This waiting did not belong to the order he had always known.

One of the shadowed presences turned, as if listening to something beyond him.

Then all at once there was another sensation—not force, not sound, but interruption. A softness passing between blade and throat. A hand laid over a decision before it could close.

The shapes withdrew.

Or the veil drew shut.

Or he fell back into himself.

Later he would never know which.

Suddenly the world slammed near again.

Pain tore through his side.

Water hit him like ice hammers.

Voices broke back into shape.

"Eirik!"

That was Astrid.

Not memory. Not dream. Astrid, raw and human and close enough now that her voice cut through everything.

Hands seized his shoulders from above the rocks. Another hand gripped the back of his belt. He tried to help and managed only a useless choking gasp as the water dragged at his legs.

"Lift when it pulls back!" Arn shouted.

Sten's voice answered, hard as iron. "Now!"

They hauled him up the stones by strength and fury together.

Eirik half woke to the sight of Sten above him, huge and red-haired against the dark, the scar white on his face, one boot braced on the rock. Arn was below, soaked to the knees and swearing at the sea as if it had cheated him. The sky had gone nearly black.

Then Astrid was there.

He did not see her come down the path. One moment Sten's hands were on him. The next Astrid knelt in the wet sand beside him, her face so still it frightened him more than panic would have.

"Move," she said to Arn, and Arn moved.

Her hands went at once to his side, pressing hard over the wound. Pain flared white and cruel. Eirik tried to turn from it and could not.

"He lives," Arn said, too quickly.

"Quiet."

That one word carried enough that even Arn obeyed.

Above them, on the rise near the shed, Leif had come despite every order given. Sigrid was with him. She had both hands locked around his sleeve as if she had dragged him only so far and no farther. In the torchlight their faces looked pale and old and very young all at once.

Leif saw the blood and stopped breathing.

Sigrid did not.

"Father?" Leif said.

Astrid never looked up. "Stay there."

Leif took one step anyway.

Sigrid caught him. "She said stay."

"He's hurt."

"Yes." Sigrid's voice shook once, then steadied. "That is why."

Leif stared, helpless, his own blood-stiffened hands hanging at his sides. Not all of it was his father's. Some of it was the dead man from the doorway. He seemed only now to know that.

Sten looked up at the children and then away again, jaw hard.

"He should be dead," Arn muttered, not softly enough.

Astrid's hands pressed harder. "Not while he is still breathing."

There was no tremor in her voice. That came later, when no one needed steadiness from her. For now she was all purpose, the way she had always been in danger—calm so sharp it left no room for anything else.

Eirik drifted.

Torchlight stretched and doubled above him. The shore tilted strangely. Once he thought he saw the ravens again on the roof beam of the boat shed, but there were too many and then too few, and one seemed larger than any bird should be. He closed his eyes and the image remained.

"Astrid," he tried to say.

It came out mostly blood and air.

"I know," she said at once, though he had not truly spoken. "Stay."

Stay.

As if he were the one choosing.

Somewhere beyond the press of bodies and firelight, the village moaned with aftermath. A woman wept. A child cried out and was hushed. Men moved the dead. Others stamped out embers where thatch had begun to catch. The smell of burned pitch mixed with salt and blood until the whole night seemed made of iron and smoke.

Leif made a choked sound. "This is because of me."

Sigrid turned on him so sharply that even Sten looked up.

"No."

"I should have—"

"No," she said again, clearer, harder. "You saved us."

Leif shook his head. "I killed him."

Sigrid's face changed then. Not softer. Sadder.

"Yes," she said. "And he would have killed us."

Leif's mouth worked without words.

Sigrid looked down at Eirik, at Astrid's blood-wet hands pressing life back into him. When she spoke again, her voice dropped almost to nothing.

"He cannot die now."

Astrid heard that. Something moved through her face at last, small and terrible. Not collapse. Not yet. Only the crack of grief beneath discipline.

"He doesn't get to."

Sten crouched near Eirik's head and laid one broad hand against the back of his neck as if grounding him to the living world by force alone.

"Do you hear me, old wolf?" the jarl said, his voice low and roughened by more than shouting. "You do not leave in a tide ditch after settling every fool's work for them."

Arn let out a breath that might have been a laugh if fear had hollowed it less.

Eirik wanted to answer. He wanted to tell Sten that the rocks had nearly taken the choice from him. That something behind the world had stood waiting and then not taken him after all. But words would not hold.

Astrid leaned over him, her braid falling forward over one shoulder, her eyes fixed on his face as if she could refuse death entry simply by watching the right place.

For one naked instant, Eirik saw what she could not hide.

Fear. Not the common kind. Not the fear of battle, which she knew well and could move within. This was older, deeper—the fear of a wife seeing her husband torn from the life between them while the children watched and the ground beneath them held too much blood.

He had feared leaving her before.

This was worse.

This was being taken while still in reach of her hands.

"Astrid," he managed again.

She bent closer. "I am here."

A simple answer. Like a rope thrown into darkness.

He held to it.

They carried him back to the house because the shore was too cold, the healer too far, and the night already too full of death. Sten and Arn took most of the weight. Eirik half walked, half hung between them. Each step jarred his side and opened the world in flashes of white. The village passed around him in broken pieces: Bjorn with blood in his beard and no boasting left in him; Hakon speaking quietly over two bodies laid side by side; a woman kneeling in the mud with both hands over her mouth; sparks drifting upward where a roof edge still smoked.

At the doorway of his own house, Eirik saw the dead man Leif had killed carried away by two others.

Leif saw it too.

The boy turned and vomited into the shadows by the fence.

Sigrid went to him at once, one hand between his shoulders, her own face gone pale but steady. She did not speak while he emptied his fear into the dirt. When he was done, she held out water.

He looked at her as if asking permission to still be himself.

She gave the slightest nod.

Inside, the house had changed shape.

A home always did when blood entered it.

The benches had been shoved aside. Blankets dragged down. A bowl of water steamed near the hearth. The smell of smoke, iron, and wet wool thickened the room. Astrid worked with the healer from the next house, their hands red almost to the wrists. Sten stood back only when made to. Arn kept moving because stillness would have broken something in him.

Leif stayed near the wall at first, his hands scrubbed raw but not clean in his own mind. Sigrid remained closer, passing cloth when asked, water when needed, saying little and seeing everything.

Once, when Astrid's hands slipped on the blood at Eirik's side, Sigrid reached in silently and held the lamp higher before anyone asked.

Another time Leif stepped forward as if to help, then stopped at the sight of the wound and went white again. Sigrid touched his sleeve, not unkindly.

"Bring more water."

He nodded too fast and fled to the bucket, grateful for something that could be done without looking too closely.

The hours blurred.

Eirik drifted in and out of them like a man standing near a door he could not decide whether to pass through. Voices came and went. Pain came and stayed. Once he opened his eyes and thought the rafters above him had become pine branches black against a winter sky. Another time he saw, quite clearly, a raven perched on the ridge beam above the hearth hole, though when he blinked there was only shadow.

He did not know when the bleeding finally slowed enough for the room's breathing to change.

He only knew that at some point Astrid's shoulders lowered by a fraction, and Sten sat down heavily as if remembering he too was flesh and bone. Arn muttered a prayer to two gods and one insult to fate. Leif, hearing the silence shift, lifted his head from where he had fallen asleep against the wall and stared at his father as if afraid to trust what he saw.

Sigrid was still awake.

Of them all, she was the one whose fear had gone deepest into stillness. She sat nearest the bed furs with both hands in her lap and her eyes fixed on Eirik's face, as if by watching him closely enough she might learn the exact moment a soul chose whether to remain.

When he finally looked at her clearly, she leaned forward at once.

"Father?"

The word was hardly louder than breath.

Eirik swallowed against the dryness in his throat. “Still here.”

It was a poor sound. Broken. But it was his.

Leif made a noise halfway between a laugh and a sob.

Astrid closed her eyes once, briefly, and bowed her head over her bloodstained hands. Not in weakness. In release. Then she looked up again, and the strength was back in her face, though now it was lined with the cost of holding.

Sigrid’s eyes filled but did not spill. “You were gone a long time.”

Eirik looked at her, at the care she tried so hard to make look like composure, and understood then that this night had wounded her too in ways no healer would bind.

“I know.”

Leif came closer, hesitating only when he reached the edge of the furs. “Father…”

He stopped there, all speed gone out of him for once.

Eirik turned his head with effort. “You did what you had to.”

Leif’s face tightened. “I didn’t mean—”

“I know.”

Leif looked as if he might break on that word alone.

Sigrid reached for his sleeve and held it. He let her.

Astrid stood and came to Eirik’s side. Her fingers touched his brow once, very lightly, as though she still half feared he might vanish if handled too roughly.

“You crossed too far,” she said quietly.

Eirik looked up at her.

For a heartbeat, neither spoke. Too much had passed between one breath and the next of this night for easy words.

Then he said, “Something waited.”

Astrid’s expression did not change. Yet something in her eyes darkened, deepened, as if he had named a thing she had long suspected but never wished to hear aloud.

“Yes.”

Not what. Not how. Only yes.

Outside, the village had gone mostly quiet again.

Not peaceful. Never that. Quiet with the weight of counting, mourning, and living on because there was no other choice.

Near dawn, when the fire had burned low and those not needed had finally drifted out to tend the wounded elsewhere, Eirik turned his head toward the hearth hole.

A raven sat on the roof beam above it.

This time he knew he was awake.

The bird was black against the paling square of sky, utterly still. Not pecking. Not cleaning its feathers. Only watching. Then, as if feeling his gaze meet it, it tilted its head once.

Another shape landed beside it.

Then a third.

They made no sound.

Cold moved through Eirik that had nothing to do with his wound.

The room around him remained ordinary—Astrid seated close but fighting sleep, Leif curled against the wall at last, Sigrid still upright though barely, Sten dozing with one arm folded over his chest, Arn snoring somewhere by the door. Yet above all of it, just beyond the reach of smoke and dawn, the three ravens sat in perfect silence.

Watching him.

As if they had not yet decided whether he belonged to the living.

Chapter Five

Mercy's Edge

That night the village slept uneasily.

The feast had long since burned down into embers and low voices. Ale had gone flat in forgotten cups. Benches stood crooked where tired men had left them. In the houses nearest the shore, women checked their door bars twice before lying down. Dogs woke at small noises and settled only after long listening. Even the fjord seemed to breathe more quietly beneath the dark.

Eirik Halvardsson lay beside Astrid and did not sleep at once.

The house had grown still around him. Leif had finally gone quiet after turning three times under his blanket and whispering one last question into the dark that no one answered. Sigrid had made less noise, but he had heard her wake once, heard the careful shift of wool as she sat up, listened, and lay down again. The fire in the hearth had sunk to a low red cradle of coals. Smoke threaded upward through the roof hole in a thin, almost invisible line.

Astrid slept on her side with one hand curled near her face.

Even in rest there was steadiness in her. Eirik had always noticed that. Some people surrendered to sleep. Astrid seemed only to enter another kind of waiting.

He lay on his back and looked into the smoke-dark rafters.

The talk with Sten still sat in him. Not like anger. That had passed. Sten had every right to challenge him. A jarl carried more than his own judgment. Eirik knew that. Yet the thing that would not leave him was not Sten's disapproval, nor Bjorn's likely barking to anyone who would listen.

It was the ravens.

Three of them at dawn, silent on the beam above the hearth hole, watching as if a man's waking meant something.

He closed his eyes.

He saw again the black shore at Ash Fjord. Hrolf on his knees. The line of blood across stone. The weight of the sword in his hand. The choice not to take the last stroke.

He had not spared the man from softness. He knew that down to the bone. He had spared him because some deaths ought to belong to battle, and some ought to belong to the gods. Hrolf had been beaten. The fury had gone from him. Killing him then would have been simple.

Simple did not always mean right.

Eirik let out a slow breath through his nose.

Beside him, Astrid stirred.

"You are thinking too loudly," she murmured, not opening her eyes.

He turned his head toward her. "I was not aware thought made sound."

"With you, it does."

That almost drew a smile.

After a moment he said, "Do you think I was wrong?"

Astrid was quiet so long he thought she might already have slipped back into sleep.

Then she said, "Wrong things are often easier to name than unfinished ones."

He watched her in the dark. "That sounds like no answer."

"No." Her eyes opened at last, catching the low red light. "It sounds like the answer you have."

Eirik looked back at the rafters.

The house settled softly around them. Wind touched the roof once and moved on.

"At times," Astrid said, her voice nearly gone to sleep again, "the gods look harder at a man who stays his hand than at one who uses it."

He turned his head toward her, but her eyes had already closed.

"Do they approve?" he asked.

Astrid's mouth moved faintly. "That depends which god is looking."

Then she said nothing more.

Eirik lay with that for a while.

He did not remember falling asleep.

Only that at some point the red glow of the coals seemed to brighten instead of dim, and the line of smoke from the hearth hole thickened into something almost silver. The roof above him deepened, rose, widened beyond what a house could contain. He knew, even within it, that he was dreaming.

But it did not feel like dream.

It felt like stepping where his feet had not moved.

The first thing to go was sound.

Not fully. Only the wrong sounds. The crackle of coals faded. The small winter groans of the house fell away. The breathing of wife and children receded until he could no longer tell whether he heard them or remembered hearing them.

Then the dark above him opened.

Not violently. Quietly. As if a curtain had been hanging in the world all this time and had now been drawn back by a hand too patient to be seen.

Eirik stood.

He was no longer in his house.

A hall stretched before him so vast that for the first few breaths he could not judge its true size. Firelight lived there, but not like firelight in mortal places. It came from long braziers set in iron stands, from wall torches that never smoked, and from some farther glow that seemed to exist without flame at all. The light was warm in color and cold in feeling. Shadows did not gather where they should. They stood where they were meant to stand, as if placed.

The roof was lost somewhere above in carved darkness.

Pillars rose like tree trunks, each one cut with knotwork, beasts, and old signs that seemed to shift at the edge of seeing. The floor beneath Eirik's feet was smooth in some places, rough in others, as though many halls had been built one atop another and all remembered at once. Far off, benches and high seats stood in ordered lines. Beyond them moved figures. Many figures.

Warriors.

The air held the smell of iron, ash, old leather, wet wool, and something else beneath it all—winter wind over open ground.

Eirik did not reach for a weapon.

He did what he always did when he did not understand a thing.

He observed.

Men stood in groups. Some looked about them as if they knew exactly where they had come. Others wore the uncertain expression of those not yet fully separated from what they had left behind. Their wounds were not hidden. A man with half his face opened by an axe stood straight beside one whose mail was black with dried blood. Another still carried a broken spear shaft through the rings at his shoulder, though it no longer seemed to pain him. They were not feasting. Not boasting. Not clashing cups and laughing into the rafters the way skalds liked to tell it.

They were waiting.

Ordered, but not unified.

The realization settled quietly in Eirik.

This was no hall of reward.

This was where men were sorted.

He moved a step forward.

No one stopped him. No one seemed surprised he was there. That troubled him more than any challenge might have.

At the far end of the hall, where the light deepened rather than brightened, two presences drew the eye whether a man wished it or not.

Eirik did not know them at once in the way stories pretended men knew gods. No thunder broke. No great voice named itself. Yet the force of them was such that the hall itself seemed to arrange around their being.

One stood taller, cloaked in dark, with a stillness that did not hide power so much as gather it inward. Ravens perched on the carved beam above him, unmoving. One black wing shifted once and settled. The figure's face was not shadowed, yet Eirik found it strangely difficult to hold in full. One eye seemed brighter than the other, or perhaps only deeper. The sense that this presence looked through men rather than at them sat on Eirik's skin like cold.

The other presence was no less commanding, but different in kind.

She stood nearer the line of the newly fallen, neither softer nor gentler, but with a steadiness that did not seem to measure men only by what they could do next. Gold lived somewhere in her, though not brightly. There was sorrow in the set of her mouth and fierceness in the stillness of her shoulders. Around her, the air held something of field flowers crushed beneath boots, of blood on silk, of a room where grief had been allowed to speak without shame.

Eirik knew then, without hearing names.

He knew because every tale he had heard since childhood rose up and failed at once before the truth of seeing.

The god of the slain.

The chooser of the fallen.

Odin and Freyja.

He did not bow.

Not from defiance. From the simple fact that his body had forgotten how in that first stunned moment.

And still neither looked toward him.

They were occupied.

Warriors came before them—not walking by choice, but drawn in the slow current of the hall as though called by names only they could hear. Some halted near the dark god beneath the ravens. Some were gathered nearer the lady whose eyes held both iron and grief. A few seemed to hesitate between one and the other until something unseen resolved it.

Eirik watched.

At first the pattern was hard to grasp. Then, slowly, it sharpened.

A skald's fragment came back to him from some winter long ago, half-heard at his father's fire:

Not every slain man feasts in one hall.

The line settled in him like a peg driven into timber.

A broad-chested warrior with a grin still fixed on his dead face stepped forward, axe in one hand, mail rent open at the belly. Even in death he carried himself like a man who had gone gladly into the crush. His eyes still burned with unfinished battle. He had no shame in him. No reflection. Only appetite and force.

The dark god's attention touched him, and the man was taken into that line.

Not with praise. Not warmly. Simply chosen.

Another came after—a thinner man with gray already in his beard and a wound through the lungs. He had died with both hands around a shield strap worn nearly through. There was no hunger in him, only exhaustion and a strange quietness. His eyes seemed still to search for someone behind him.

He was not drawn beneath the ravens.

He went to Freyja.

Then another. Then another.

A youth who had died in first fury, laughing through blood.

A scarred veteran whose hands still curled as if around a child he had pushed behind him before the last blow.

A raider with sharp teeth bared even in death.

A defender with a farmer's shoulders and fear still on him, though he had stood where fear told him not to stand.

Eirik's unease deepened.

It was not random.

Nor was it simple.

The god beneath the ravens seemed to choose for strength, ferocity, and men whose will cut forward even through death—those who would be useful again where war had not ended, only paused. Not the reckless alone. Not fools. Usefulness sat in the choosing, cold and far-sighted.

Freyja chose differently.

Not weak men. Never weak men. But those in whom something else had burned beside courage. Those who had held. Those who had sacrificed. Those whose deaths had not been the loudest in the field, but whose meaning ran deeper than noise. Not all protectors. Not all gentle. Yet again and again Eirik saw her attention settle where a man had died for more than his own name.

He thought of the stories told by winter fires. Of men speaking as if honor were one road with one gate.

He felt the old certainty shift under him.

The gods themselves did not seem to agree on what made a death worthy.

Or perhaps they agreed only that worth had more than one face.

A movement among the waiting dead caught his eye.

Two warriors stood near one another, not touching, not speaking.

One wore the look Eirik knew too well from shore fights and surprise raids—a hard-mouthed Norseman, broad through the chest, beard braided with rings, one ear torn, blood dried along the edge of his jaw. Even dead, there was challenge in him. He had died weapon-forward, that much was plain. Rage and daring still clung to him like old smoke.

Beside him stood a younger man with no rings and poorer gear. His tunic was plain beneath the blood. One hand was broken. The side of his skull had been caved in. Yet his body remained turned, even now, as if he had fallen while shielding someone behind him.

The first would have fit any skald's easy tale.

The second would barely have made the song.

The dark god's regard went first to the raider.

Freyja's went to the defender.

Neither hurried. Neither contended openly. Yet the difference between them rang louder than argument.

Eirik stared.

A thought came to him—not in words at first, only as a deep inner turn.

The world is not ruled by one measure.

He felt then, with sudden clarity, that what he had done on the shore had not vanished into the wind between men. It had landed somewhere beyond mortal judgment. That was why the ravens watched. That was why the unease had not left him. He had chosen in a way that cut across expectation, not only among men like Sten and Bjorn, but perhaps among powers higher still.

His mercy had not gone unseen.

That did not mean it had been approved.

A chill moved through him at that.

He thought of Hrolf.

Of the open throat he had spared.

Of the chance left unfinished.

Would the dark god have called that weakness?

Would Freyja have called it restraint?

Would either have cared for the reasons in his heart, or only for the shape of the deed itself?

Eirik looked from one power to the other and understood less than before, yet more truly.

A man might live his whole life believing the gods wanted one thing from him. Then, if he looked hard enough, he might find that heaven itself held more tension than the sagas admitted.

He became aware then that the waiting warriors nearest him had drawn subtly aside.

Not out of fear. Out of allowance.

Space had opened around him.

No one had told him to step forward, yet the hall seemed to know where he stood.

Eirik stayed where he was.

A line of the newly dead passed between him and the far end of the hall—men from different shores, different deaths, all still wearing the last truth of themselves. One glanced at Eirik as he went by and frowned faintly, as if puzzled to see a man there who still held the warmth of life.

Warmth.

Eirik looked down at his own hands.

They were not as the others' hands were.

He bore no death wound. No opened throat. No crushed helm. No blood frozen black in his beard.

He was present in the hall, but not of it.

That realization should have frightened him. It did not. It only made the unease clearer.

He was not supposed to be here.

And yet no one challenged his presence.

Above the dark god, the ravens shifted.

One spread its wings and settled again.

The sound of the feathers was soft as cloth dragged over bone.

At last, slowly, deliberately, the figure beneath them turned.

Not fully. Only enough.

The hall did not fall silent because it had never truly been noisy. Yet something in it tightened all the same.

Eirik felt the regard before it landed.

When it did, it was like standing bareheaded in winter wind on a high ridge—nothing touching him, yet everything in him known. Not judged all at once. Not condemned. Seen. Measured for what he had been, what he was, and perhaps what he might yet be asked to become.

The one bright-deep eye held him.

No surprise lived there.

That was the strangest part.

Not surprise. Recognition.

As if this looking had begun before the hall, before the ravens, before even the shore at Ash Fjord, and Eirik had only now become aware of it.

He did not lower his gaze.

That would have been disrespect from some men, perhaps. From others, cowardice. Here it felt simply impossible to do anything but stand as he was and endure being known.

Then, before the moment could sharpen further, another attention touched the edge of it.

Freyja had seen him too.

Her regard was not less penetrating, only different. Where Odin's felt like weight laid upon iron to test its true strength, hers felt like the sudden knowing of a wound one had not named aloud. Not pity. Never that. Understanding without softness.

For the first time in the hall, Eirik felt something almost like danger.

Not because either would strike him.

Because they looked at him differently.

The same man.

Two different measures.

Between those two gazes, Eirik understood with a clarity that left no room for comfort that his life had stepped into a place where simple answers would not hold.

He thought of Astrid's voice in the dark.

That depends which god is looking.

A warrior passed before Freyja then, drawing her attention away—an old woman in mail, spear still in hand, death written clear across her ribs and calm upon her face. Freyja took her into her line without hesitation.

Odin's gaze lingered on Eirik one heartbeat longer.

Then he too turned back to the dead.

The hall resumed its vast, ordered motion.

Eirik stood very still.

He had not been summoned.

He had not been spoken to.

He had not been dismissed.

And yet something final had happened in that shared looking.

He did not belong among the dead.

But he had been seen where the dead were chosen.

That knowledge sat in him like cold iron.

Far off in the hall, for just an instant, he thought he saw another figure among the waiting lines—a Norseman broad of shoulder, scar-drawn at the jaw, carrying shame like a second wound. Hrolf, perhaps. Or only the shape of him made from Eirik's own thought. Before he could be certain, the line shifted and the figure was gone.

Not chosen.

Not present.

Or simply not his to see.

The uncertainty bit deeper than certainty might have.

Then the hall began to thin around the edges.

Not vanish. Recede.

The pillars seemed farther apart. The torches dimmer. The smell of iron and winter gave way to peat smoke, banked coals, wool, and the human warmth of a lived-in house. The braziers became red eyes of a hearth. The carved beams above him shrank, lowered, became his own rafters blackened by years of smoke.

He was lying down.

Astrid slept beside him, one hand near her face as before.

The fire had burned lower, not higher. The roof hole showed only a narrow slice of paling night. No sound of warriors. No hall. No gods.

Only the soft winter creak of the house and the distant wash of the fjord.

Eirik did not move at once.

His heart beat steadily. His hands were warm. The furs beneath him were real. Yet every part of him knew he had not merely dreamed as men usually dream.

He lay listening until he heard it.

A soft scrape above.

He turned his head toward the hearth hole.

Three ravens sat along the roof beam beyond it, black against the paling sky.

They were utterly still.

One tilted its head, as if in greeting.

Or judgment.

Or simple notice.

Eirik watched them, and for the first time since Ash Fjord, he knew this much with certainty:

Men might argue what honor demanded.

The gods were still arguing it too.

Chapter Six

The Weight of Honor

Eirik did not move when he woke.

The house was still dark, though not fully. A little gray had begun to gather at the hearth hole above, enough to separate beam from shadow and roof smoke from night. Beside him, Astrid's breathing remained slow and even. Farther off, under their blankets, Leif shifted once and settled. Sigrid made no sound at all.

The ravens were still there.

Three black shapes along the beam beyond the hearth hole, unmoving against the paling sky.

Eirik lay on his back and watched them without blinking. He did not rise. He did not call out. He did not yet trust his own voice.

The dream—or whatever it had been—still sat in him with a weight ordinary sleep never left behind. He could still see the hall if he let himself. The pillars. The warriors. The ordered waiting. The two different lines of judgment. He could still feel the cold attention that had touched him there, one gaze like winter iron, the other like a wound known before it was spoken.

He had spent his life thinking of honor as men spoke of it.

A man upheld it.

Or failed it.

A man stood.

Or broke.

A man met death rightly.

Or did not.

It had seemed clean enough when spoken aloud in halls, near fires, over ale, with blades oiled and laid within reach. Men preferred such things simple. Simplicity made choices easier to praise and easier to condemn.

But what he had seen in that hall had not been simple.

The gods themselves did not seem to weigh men on a single scale.

One chose for strength, for will, for use not yet spent.

The other chose for sacrifice, for what had been given rather than merely taken, for worth that men might overlook because it did not shine loudly enough.

Eirik stared at the ravens and thought: *Then what have I done?*

Not only on the shore with Hrolf.

Deeper than that.

What sort of man had he been building, all these years, beneath habit, duty, battle, marriage, fatherhood? If the gods looked at different truths inside the same death, then perhaps they looked at different truths inside the same life.

The thought left him colder than the dawn.

One of the ravens tilted its head.

That small movement broke the stillness enough that Astrid stirred beside him.

She did not sit up at once. She only shifted onto her back and looked where he was looking. Her hair had loosened in sleep, one pale strand crossing her cheek. She watched the birds a moment, then let her eyes slide back to him.

"You have the look of a man," she murmured, her voice rough with sleep, "who has seen a door and dislikes what waited behind it."

Eirik let out a slow breath.

"That plain on my face?"

"With you, most things are." She glanced once more toward the ravens. "Except when they are not."

He almost smiled, but the feeling did not hold.

Astrid noticed that too. Of course she did.

For a little while neither spoke. The house breathed around them. A coal shifted in the ash and gave a dim red blink. Wind moved softly over the roof and was gone.

At last Eirik said, "I saw where the dead are judged."

Astrid was very still.

She did not ask if he had dreamed it. She did not laugh. She did not tell him dawn thoughts were strange things and best left to daylight. That was one of the reasons he trusted her more than anyone living. She never rushed to make the unknown smaller merely because it was unsettling.

Instead she asked, "And was it what men claim?"

"No."

The answer came too quickly to be mistaken.

He turned his head toward the rafters, though what he truly saw was the hall again.

"They were not feasting," he said. "They were waiting."

Astrid's eyes stayed on him, quiet and unreadable.

"There were lines," he went on. "Not made with rope or walls. Only formed. As if each dead man had already begun to lean toward one place or another before he knew what called him." He swallowed once. "And they were not chosen the same way."

Now Astrid sat up slowly, drawing the blanket around her shoulders. The dim light caught the line of her face, the calm set of her mouth.

"Tell me."

So he did.

Not every carved pillar. Not every face among the dead. Only the things that mattered.

He told her of the hall's strange order. Of the waiting warriors. Of the two presences at the far end. Of the choosing—how one kind of worth was gathered one way, and another elsewhere. Of being seen there himself, though he had no place among the dead.

Astrid listened without interruption, her hands folded loosely in the blanket.

When he finished, the silence between them felt different than before. Not empty. Measured.

"At times," she said at last, "men speak of honor as though they forged it themselves."

Eirik looked toward her.

"But iron remembers the mountain," she went on. "And even a blade may be wanted for different hands."

He frowned faintly. "That sounds wise enough to be irritating."

Astrid's mouth moved, almost a smile. "Then it is likely true."

He turned back toward the hearth hole. The ravens had not moved.

"I thought honor was a road," he said. "Hard, maybe. But a road."

"And now?"

"Now it looks more like a weighing."

Astrid considered that. "That is worse."

"Yes."

"Good."

He looked at her fully then.

She shrugged one shoulder beneath the blanket. "A narrow answer comforts a man only until a wider truth reaches him. Better discomfort than stupidity."

That drew the smallest breath of laughter from him.

It faded quickly.

"The gods do not agree," he said.

Astrid was quiet a moment. "No."

He studied her. She had said it without hesitation.

"You speak as if you knew."

"I suspected." She adjusted the blanket at her shoulder. "The world has never behaved as if one voice ruled all judgments. Men only prefer pretending it does."

Eirik lay with that awhile.

Outside, some early sound reached them from the village. A door bar lifted. Someone coughed. Somewhere farther off, a goat made a thin complaining cry. Morning was coming whether men welcomed it or not.

"I spared Hrolf," Eirik said, more to the dim roof than to Astrid herself. "Not because I feared the last stroke. Not because I wanted praise for mercy. I simply…" He stopped and searched for the truest shape of it. "I did not want to kill a beaten Norseman with no fight left in him."

Astrid's gaze stayed steady. "I know."

"But what if one god calls that restraint, and another calls it waste?"

"Then you have displeased at least one power worth displeasing."

He huffed a quiet breath through his nose. "You make it sound simple."

"No," she said. "I make it sound survivable."

That stayed with him.

The ravens shifted at last. Not flying, only resettling on the beam, black claws scraping wood softly enough that the sound felt louder than it was.

Eirik watched them and said, "It was not only the dead being judged."

Astrid did not answer at once.

Then, softly: "No."

He turned toward her. "They looked at me."

"Yes."

The word rested there as though it had been waiting since he woke.

Eirik pushed himself up onto one elbow despite the heaviness in his chest. "You knew that too?"

"I did not know." Astrid drew one knee up beneath the blanket and rested an arm over it. "But a man is rarely stared at by ravens for his beauty."

"That is cruel."

"It is accurate." Her eyes flicked once toward the hearth hole. "If the gods are watching, I doubt they were there for the fire."

Eirik almost smiled again. This time it held a moment longer.

Then he sat fully up and swung his legs over the side of the bed furs.

The floor was cold beneath his feet.

He rested his forearms on his knees and stared into the ash-cradled hearth. Sleep had left him, but not heavily. More as if some deeper waking had taken its place.

Behind him, Astrid shifted closer. He felt her hand rest lightly between his shoulders.

Not urging. Not questioning. Only there.

"Tell me true," she said. "What troubles you most?"

Eirik thought before answering.

Not the ravens.

Not even the hall.

What troubled him most was simpler and therefore harder to escape.

"I do not know whether the thing I did on the shore was wisdom or pride."

Astrid's hand remained still.

He went on, his voice low so as not to wake the children. "I told Sten I would not butcher a beaten man like a dog in surf. I believed that when I said it. I still do. Yet part of me wonders whether I spared Hrolf because I wanted to remain a certain kind of man in my own eyes." He looked down at his scarred hands. "That is not the same as being right."

The words, once spoken, left a quiet ache behind them.

Astrid's fingers moved once against his back, a grounding touch.

"A man who never questions his own virtue is already halfway rotten," she said.

"That is not comfort."

"No." Her tone stayed dry and calm. "Comfort is often lazy."

He let out another small breath that might have been a laugh.

Then he grew serious again. "Sten weighed the danger. I weighed the man before me. The gods…" He shook his head once. "The gods weighed something else entirely."

"Perhaps." Astrid's hand left his back. "Or perhaps they weighed the same thing and valued different parts."

That landed more sharply than he expected.

He turned it over in silence.

Different parts.

Strength, purpose, sacrifice, protection, future use, hidden worth. All of it within one life. All of it possible within one death.

If that was true, then honor was not only the loud courage men boasted of. It was also the quieter choices that left no song behind, the ones made in a heartbeat with no witness but one's own conscience—and perhaps, it now seemed, a few patient gods.

Leif mumbled in his sleep then and rolled onto his back, one blanket half kicked away. Sigrid, without waking fully, reached across the furs between them and dragged the edge of it back over him.

Eirik watched.

Even half asleep, she was correcting his carelessness.

He felt something loosen in him at the sight.

There it was again—that other kind of worth. Not glorious. Not sung. Yet no less real for it.

He looked back toward Astrid. She had seen it too.

"The gods would disagree about children as well, I expect," she said.

He gave her a sideways look. "How?"

"One would admire Leif for running headfirst into whatever future wished to hit him." Her mouth curved faintly. "The other would notice that Sigrid keeps him from dying of enthusiasm."

This time he did smile, properly.

It faded into reflection rather than disappearing.

When dawn grew strong enough to gray the whole room, Eirik rose and crossed to the doorway. He lifted the latch carefully so as not to wake the others and stepped outside.

The air struck cold and clean against his face.

The village was only beginning to stir. Smoke rose in pale lines from a handful of houses. Frost silvered the yard fence and the edges of the woodpile. Down by the fjord, the water lay dark and quiet, not yet broken by work boats or voices. The world looked ordinary in the way only early morning can make it look.

Yet nothing felt ordinary to him.

He stood in the yard with his hands loose at his sides and looked up.

The ravens had left the beam above the hearth hole.

For a moment he thought they were gone.

Then he saw them on the roof ridge instead, three black shapes in a row, silent and still, facing him.

Not scavengers this morning.

Witnesses.

Eirik held their gaze.

He thought of Odin's cold selection. Of Freyja's different, no less deliberate choosing. Of Sten's anger, earned and human. Of Hrolf kneeling on the shore with blood in his beard. Of the road left unfinished. Of the weight of deciding where a man stops his hand and where he does not.

He could no longer pretend the matter belonged only to mortal judgment.

Whatever his mercy had been—wisdom, pride, restraint, folly, some knot of all four—it had been seen beyond the sight of men.

And the seeing was not done.

Behind him, he heard the door open. Astrid came out wrapped in her cloak, her hair still loose from sleep. She stepped beside him and followed his gaze to the roof ridge.

"They're stubborn," she said.

"So am I."

"Yes." Her tone was mild. "That is why I mentioned it."

For a while they stood together in the morning cold.

Then Eirik said, "I thought what I saw would answer something."

Astrid looked up at the ravens. "Did it?"

"No." He watched the birds. "It made the question larger."

"That is often the more honest gift."

He turned her words over and found, to his own irritation, that he believed them.

The village began to wake in earnest around them now—doors opening, footsteps in frost, the first call from the lower sheds, a dog shaking itself awake. Life pressed forward because it always did. Yet above them the ravens remained, black and unblinking on the roof ridge, watching the yard as if they had chosen it for their perch and would not easily be moved.

Eirik stood in the cold a moment longer.

Then he said quietly, "Bring the mead."

Astrid looked at him.

Not with surprise. Only with the stillness of someone who understood at once that a thing had shifted from thought into action.

"Ale?" she asked, though her voice already carried the answer.

Eirik kept his eyes on the ravens. "Ale is not enough for Odin."

The words were plain. He did not dress them. He had no wish to sound greater than himself before gods who would know his measure regardless.

Astrid nodded once and turned back toward the house.

Behind them, a door opened farther down the lane. Someone called for kindling. The village was waking into another ordinary morning, but the space around Eirik no longer felt ordinary. The cold seemed sharper. The silence between sounds deeper.

Leif came into the yard still half wrapped in his blanket, hair wild from sleep. He stopped when he saw his father standing still beneath the ravens and his mother already moving with purpose back inside.

"What is it?" he asked.

Sigrid followed him more quietly, fastening her cloak at the throat. She looked from Eirik to the roof ridge and said nothing.

Eirik turned toward them. "We make an offering."

Leif straightened at once, excitement rising before he remembered to hold it. "To Odin?"

"Yes."

The boy's face sharpened with curiosity and something close to pride, though he kept still. That in itself told Eirik he understood the weight of it more than he might once have.

Sigrid's eyes lifted to the ravens. "Because of them?"

Eirik looked at her. "Because of what has been seen."

She took that in without asking further.

Astrid came out carrying the mead jug wrapped in cloth against the morning chill. It was the better drink, saved carefully, not taken up lightly. The sight of it in her hands changed the air of the yard more surely than any spoken prayer could have done.

She stopped near Eirik and held it out.

He took it with both hands.

For a breath, no one moved.

Then Eirik said, "Fetch the goat."

Leif blinked once, his excitement fading into seriousness. Sigrid lowered her gaze slightly, as if the words themselves required space.

Astrid did not question it. "From the pen behind the longhouse?"

Eirik nodded.

That was answer enough.

The four of them went together around the back path where the frost lay thicker in the shadow of the wall. Their boots pressed dark marks into the whitening grass. The village sounds seemed farther there—muffled by turf, fence, and the low morning air. A few hens scratched beneath the woodpile. From the lower yards came the soft complaint of cattle and the creak of a gate being opened.

The goat pen stood behind the store shed, rough-posted and rimmed with old straw gone stiff in the cold. The animals stirred when they approached, stamping lightly, breath steaming. One turned its head toward them with pale eyes and went still.

Leif started forward first, then checked himself and looked to Eirik.

“Which one?” he asked.

Eirik studied the small herd, then pointed. “That one.”

It was a broad-shouldered brown buck with a white mark down the bridge of its nose. Healthy. Strong. Not the easiest one to lose.

Leif nodded and climbed into the pen, slower than usual now.

Sigrid moved to the gate before he asked, lifting the latch and holding it ready. When the buck tried to turn away, Leif reached too fast and nearly lost the collar rope.

“The rope first,” Sigrid said.

Leif caught it properly the second time. He did not answer her, but his jaw tightened in that familiar way.

Even here, even now, the old shape of them remained. Chaos and correction. Movement and measure. Eirik felt a strange quiet gratitude for that.

They led the buck back toward the house.

Smoke from the hearth drifted low through the yard. The ravens had not left the roof ridge. Firelight flickered faintly from inside through the half-open door. The warmth of the house met the cold morning at the threshold and held there, neither yielding.

Astrid went in first and stirred the hearth up from its coals into a steadier flame. Dry kindling caught. Thin fire licked upward through the older wood, and soon the room held that living light that made every carved beam and wool blanket seem more real. Sacred fire was still fire. It warmed, cooked, dried, protected. That was part of its holiness.

Eirik brought the mead inside and set it near the hearth.

Leif and Sigrid led the buck as far as the packed earth near the doorway. The animal resisted the change in light and smell, then settled with one rough pull on the rope. Its breath smoked. Its hooves knocked once against the threshold wood.

No one raised a voice.

No one hurried.

The seriousness of the thing lived in the silence, in the way each person moved as though stepping into something already old.

Astrid fetched a bowl and a cloth without being told. Sigrid took the rope from Leif and held it nearer the horn base, firm and calm. Leif stood close enough to help if asked, but no longer pushed himself forward merely because he wished to be useful.

The fire brightened.

Its light struck Eirik's face and hands, turning the mead in the jug neck to dark gold. Outside, the yard remained pale with frost, and above that cold stillness the ravens watched from the ridge without a sound.

Eirik rested one hand briefly against the goat's neck.

Then he looked once toward the hearth, once toward the roof hole, and once toward the birds beyond it.

"Let this be given properly."

That was all.

No grand speech followed. No pleading. No boast.

Only the plain acknowledgment that he had been seen, and that seeing deserved an answer.

Astrid lifted the bowl into place. Leif held his breath without meaning to. Sigrid's grip stayed steady on the rope.

The fire cracked softly behind them.

When the offering was done, Eirik poured the first mead into a smaller cup and tipped it carefully into the flames. The fire caught it with a low hiss and a brief bright leap, sweet smoke rising into the dim air above the hearth.

Then the house fell still again.

The goat lay quiet.

The mead shone in the cup.

The fire burned warm against the cold.

And on the roof above, the three ravens remained black and motionless, as if the gods had accepted the courtesy of being answered.

Chapter Seven

The Thunderer's Truth

The smell of mead lingered in the house long after the fire had swallowed its share.

It clung to the warmth near the hearth and to the rough wood of the cup still standing near the ash. Under it lay the darker smells of goat blood, smoke, damp wool, and the faint clean bite of frost that had come in through the opened door and not yet fully left. Morning had widened by then. Pale light entered through the roof hole and the door seam, flattening the corners of the room and making everything look both ordinary and newly exposed.

Eirik stood near the hearth with his hands loose at his sides and looked at the place where the offering had been made.

The house had settled again. That was the strange part.

Astrid had cleaned the blade. Sigrid had scrubbed the threshold. Leif had carried the carcass where he was told and done so with more care than usual, no boyish boasting in him at all. The fire still burned. The walls still held. The day had not stopped for what had happened in the half-light of morning.

Yet nothing in Eirik felt settled.

He did not doubt the offering. That had been necessary. Not because he believed the gods could be bribed like small men with wounded pride, but because being watched required an answer. A man did not ignore a gaze from beyond the world and call that strength.

Still, Odin's ravens had remained what they were—witnesses, not comfort.

Leif sat on the bench nearest the wall, whittling a stick too quickly until the knife slipped and bit deeper than he intended.

Sigrid looked up at once. "Too fast."

"I know."

"You always say that after."

"That is when it becomes useful."

Sigrid folded the cloth in her lap with patient care. "No. That is when it becomes true."

Leif frowned at the stick, then deliberately slowed his hand. He did not argue further. That, more than any words, told Eirik the morning still weighed on him.

Astrid came from the storage chest with a fresh strip of wool in one hand and set it beside Sigrid. Her eyes went first to Leif's knife, then to Eirik, then to the hearth.

No word passed between them.

She understood he was not yet finished with what the morning had begun.

"Take the smaller axe and split the birch stack," she said to Leif.

The boy looked up. "All of it?"

"What I said was not hidden."

Leif nodded and rose, eager for labor because labor gave the hands somewhere to put thought. He took the axe from its peg.

"I'll do the kindling too," he said.

"You'll do the birch stack first," Sigrid answered before Astrid could.

Leif gave her a look. "I know the order of wood."

"That would be more convincing if you hadn't once stacked the wet wood by the driest wall."

"That was one time."

"It was a memorable time."

Leif snorted, but some of the tension left his shoulders as he went out.

Sigrid watched him through the half-open door until he crossed the yard safely, then lowered her eyes to the wool again.

Astrid saw that too. She always saw that too.

Eirik stepped outside not long after, drawn less by intention than by the need for air that had not passed through blood, mead, and fire.

The day had sharpened into cold brightness. Frost still silvered the north side of the fence posts, though the sun had begun to bite it away from the open yard. Down by the fjord, the water lay dark and broad beneath a sky washed nearly white. The longboats rested high on the shore, their hulls scarred and honest in the light. Smoke rose from other houses in pale lines. The village had resumed itself, but carefully, as a man favors an arm after an old break.

Leif was at the woodpile with the smaller axe, breathing in visible bursts, jaw tight with effort. He struck hard—too hard on the first swing, burying the blade and nearly losing his balance. He caught himself, glanced toward the house to see whether anyone had noticed, then reset his feet and tried again with more care.

Eirik watched him a moment.

He could see the boy trying to work something out through muscle and repetition. Fear. Pride. Shame. The strange new knowledge of blood. Labor would not solve it. But it would keep it from souring into helplessness too soon.

Near the doorway, Sigrid sat on the low step with the wool in her lap, not spinning yet, only sorting, her fingers choosing one strand from another. Her eyes moved between Leif, the lane, and the roof ridge where the ravens had been.

They were gone now.

That, somehow, unsettled Eirik more than if they had stayed.

Arn came through the side path as if he had been blown there by weather rather than choice. He carried no shield, of course, only the twin bearded axes at his hips and a split rail over one shoulder as though it weighed no more than a staff. He saw Eirik in the yard and grinned.

“I heard you fed Odin better than the rest of us breakfast.”

Eirik leaned one shoulder against the fence post. “You hear too much.”

“No. I hear exactly enough and invent the rest where needed.” Arn let the rail drop beside the goat pen and tipped his head toward the house. “How heavy is the mood in there?”

“Heavy enough that even you would improve it by leaving.”

“That is grave indeed.”

Eirik smiled faintly.

Arn saw it and narrowed one eye. “There. That means something’s wrong. Men don’t smile at my wisdom unless the gods have touched them or the head wound is worse than it looks.”

“I have no head wound.”

“Not one others can see.”

Arn reached for one axe, checked the edge with his thumb, then glanced toward the fields beyond the village. “Come help me with the north fence after midday. The wind dropped a section and Hrolf’s goats have more ambition than sense.”

At the name, brief and accidental, something tightened in the yard. Leif’s axe paused in mid-lift. Sigrid’s gaze flicked up sharply. Arn noticed it a heartbeat too late and made a face at himself.

“I should choose my dead men more carefully,” he muttered.

Astrid appeared in the doorway then with a bowl in her hands. “It would be a good first habit.”

Arn straightened as if her words had struck him with an unseen rod. “I came to offer labor, not insight.”

“That is safer,” Astrid said.

Arn bowed his head in mock submission, though he looked relieved to have the sting turned aside without ceremony. "Midday, then," he said to Eirik. "If Thor wishes the fence upright, he may as well use men already here."

There was something in the way he said *Thor* that made Eirik look at him more closely.

Arn caught the look and shrugged one shoulder. "Someone has to keep the world standing while Odin goes about thinking too much."

Astrid's mouth moved faintly. "Blasphemy before breakfast."

Arn grinned. "Not blasphemy. Division of labor."

He went off before more could be said, calling some nonsense to Leif about keeping all ten toes if he meant to impress girls before spring. Leif shouted back automatically, though the color rose in his face.

By midday the sky had changed.

Not darkened, exactly. Thickened.

Cloud came in from the west in a long gray mass that rolled over the hills and lowered itself across the fjord. Wind followed after, cold and steady, flattening the smoke trails and setting the bare branches of the birch grove to whispering. Men glanced up from their work. Women gathered what could not be left to weather. Hens were called into sheds. The world shifted from clear winter morning toward something larger and rougher.

Eirik went with Arn to the north fence line above the store plots where the ground broke open toward the pasture. The section that had fallen lay half twisted in frozen mud, one post snapped low and the rails kicked loose by the weather. Beyond it, the winter field stretched hard and pale, the stubble of the last cut crop flattened under frost.

Arn set his rail down and spat into his palms.

"There," he said. "A battle worth winning. Wood against wind. Thor loves this sort of thing."

Eirik took hold of the broken post and dragged it clear. "You speak for him often."

"Only because he's sensible enough to agree with me." Arn wedged one foot against the fallen rails and tugged them free. "Besides, men speak of Thor like he wakes every morning hungry to split giants and crack skulls. But winter would eat us quicker than most giants, and he still bothers to hold the sky in place."

Eirik worked in silence a while, setting the new post, tamping hard earth and stone around it with the back of the maul.

The wind strengthened. It came over the field in visible shivers through the dead grass, then struck them full in the face with the smell of cold earth and water.

Arn glanced up at the darkening west. "There. He's close."

Eirik did not ask whether he meant storm or god. With Arn, there was often little use in separating them too quickly.

They worked until their hands were numb and their shoulders warm beneath wool and fur. Practical labor steadied Eirik more than thought did. Lift. Set. Brace. Strike. The body understood such things honestly. Yet under the labor, the morning remained with him—Odin's ravens, the offering, the hall beyond sleep, the weight of being seen.

By the time the broken section stood upright again, the first low growl of thunder rolled across the fjord.

It was too early in the season for such a sound.

Both men stopped.

The thunder was not loud. That made it worse. It came deep, as if from beneath the hills rather than above them.

Arn broke into a grin too quick and too reverent to be mockery. “Now that,” he said softly, “is a man arriving without asking whether the door is open.”

Eirik straightened slowly.

The sky over the western hills had grown heavy and dark, but not with common winter storm. The cloud there seemed layered, alive with pressure. Wind flattened the fur at his collar and moved through the field in long bent lines. Somewhere behind them a gate banged once, twice, and then held.

Another roll of thunder crossed the land.

This time Eirik felt it under his boots.

Arn stepped back from the fence and lifted his chin, as though listening to words not meant for all ears.

“You feel that?” he asked.

“Yes.”

“Good,” Arn said, and the grin had gone from him. “Then he did not come only for me.”

The world shifted.

Not with light. Not with blindness or dream.

With presence.

One moment the field was field, wind, dark cloud, broken fence mended by labor. The next it was all those things still, but greater somehow, filled past its mortal edges by a force that made every simple object seem newly significant. The post in Eirik’s hand felt heavier. The cold earth beneath his boots felt deeper. The air smelled suddenly of rain on stone, iron, churned soil, and oak split fresh.

A figure stood beyond the fence line where no man had been an instant before.

He was broad enough to make Arn seem merely lean. Red-bearded, though not in the ringed careful way of Sten. This beard was rougher, fuller, lit at the edges by the strange gray light. His shoulders filled the air beneath a heavy cloak the color of storm cloud, and his hands looked made more for hammer haft and plow beam than for courtly gesture. There was no softness in him. Yet neither was there the cold distance Eirik had felt in Odin.

This presence was immediate. Weight on the land. Strength in the weather. A force that could break, yes—but built first to hold.

The figure looked at the fence.

Then at the field.

Then at Eirik.

No hall. No waiting lines. No ordered distance.

Thor, Eirik thought, and the thought did not feel borrowed from any skald.

Arn had gone utterly still. For perhaps the first time in his life, no quick remark came to him.

The god stepped to the broken section they had just raised, gripped the top rail once, and shoved it with casual force.

The whole fence held.

Thor grunted.

It was approval of a kind.

Then he looked at Eirik and said, in a voice that sounded like oak splitting in winter, "You thought war was the heavy work."

It was not a question.

Eirik felt the wind press through him and somehow managed not to step back. "Much of it is."

Thor's mouth shifted beneath the beard. Not quite a smile. "Much of it is noise."

Arn let out a breath through his nose. "There. I've been saying that for years. No one listens when I say it."

Thor ignored him.

He looked out across the field toward the village below. Smoke bent under the wind. Roofs held. Men and women moved between house and shed, gathering, storing, carrying, mending.

"That," Thor said, "is the heavy work."

Eirik followed his gaze.

From here the village looked smaller than it ever did from inside it. A cluster of turf roofs and smoke. Fences, sheds, paths, pens, shore. Children somewhere below. Women with bundles under one arm. Men hauling what weather might ruin if left. No song. No boasting. Only the plain labor of staying alive.

Thunder sounded again, farther off.

Thor rested one huge hand on the fence post they had just set. The wood creaked under the weight and did not give.

"Any fool can break," he said. "Winter breaks. Sea breaks. Hunger breaks. Raiders break. Fire breaks." His eyes came back to Eirik, blue-gray and steady as stormwater under ice. "The question is who still stands when the breaking is done."

The words struck deeper than their plainness suggested.

He had expected, perhaps without knowing it, a god of battle to speak first of courage, enemies, the strike of hammer and the joy of contest. But Thor's voice held none of that hunger. Strength, yes. Great strength. But yoked to use, not glory.

"To fight is not hard," Thor went on. "Not for men built for it. Hard is what comes after. Hard is what must still be roofed, planted, fed, guarded." He nodded once toward the village. "Hard is keeping them through the winter."

Arn made a quiet sound then, almost relief. It might have been the first prayer he had ever spoken without swagger.

Eirik said, "Men praise the kill more easily."

"Men are often stupid," Thor replied.

Arn closed his eyes briefly as if in gratitude.

Despite himself, Eirik felt the edge of a smile.

Thor saw it and gave him a look that was almost human in its blunt amusement. "There. You've enough wit for honesty. Use it."

The wind rose, flattening the dead grass and snapping Arn's cloak against his legs. The cloud bank above the fjord rolled dark and heavy, yet no rain fell.

Eirik thought of Odin's hall. Of lines of warriors chosen for different ends. Of Freyja's grave regard. Of the way divine things had seemed layered and uncertain there.

This was not uncertain.

Not simple, no. But plain.

"What do you value?" he asked before caution could stop him.

Arn flicked him a sidelong look that said the question was either brave or stupid, and perhaps both.

Thor did not take offense.

“Weight that can be carried,” he said. “Hands that do not drop what depends on them. Men who strike when striking is needed and build when building is needed.” He looked again at the fence, then at Eirik’s hands. “Not all strength is for killing.”

The field seemed to grow quieter around them.

Eirik heard, somewhere far below, the faint bark of a dog and the answering cry of a woman calling two children home from the lane. The ordinary sounds of a settlement. They did not diminish the moment. They deepened it.

He watched Leif in his mind not as an idea, but as he had stood that morning, jaw tight over the birch stack, trying to work fear out through labor and bad swings. That image came before all the rest and held.

He looked back at Thor.

“I was taught battle is what keeps a people alive.”

Thor’s brows drew slightly, as if the statement were incomplete rather than false.

“Battle keeps wolves from the door,” he said. “It does not fill the grain bins.”

The words landed with the weight of stone.

A man could fight a hundred fights and still lose his household to one bitter winter, one failed harvest, one sickness left untended, one roof left weak when the snows came. Eirik had known all of that in the way men know truths they live beside. Yet hearing it spoken from such a mouth changed the shape of it.

Strength was not less holy when bent to simple use.

It was more necessary.

Thor turned then and looked directly at Arn.

"You." The god's voice carried no ridicule, yet Arn straightened as if struck. "Tell him what men forget."

Arn swallowed once. For perhaps the first time since Eirik had known him, he looked like a boy caught before his elders.

"They forget," Arn said slowly, "that thunder comes before rain."

Thor's beard shifted as the almost-smile returned.

"They forget," Arn went on, gaining a little ground under his own feet, "that a strong arm is wasted if it guards nothing. That a hammer is not only for skulls. That if the fields fail, no one reaches old age to tell brave lies."

Thor grunted again.

Approval.

Arn let out the breath he had been holding and looked half ready to laugh from sheer relief.

Eirik saw then why Arn had always spoken of Thor with a devotion different from mere battle lust. Arn loved force, yes, and speed, and the clean rightness of axes in motion. But beneath that, he revered the god who did not pretend strength existed only for songs.

The first spatter of rain struck the hard ground at last. Then another. Not much. Only enough to darken the dust and lift the scent of earth.

Thor rested his hand once more on the fence rail they had repaired.

"Storm breaks," he said. "Storm also feeds."

Then he looked at Eirik, and for a moment the whole field seemed to narrow to that gaze alone.

"You are not being weighed only for what you can kill."

This time the truth of it settled more slowly, and deeper.

Odin's ravens. Freyja's silence. Sten's challenge. Hrolf's spared life. The blood at his own hearth. The blót. All of it shifted under that one plain truth.

Not excused.

Not solved.

But widened.

Eirik had felt himself caught between human honor and divine judgment. Now he saw another line beneath both: purpose. Not glory, not merely restraint, but what a man's strength was for.

He opened his mouth to answer, but thunder cracked overhead so near that the whole field jumped under it.

When his sight cleared from the flash, Thor was farther away.

Not vanished entirely. Only already becoming storm, weather, pressure, presence less bound to one shape than Eirik had first believed. The cloak moved like low cloud. The red of the beard became a streak in gray light. Then even that was only rain, dark sky, and the feeling of a great force withdrawing along the ridge of the world.

The fence stood straight.

The field bent under wind and then lifted again.

Arn exhaled hard. "Well."

"That is all you have?" Eirik asked.

Arn wiped rain from his face. "No. I have many better words. None of them seem worth using now."

That, from Arn, was nearly reverence in itself.

They stood in the rain a little longer, neither eager to be first to speak as an ordinary man again.

At last Arn said, quieter, "I told you he wasn't all skulls and thunder."

"You mostly said he liked your axes."

"He does like my axes."

Eirik gave him a look.

Arn spread both hands. "I choose to hear no contradiction in what just happened."

That loosened something in Eirik, enough for a low laugh.

The sound felt right in his chest.

They went back toward the village under the growing rain. Not hurriedly. Men still had work in weather. If anything, more of it. A woman near the lower path was wrestling blankets off a line before they soaked through. Two boys ran laughing under a cart until some mother shouted them home. Leif had abandoned the woodpile and was dragging a grain sack away from the open lane with more effort than grace. Sigrid, of course, had already thought to prop the shed door against the gusting wind with a stone.

Eirik slowed as he saw them.

Thor's words remained in him not like mystery, but like something struck true in iron and left ringing.

Battle keeps wolves from the door. It does not fill the grain bins.

Leif saw him coming and straightened, hair wet against his forehead. "The rain came too fast."

"Yes," Eirik said.

"I was moving the sack."

"I can see that."

Leif glanced down at the mud on his boots, then back up. "I thought it would stay clear longer."

Sigrid came from the shed with her cloak already darkened by rain. "You always think that when the clouds are thick."

Leif frowned. "Not always."

"Often enough that I no longer count it as surprise."

Eirik looked at them both and, for the first time since dawn, the sight of their ordinary labor did not feel small compared to what he had seen. It felt bound to it.

He stepped forward, took the heavier end of the grain sack from Leif without ceremony, and nodded toward the house. "Move."

Leif obeyed at once, grabbing the other end. Sigrid ran ahead to clear the threshold and kick the door wider before they reached it.

Inside, Astrid had already shifted the drying wood farther from the draft and laid cloth over the open basket of meal. She looked once at Eirik, once at Arn behind him, and whatever she saw in their faces made her set down the bowl in her hands more carefully than before.

"Well," she said.

Arn spread his arms slightly, soaked and grinning and still somehow reverent beneath it. "The fence stands. The sky objected. Thor gave instruction. Eirik became even harder to live with."

Astrid nodded. "So a useful afternoon, then."

Arn laughed and shook rain from his hair like a dog. "I'll leave before you make me earn supper."

He did, though not before stealing a strip of dried fish from the peg line and claiming Thor would approve of strength maintained by theft among friends.

When he was gone, the house settled into the warm close hush of rain against turf and wood. Leif went back out to stack the rescued birch under cover. Sigrid sorted the damp wool from the dry with her usual exactness. Astrid hung Eirik's wet cloak near the hearth and gave him a long look without speaking.

He knew that look.

He said, "I saw Thor."

Astrid did not start. She only tilted her head slightly. "And was he disappointed in the fence?"

"No."

"That is kind of him."

Eirik's mouth moved faintly. Then he grew serious. "He said battle keeps wolves from the door. It does not fill the grain bins."

Astrid's gaze sharpened, not in surprise, but recognition.

"Yes," she said softly.

He looked toward the children—Leif in the yard beyond the open door, straining with wet wood; Sigrid inside, sorting, storing, preserving what could still be preserved.

A father.

A mother.

A son.

A daughter.

A house against weather.

Food against winter.

Work against loss.

All of it was under protection greater than walls and smaller than songs.

He had thought the gods looked mostly toward battle because battle was where men shouted loudest of them. But perhaps that had been mortal vanity more than divine truth.

Thor guarded storm and field, roof and road, labor and survival. Not because such things were lesser than war.

Because they were what war was supposed to serve.

Eirik stood in the hearth warmth and let that settle into him.

Not enlightenment. Not peace.

Something sturdier.

A new measure.

When evening came and the rain finally eased, he stepped out once more into the yard. The field beyond the village lay dark and fed. The repaired north fence stood straight against the dim light. Smoke rose from the roof vents in calm gray lines. Inside his own house, he could hear Leif talking too quickly about some future he wanted to run toward and Sigrid cutting across him with precise doubt. Astrid's lower voice moved beneath them both like a steady hand under rough timber.

Eirik looked over the village and understood, not fully but enough, that strength was holy not only when it struck.

It was holy when it held.

And as the last thunder rolled far off beyond the fjord, fading into the night, Thor's blunt truth remained with him like the weight of a good hammer in the hand—plain, useful, and made for more than one kind of work.

Chapter Eight
The Mother Revealed

The days after the rain settled into a quieter rhythm.

Not peace exactly. Peace was too clean a word for what the village lived with now. Men still looked twice toward the hills when dogs barked in the wrong direction. Women still barred their doors with more care after sunset. The burned places had been mended, but not forgotten. A fence rail replaced did not mean the hand that broke it vanished from memory.

Still, life had returned to its work.

Wood had to be split. Nets had to be checked. A roof patch over Bjorn's shed had to be tied down before the next hard weather came. The goats needed watching because goats always needed watching, and because one creature in the world was never enough trouble by itself if it could find a second to join it.

The morning was pale and cold, the sky a hard white over the fjord. Thin frost clung where the sun had not yet reached. Smoke rose slowly from the houses, and the shore below gave back the dull knock of wood against wood where the boats rested at their moorings.

Eirik Halvardsson stood in the yard with a length of rope in his hand, repairing the strap on a grain sled that had frayed near one corner. He worked with his head bent and his thoughts turned inward, though not so deeply that he failed to hear the world around him.

Leif was near the chopping block with a practice sword in hand, moving through the same sequence of cuts Eirik had shown him the day before. The boy was still too quick on the turn and too eager in the shoulders, but he had begun, at last, to understand that speed without balance was only a better way to fall.

Again and again he stepped, cut, reset.

This time, after the third strike, he held his footing.

Sigrid sat on the low step by the doorway with a basket of mending in her lap. She looked up from her stitching and said, "That one was less foolish."

Leif lowered the sword and frowned. "You could have just said it was good."

"I could have," she said. "But this is more accurate."

Leif opened his mouth, shut it, then nodded once. "It was better than before."

"Yes."

He looked toward Eirik. "Father?"

Eirik glanced up. "Your left foot stayed honest."

Leif tried not to smile too broadly and failed at once. "I told you."

"You told the air," Sigrid said. "It was not arguing."

Leif pointed the practice sword toward her in outrage.

She did not even blink. "You are doing it again."

He lowered it at once.

Astrid came from the house carrying a bucket of rinse water, one shoulder set against the weight of it. The morning light caught in the pale strands that had slipped loose from her braid. She looked from Leif's stance to the sword tip lowering and then to Sigrid's expression.

"I see the lesson is thriving," she said.

"It was," Leif muttered, "until she began helping."

Sigrid threaded her needle through the wool strip in her lap. "You say that as if my help was the injury."

"It usually is."

Astrid set the bucket down by the door. "That is because truth bruises more cleanly than wood."

Even Eirik smiled at that.

He worked the rope through the sled ring and pulled it taut. His hands knew the motion better than his mind needed to. That had become more common since the blót and the storm and the field where Thor had stood like weather taking shape. His body still went where the day asked of it, but some deeper part of him remained elsewhere half the time, turning over what he had seen and heard and not yet fully made peace with.

Odin had shown him that honor was not simple.

Thor had shown him that strength was not only for killing.

And between those truths something in Eirik's old understanding had broken open.

He was not sorry for it.

But neither was he comfortable.

That, he thought, was often how truth arrived.

By midday the work had scattered them in small directions.

Leif was sent with two sacks of kindling to Sten's hall and told not to race the path or trip over his own ambition. Sigrid went with Astrid to check the herb drying near the southern wall and to speak with old Runa about winter stores. Eirik stayed behind a little longer to mend the sled and stack the split birch under the awning before the sky changed again.

The village lay quiet in the thin light, busy without noise. Somewhere down near the shore, Arn was laughing too loud at something only half worth hearing. Hakon's dog barked once and was silent. A gull wheeled across the fjord and vanished into the white.

When the rope was tied and the sled set right, Eirik did not rise at once.

His hands remained on the wood.

The strap he had repaired was plain enough—rope through ring, knot cinched hard, weight made bearable by being distributed where it must be. It would hold because he had made it hold. No one would sing of it. No one would name the morning by the mending of one sled corner.

Yet grain would ride on it.

Winter would lean on it.

A household might pass through one harder week because a small thing had been repaired before it failed.

The thought did not come grandly. It came in the plain way truth often did when a man's hands were occupied honestly.

He thought then of Astrid counting stores without complaint. Of Sigrid mending what others wore through. Of Leif, still clumsy with force, trying to grow into strength without yet knowing what it was for. Of the dead whose names would never enter a skald's mouth though their labor had carried whole winters on its back.

The yard around him had grown very still.

Not empty. Not silent. Still in the way a room sometimes grows still when someone enters whose presence all others feel before they understand it.

Eirik lifted his head.

The little sounds had not vanished. They had only drawn farther off. The creak of the gate. The far-off laughter near the shore. The scrape of his own boot against frozen earth. All of it remained, but less near than before.

He looked toward the house.

Nothing moved.

He looked toward the ridge beyond the village.

Nothing there either.

And yet he knew, with the same quiet certainty that had come to him on darker days, that he was not alone.

Eirik set the coil of spare rope down on the sled rail.

He did not reach for his knife.

He had begun to learn the difference between danger and presence.

The world did not open this time. No hall, no storm, no force pressing itself into shape. Instead it was as if the edges of things grew clearer and softer at once, the way the world sometimes looked after a snowfall when all harshness had been covered but not erased.

The air smelled faintly of clean wool, fire ash, and something older than either—something like cold linen folded away for a long winter and then brought into light again.

When he turned, she was standing near the fence.

He had not seen her arrive.

That unsettled him more than any thunderclap would have done.

She was not dressed like some skald's painted dream of a goddess. No great blaze of jewels. No impossible armor. No crown fit for songs. She wore a long gray-blue mantle that fell in still lines, and beneath it a dress the color of winter sky where it pales just above the snow. Her hair was bound back, though not tightly, and the light seemed to rest on it rather than strike it. Her face was not young and not old. Beautiful, yes, but the beauty of her was not what held him.

It was the sense that she saw everything at once.

Not only him.

Not only the yard.

Everything that had led here and might yet follow.

Her presence did not crowd the world.

It deepened it.

Eirik stood very still.

He knew her.

Not because he had seen her before in any clear way, but because something in him recognized the shape of that quiet. This was not Odin's weighing gaze or Thor's plain force. This was a stillness with no weakness in it. A stillness vast enough to hold grief, patience, memory, and all the threads men thought themselves too simple to notice.

Frigg.

He bowed his head then, not from fear, but because anything else would have felt small and foolish.

When he lifted his eyes again, she had not moved.

For a while neither spoke.

The wind touched the fence once and went on.

At last she said, "You expected answers to grow easier."

Her voice was low and even, with no strain in it at all. It did not echo, yet it seemed to settle into the yard more completely than mortal speech.

Eirik answered honestly. "I had hoped they might."

"And are you disappointed?"

He considered that before speaking. "No."

Her gaze stayed on him, waiting.

He let out a slow breath. "Only less certain."

"That is often the wiser beginning."

He almost smiled at that, though the weight of her presence kept the humor quiet in him.

She looked past him then, toward the house, toward the half-open door where warmth lay just beyond sight. Her eyes moved over the woodpile, the sled, the fence line, the hanging fish strips near the wall. Nothing in her expression changed, yet Eirik felt as though each humble thing had been seen and kept.

"You have been taught," she said, "to look where men make the most noise."

He followed her gaze to the house and back again. "Most men do."

"Yes."

The single word held no contempt. Only truth.

He waited.

Frigg rested one hand lightly on the fence rail. Her fingers were bare. The frost beneath them did not melt, but the wood seemed somehow steadier for being touched.

"Men speak of glory as if it were the center of the world," she said. "Warriors sing of battle, kings of land, and the dying of worthy deaths. Even the gods are not all free of that hunger." Her eyes came back to him. "But the world does not endure on battle alone."

Thor had said as much, though more roughly.

Yet hearing it from her made it something wider than labor and weather. It reached into the house behind him, into memory, into what remained after the strong had fallen and the songs had thinned.

Eirik said, "No."

"You know that."

"Yes."

"Then why does it trouble you to know the gods know it too?"

The question struck deeper than he liked.

He did not answer at once.

Because the truth of it was not comfortable. If gods saw the same things he was beginning to see—the worth of restraint, of protection, of keeping rather than taking—then his life had been judged more closely than he had once imagined. Not only his courage. Not only his skill. The shape of his heart. The uses of his strength. The world he was helping to preserve.

Eirik looked at the house.

He thought of Astrid's hands at the hearth, never idle unless she chose them so. Of Leif rushing too quickly toward manhood and not yet knowing what it cost. Of Sigrid seeing more than children ought and bearing it with too much calm. Of the long winters behind them and ahead. Of the names forgotten in most sagas because they had built, carried, mended, and buried instead of raided.

When he spoke, his voice had gone quieter.

"Because men know how to be judged for what they do with a blade." He looked back at her. "It is harder to be judged for what they fail to keep."

Frigg's face did not soften. It deepened.

"There," she said. "That is nearer."

The yard seemed very still.

Eirik felt, for a strange moment, not awe exactly, but the deep human unease of standing before someone who had already reached the thought he had only just begun to name.

Frigg went on, and now her words narrowed rather than broadened.

"A man's worth is not measured only by what he can end."

Her voice did not rise. It did not need to.

“It is measured also by what he refuses to destroy when destruction would be easier. By what he carries when no song will remember it. By whether the world behind him is more fit for life because he stood in it.”

Eirik felt the words settle into him one by one.

Not like command.

Like recognition.

That was the part that unnerved him most. She was not telling him what to become. She was naming what in him had already struggled toward shape.

He said, after a long quiet, “Men do not speak of such things in halls.”

“No,” Frigg said. “Men in halls often prefer to sound simpler than they are.”

That might almost have been Astrid speaking.

The thought touched him and passed.

He looked toward the doorway again and imagined Astrid inside, seeing the room and the day and the children at once, as she always did. He imagined Leif returning in a rush and Sigrid arriving more quietly, each carrying what they understood differently. He thought of the way a household held more than one life under its roof and how easily men called such keeping ordinary simply because it was constant.

Frigg followed his gaze.

“You know this already,” she said. “You have known it in your hands longer than in your thoughts.”

Eirik frowned faintly. “What do you mean?”

"You build. You mend. You teach. You hold your strength back from waste when you can. You do not mistake killing for greatness, though the world around you often tries to make that mistake for you." Her eyes returned to his. "Why else would you be troubled?"

He could not answer that.

Not because she was wrong.

Because she was too near the truth of it.

The wind shifted and brought the smell of baking barley from some nearby hearth. Down by the fjord, a gull cried sharply and was answered by another. The village remained itself even with a goddess standing in one yard, and that too seemed somehow part of her meaning.

Frigg stepped away from the fence then and moved a little nearer.

Not enough to threaten.

Enough to deepen the silence between them.

For the first time, Eirik felt something in her presence that reminded him not of gods, but of mothers. Not one mother only. Something broader than that. The part of the world that endured loss without surrendering to it. The part that remembered who had been born, buried, married, named, and fed when men returned from battle eager to speak first of blood.

It did not make her softer.

It made her larger.

He understood then, dimly and with a chill of awe, that to call her only Odin's wife would be like calling the sea a bucket of water. Not untrue. Only painfully insufficient.

Frigg said, "The future does not belong only to warriors."

Eirik held her gaze.

"It belongs to what they leave unbroken."

He drew breath slowly.

The words were plain enough. Yet they reached past the yard and the village and the present moment into something he could not wholly see.

Leif and Sigrid.

Astrid.

The unborn.

The winters still to come.

The names that would outlast their bones.

The stories that would change shape in other mouths and still carry some hidden truth of them.

Frigg looked toward the house once more, and when she spoke again her voice had gone quieter, not weaker.

"You will suffer for what you protect."

The sentence fell between them with no heat in it and no cruelty.

Only certainty.

Eirik felt that more sharply than any prophecy screamed in storm or hall could have touched him.

He thought of Astrid waiting through his absences.

Of Leif growing toward danger because boys admired what they did not yet understand.

Of Sigrid learning steadiness too young.

Of every fence, roof, field, and living tie that made a man vulnerable simply by giving him something worth losing.

He said, after a moment, "That sounds more like warning than blessing."

Frigg's expression changed then, though only slightly. There was compassion in it, but not the kind that lied.

"At times," she said, "they are the same thing."

They stood together in the cold yard while the village carried on around them, ignorant and blessed in its ignorance.

Then Eirik heard footsteps on the path.

Quick ones. Uneven with hurry.

Leif.

A second, lighter pace behind him.

Sigrid.

Before he turned, he saw the smallest change in Frigg.

Not retreat. Attention.

As though she had felt them before they crossed the corner of the house and had already included them in whatever measure she carried.

Leif came around the side of the house with a coil of cord over one shoulder and nearly ran straight into the yard before seeing his father standing still and stopping short.

Sigrid caught up a heartbeat later and looked from Eirik to the fence line.

For an instant she went very still.

Not in full understanding. In recognition of presence, or its passing.

Her eyes narrowed slightly, not with fear but with the precision of someone noticing that the world had not remained entirely ordinary in her absence.

"What is it?" Leif asked.

Eirik glanced once toward Frigg.

She stood where she had been, but the world around her had begun to take her back into itself. Not with brightness. With stillness. Her outline seemed less bound to the air, more to the sense of her.

Then the place by the fence held only pale light, frost-dark wood, and the drifting smell of clean air.

Leif frowned. "Father?"

Eirik looked at his son, then at his daughter.

Leif was flushed from running, eager and alive and still too ready to throw himself into whatever road lay nearest. Sigrid stood calmer, the hem of her cloak damp from the frost, her eyes still searching the fence line before they came back to his face.

"Nothing is wrong," he said.

Leif looked unconvinced. "That is not the face you make when nothing is wrong."

Sigrid adjusted the cord on her brother's shoulder before it could slip. "He means nothing is immediately on fire."

"That would be a clearer answer," Leif said.

Eirik smiled despite himself.

There was warmth in it this time, but also something new beneath it. Not comfort. Not ease.

Recognition.

He looked once more toward the fence where Frigg had stood.

Nothing remained there to prove the moment. No mark in the frost. No bending of light. No scent beyond what a winter day already held.

Yet the yard felt fuller than before, as if a presence could leave without departing.

Sigrid followed his gaze. "Did someone come?"

Eirik thought of answering as men often did when children asked what was harder than they yet should bear. With a half-truth. With a turning aside. But he found he had no wish to shrink the world for them more than it already would on its own.

"Yes," he said.

Leif's eyes brightened at once. "Who?"

Eirik looked at him a moment, then at Sigrid.

"Someone who thinks your mother should not be forced to do all the wisdom in this house."

From behind them, Astrid's voice came dry and even from the doorway.

"Then that someone is finally showing sound judgment."

Leif turned so fast the cord nearly slid from his shoulder. Sigrid caught it before it fell.

"I had it," he muttered.

"You nearly had it," she replied.

Astrid stepped into the yard, her eyes moving over all three of them and then, very briefly, to the place by the fence.

That was enough to tell Eirik she understood more than she would say.

Of course she did.

He found himself thinking, as he often did after being near her in any truth worth bearing, that even silence shared with Astrid left him steadier than loud certainty from other people.

Leif came forward with his usual urgency. “Was it one of the gods?”

Astrid lifted one brow. “You ask that as if expecting a guest list.”

Leif flushed. “I only mean—”

“I know what you mean.”

Sigrid looked at Eirik. “Will you say?”

Eirik held her gaze. Then he said, simply, “Frigg.”

Leif blinked.

Sigrid went very still.

Astrid said nothing at all.

The wind moved once across the yard and was gone.

Leif lowered his voice without meaning to. “What did she want?”

Eirik looked toward the house, toward the village beyond, toward the work still waiting because life did not stop for revelation.

“To remind me,” he said, “that battle is not the only thing that keeps a people alive.”

Sigrid took that in first.

Leif, as usual, reached toward it by another path. “Thor already said something like that.”

“Yes.”

“Then why did she need to?”

Eirik almost laughed softly at the directness of it. Instead he answered honestly.

“Because some truths have more than one root.”

That quieted the boy.

Astrid came nearer and took the cord from Leif's shoulder before he forgot to hold it properly. "Good. Since the gods are finished improving you for the moment, the lower rack still needs tying before dark."

Leif let out a breath, half disappointed and half relieved. "I was already doing that."

Sigrid looked at the slipping cord in Astrid's hand. "Poorly."

"I was not."

"You were drifting."

"I was thinking."

"That is what I said."

Eirik watched them turn toward the house and work again—Astrid steady and sharp, Leif quick and eager, Sigrid correcting without cruelty, all of them alive within the small daily motions men so often failed to count among sacred things.

He stood a moment longer in the yard.

Frigg's words had not solved him. They had not absolved him either. But they had done something perhaps more difficult.

They had shown him that the world he fought for was larger than fields and walls, and that the gods were not merely watching who won and who fell. They were watching what kind of life men preserved by their choices, and what kind of future those choices left behind.

Not only warriors.

Not only glory.

Not only fate.

Memory.

Children.

Households.

Continuance.

And beneath all of it, the older suffering that men praised too little because it did not shine.

He looked toward the doorway where Astrid had paused to lift the lower rack cord from the peg and hand it wordlessly to Leif when the boy forgot where it hung. Such a small thing. Such a common thing. Yet there it was again: the shape of what endured.

Frigg had said, *You will suffer for what you protect.*

The sentence had not left him.

Until now he had carried it mostly as a warning.

Now, watching the life around him move and depend and fray and hold, he understood the harder part of it.

The suffering was not proof that such things were too costly to love.

It was proof that they mattered enough to wound.

He bent then, took up the spare cord Astrid had left coiled on the sled rail, and went to help with the lower rack before the weather turned again.

And as he worked beside the life he had built—wife, children, wood, cord, roof, breath—Frigg's last truth stayed with him not as a burden, but as a quiet widening of the soul:

The future did not belong only to the men willing to die for it.

It belonged also to those who kept something living long enough to reach it.

Chapter Nine

Fractures Among Gods

That night the wind did not settle.

It moved around the village in long, cold breaths, worrying the roof edges, stirring the hanging fish strips, and pressing smoke low over the fjord. The dogs slept badly. A shutter somewhere down the lane struck wood, then struck it again until someone cursed and tied it fast. Frost took the paths by midnight and silvered the fence rails by morning's edge.

Eirik woke before dawn.

Not all at once. He rose from sleep the way a man rises from cold water, aware first of discomfort, then of stillness, then of the shape of the dark around him. The fire had burned low. Astrid lay beside him, one hand half-curled near her face, her breathing slow and even. Leif had kicked his blanket almost free again. Sigrid, sleeping near him, had caught one corner of it in her hand without waking.

Eirik watched them for a while.

The house smelled of peat smoke, wool, and the faint lingering sweetness of the mead from the blót. Beyond the walls, the wind moved over the village and away again. It should have been an ordinary hour.

It did not feel like one.

That uneasy knowing had come to him often now, enough that he no longer mistook it for simple restlessness. Something in the world had shifted since Ash Fjord. Since the ravens. Since the hall. Since Thor. Since Frigg.

He had thought, foolishly perhaps, that one revelation might settle the last. That if a man saw far enough into a thing, the pieces would come to rest and show him the truth cleanly.

Instead each new truth had widened the wound in what he thought he knew.

Honor was not one thing.

Strength was not one thing.

The gods were not one voice.

He closed his eyes, meaning only to listen to the wind a while longer.

When he opened them, he was no longer in his house.

He stood beneath a sky with no dawn in it.

There was light, but not of sun or fire. It lay over the land like old steel—dim, gray, without warmth, yet clear enough to show every shape. Before him stretched a place that seemed part hall, part open ground, and part something older than either. Great stones rose from the earth in a wide half-circle, their faces carved with runes so worn they looked less cut than remembered. Beyond them lay a dark plain without end, its edges lost in mist. No tree moved there. No bird crossed it. Even the air felt as though it were holding its breath.

Eirik stood still and let his eyes work.

He had learned by now that rushing at divine things with mortal questions only made a man look smaller than he already was.

A long hall stood ahead, but not enclosed as mortal halls were. Its roof beams rose into dark emptiness without full walls to contain them. Wind moved through its pillars. Fire burned in iron bowls, though the flames leaned in no direction. Benches stood along the edges, empty. The place did not wait for men. It endured them.

He was not alone.

At the far end, beneath the highest beam, stood Odin.

There was no mistaking him now. No need for recognition to arrive slowly, as it had before. The god seemed cut from purpose itself. His cloak fell dark and heavy. Ravens perched above him, motionless, black shapes against the beam. His face was not severe in the ordinary way men were severe. It was worse than that—contained, measured, carrying so much will that even his stillness felt like a choice made against violence. The single keen brightness of his gaze held the room as if it belonged there because he had decided it should.

Freyja stood some paces away, not below him, not behind him, but apart in a way that made the distance between them feel more deliberate than any wall.

She wore gold, though not the kind men used to boast of wealth. This was older, deeper, like the warmth in amber or the hidden fire in polished bronze. Her beauty was not ornamental. It had edge. Pride lived in the set of her head and in the steadiness of her shoulders. She looked as if grief would not diminish her and power would not sweeten her. The force in her was not borrowed from any hall, husband, or battle. It was her own.

And nearer the stones, turned half toward both of them and fully toward neither, stood Frigg.

No crown marked her greater than the others. None was needed. She seemed quieter than power should have been and therefore more difficult to ignore. Her mantle moved only where the unseen air touched it, and her gaze held the strange unsettling calm of one who saw beyond the room, beyond the plain, beyond even the argument already gathering between those present.

No Thor had come.

That absence carried its own shape. Not neglect. Not ignorance. More like refusal to stand inside this particular fracture while roofs still needed mending somewhere beneath the weather.

Eirik felt then that he had not stumbled into a chance moment.

He had been brought.

The thought ran cold through him.

None of the three seemed surprised that he stood there.

That troubled him most.

For a long breath, no one spoke.

Then Odin said, "You keep drawing him nearer."

His voice did not rise. It did not need to. It carried the way a drawn blade carries its edge without flashing it.

Frigg answered first. "He keeps walking."

Odin's eye shifted to her. "Men walk many roads."

"Yes," she said. "And not all of them lead where you prefer."

The words were calm. Their effect was not.

Freyja's mouth curved faintly—not amusement exactly, but the recognition of a true strike cleanly placed.

Odin turned then, not toward Eirik, but toward the dark plain beyond the hall. "Preference has little to do with it."

"No," Freyja said. "Only sacrifice. Cost. Use. You name those things often enough."

Her voice was sharp but never shrill. She did not challenge like a lesser being seeking permission to speak. She challenged like one power addressing another on ground neither fully owned.

Eirik stood in silence and understood, with a deep tightening in his chest, that what he had glimpsed before had not been uncertainty among separate gods moving about their roles.

It was fracture.

Not hatred. Not chaos. Something older and perhaps more dangerous than either: conviction without agreement.

Odin's hand rested lightly on the carved arm of the high seat beside him. "The world does not survive because men wish it kindly."

"No," Freyja said. "But neither does it survive because every life is weighed like iron for a forge you alone have chosen."

That landed in the air between them like a spear driven upright into earth.

Eirik's thoughts flashed at once to the hall of the dead, to the warriors chosen under Odin's ravens, and to the different line beneath Freyja's gaze.

Use.

Worth.

Future purpose.

Hidden cost.

Odin looked at her, and the stillness in the hall grew sharper. "You mistake preparation for cruelty."

"And you mistake necessity for wisdom."

The answer came at once.

Frigg's gaze rested on neither of them fully. She seemed to hold both argument and aftermath in a single quiet regard.

Eirik thought of Thor then, of the field fence standing in cold mud, of storm held in a hammer hand, of plain words about grain bins and wolves. Thor had felt solid as earth. This felt like standing between blades no man had drawn and no man could stop.

Odin spoke again, and now his gaze turned, briefly, to Eirik.

"The lives of men are not outside what is coming."

Eirik said nothing. He doubted the statement asked anything of him yet.

"The world narrows," Odin went on. "Threads tighten. Fate does not soften because men would prefer comfort."

Freyja's eyes flashed. "And so you sharpen them for slaughter? Is that your answer to every narrowing path?"

"My answer," Odin said, "is to prepare for what will not be turned aside."

His voice remained measured. That made it heavier.

Freyja took a step closer—not toward him, not toward Frigg, but toward the center of the hall. "You see men for what they may become in death. I see them for what they were willing to lose while still alive."

Odin did not move. "I do not ignore that."

"No," she said. "You spend it."

Frigg closed her eyes once, briefly, as if hearing an old wound touched again.

Eirik's heart beat hard once and then seemed to slow.

It was no longer enough for him to say the gods differed.

They judged each other.

Not loudly. Not with mortal pettiness. But truly. Deeply. On the meaning of sacrifice, the shape of fate, the worth of human life.

And he—warrior, husband, father, man who had spared Hrolf against the cleaner logic of the moment—stood somewhere in the space between their measures.

Frigg spoke then, and though her voice remained low, both Odin and Freyja turned enough to hear her fully.

"You speak as if men exist for the future."

Odin answered first. "They do."

Freyja, at nearly the same instant, said, "They do not."

The two responses crossed and hung in the hall together.

That, more than any sharp phrase before it, made the fracture plain.

Frigg opened her eyes.

"There," she said softly. "And that is the heart of it."

No one in the hall moved.

The god of fate and sacrifice.

The chooser who saw the worth in what did not fit war's narrow measure.

And between them, or above them in some older way, the Mother who refused the boundaries that made the argument manageable.

Eirik felt suddenly very mortal.

Frigg looked toward him then—not to draw him in, but because the truth under dispute had already taken root in his life.

"You ask," she said, "what his mercy means."

Odin's gaze hardened slightly. Freyja's sharpened.

Eirik understood that they had been speaking of him all along, whether or not his name had been used.

Not only him. What he represented. What kind of man he might yet become beneath their different judgments.

Odin said, “Mercy without foresight can kill more than cruelty.”

That was Sten’s warning, raised into something colder and larger.

Freyja answered almost over him, “And foresight without mercy breeds a world not worth preserving.”

Odin’s jaw shifted. A tiny movement. But it was the first crack Eirik had seen in the iron composure.

“And what would you preserve?” Odin asked, and now there was something else in him—not heat exactly, but old strain drawn near the surface. “A people unblooded? A future kept clean by wishing? You speak of worth as if the world were inclined to spare it.”

Freyja did not yield. “I speak of worth because you are too willing to spend it.”

The answer came like a cut, not an argument.

Eirik felt the words in separate weights laid into either hand.

He thought of Hrolf spared on the shore and of the blood later spilled at his own hearth. He thought of Leif’s shocked face after his first kill. Of Sigrid going pale but steady. Of Astrid standing in blood and silence, refusing to let him die. Of Thor naming battle only one part of survival. Of Frigg reminding him that the future belonged also to what men left unbroken.

Odin looked directly at him.

“What you spare is not spared from consequence.”

The sentence was plain enough to be mistaken for mere truth. Yet in Odin’s mouth it carried warning. Perhaps accusation too.

Eirik took a slow breath.

He did not want to speak. Mortal words felt thin there. But silence had its own cowardice if held too long in the face of being measured.

"I know," he said.

His voice seemed smaller than theirs, but not lost.

Freyja asked, "Do you?"

That question held different weight. It was not about tactics or destiny. It was about grief. About whether he truly understood what mercy cost the living when it failed to turn the spared man toward honor.

Eirik met her gaze. "More than I did."

The answer satisfied nothing.

That, he thought grimly, was likely the truest answer he had given in some time.

Frigg turned slightly, the light along her mantle paling and deepening with the motion. "He is not the only one learning."

That made both the others stiller than before.

Frigg looked toward the stones at the edge of the hall, toward the dark plain beyond, toward whatever lay further still.

"You prepare for what is coming," she said to Odin. "You gather. You shape. You harden."

"I do."

She turned to Freyja. "You keep what would otherwise be cast aside by that hardening."

Freyja lifted her chin slightly. "I do."

Frigg's gaze settled somewhere beyond both of them. "And still neither of you holds all of what must endure."

The line fell quietly.

Yet it seemed to go deeper than anything else spoken there.

Odin's eye narrowed, not in anger, but in refusal. "What must endure is decided by what survives."

Frigg looked at him with a calm so complete it was almost terrible. "No. What survives is often only what was most willing to consume."

Freyja's mouth tightened. Not because she disagreed. Because she understood the cost of the distinction.

Eirik stood utterly still.

He had never heard the divine made so plain and so dangerous.

Not in power.

In conviction.

The gods were not merely guiding men from separate corners of one design. They were contending over what the design itself should serve.

Odin saw future war, sacrifice, necessity.

Freyja saw the lives and deaths that would be crushed if only usefulness ruled.

Frigg saw beyond both—to lineage, memory, continuance, the long life of a people not reducible to battle or even to glorious death.

And Thor, Eirik thought, had chosen his own counsel. Not because it did not matter, but because roofs still needed mending while higher powers disputed the shape of fate.

The thought would almost have made him smile if the hall had not felt so sharp.

He became aware then that the argument was not only about abstract men or whole peoples. It had narrowed around him in ways none of them needed to name aloud.

Warrior.

Husband.

Father.

Protector.

Man of restraint where death would have been simpler.

Odin said, not looking away from Frigg, “You would leave more to chance than I can allow.”

Frigg answered, “And you would bind more by fear than I can trust.”

Freyja stepped nearer the center. “And both of you speak as though men are pieces already moved.”

Odin’s gaze shifted to her. “They are moved.”

“They are not only moved.”

The pride in her voice did not make it less true.

Eirik thought then of every choice he had struggled through since Ash Fjord. None of them had felt clean. None of them had felt wholly his or wholly compelled. Men lived in that uneasy place between choosing and being carried. Perhaps the gods did too, though on some greater and stranger scale.

He had the sudden, unsettling sense that the room itself knew this and had known it long before any of them spoke.

Freyja’s eyes moved once to Eirik. “He is not useful to you because he kills.”

That was not a question, but it landed near one.

Odin gave no answer for a heartbeat.

Then: “No.”

Even Frigg seemed to listen more sharply.

Odin’s next words were slower, as if drawn from further inward. “He is useful because he chooses against easier paths and still stands in the cost of them.”

The truth of that struck Eirik harder than praise would have.

Useful.

Still a hard word.

Yet not for killing.

For choosing under burden.

Freyja studied Odin, and something unreadable passed through her expression. “Then perhaps you see more than you enjoy.”

This time Odin did not let the line pass.

His composure did not break. It changed.

When he answered, the restraint remained, but underneath it Eirik heard something harsher, older, less kingly and more dangerous—the voice of one who had gone to wisdom through loss, through cunning, through wounds willingly taken and never regretted.

“Enjoyment,” Odin said, “has little place in seeing clearly.”

The words were not loud. Yet the ravens above him shifted together, and the dark beyond the hall seemed to draw one breath inward.

For the first time, Eirik understood that Odin’s calm was not peace.

It was control.

And that beneath it lived things older than any mortal hall could safely name.

Frigg's gaze came to Eirik once more, and there was in it the same unsettling awareness he had felt before—the sense of being seen not only in action, but in root and consequence.

"You are listening," she said.

It was more statement than question.

"Yes," Eirik answered.

"Good."

The word was simple. It carried no comfort.

Then Frigg looked from one to the other, from Odin to Freyja, and for the first time Eirik felt that her patience itself might be the largest force in the room. Not passive patience. Not yielding. The kind that outlasted storms, kings, feuds, and songs. The kind that remembered what others forgot because they were too intent on winning their part of the truth.

"Men think the gods judge them," she said.

Odin's ravens did not stir.

Freyja did not lower her gaze.

Frigg went on, "And we do. But not only them."

The stillness after that felt like the edge of a blade drawn slowly from a sheath.

Eirik understood then, with a clarity that left him cold all through, that he had not merely wandered into divine revelation.

He had witnessed divine judgment turned inward.

Not temporary irritation.

Not a passing difference of method.

A fracture older than his life and carried further than he could see.

The gods were not only weighing men.

They were weighing each other's visions of the world.

No agreement came.

No final word settled the matter.

Odin turned first, though not in retreat. More as a man might turn from a fire whose heat he had chosen not to answer further. The ravens above him shifted once, then went still again.

Freyja held her ground a moment longer, then inclined her head—not in surrender, but in cold acknowledgment that truth had been spoken and not resolved.

Frigg remained where she was.

That, more than anything, made the ending of the exchange feel unfinished rather than complete.

Eirik's breath felt loud in his own chest.

He thought suddenly of Astrid. Of how she would listen to such a thing with her head slightly bent, saying little, and then in one dry line lay her hand on the hidden center of it. He wished, strangely and sharply, that she were there beside him.

Perhaps that human wish was what pulled him loose.

The hall dimmed not in light, but in hold. The stones grew more distant. The plain beyond them lost definition. The fires thinned to red points, then to the memory of warmth.

He woke seated against the wall of his own house, not in the bed furs but on the bench near the dying hearth.

His neck ached from the angle of sleep. One arm had gone numb beneath his cloak.

The fire had burned nearly out.

For one breath he did not move.

The fracture remained in him.

Not as vision. As knowledge.

Astrid sat across from him, awake, a mending knife in one hand and half a torn seam in her lap. The room was dim, the air thick with late-night quiet. She looked up the instant his eyes focused.

"You have the face again," she said.

Eirik rubbed one hand over his jaw. "Which face?"

"The one that says the world has grown larger while you were sitting still."

That drew the faintest breath of laughter from him, though it carried no ease.

Astrid set the knife down. "Was it worse than last time?"

Eirik leaned forward, forearms on his knees. He stared into the coals and watched one red line collapse into ash.

"Yes," he said.

Astrid waited.

He told her enough.

Not every word. Not every presence. Only the shape of it: Odin and Freyja openly divided. Frigg between and beyond them. No simple harmony. No final answer. The gods themselves contending over destiny, worth, survival, and what the future of their people should require.

Astrid listened without interruption, the way she always did when a thing mattered too much for hasty comfort.

When he finished, she was silent a long time.

Then she said, "That explains the ravens."

He looked up. "Does it?"

"No." Her mouth moved faintly. "But it explains why they look so pleased with themselves."

That might almost have made him smile.

It did not last.

Astrid studied him a moment longer. "You thought the gods stood above the same argument men have below."

"Yes."

"And now?"

"Now I think men may only be repeating a fracture older than they know."

Astrid nodded slowly, as if the answer fit some shape she had long suspected.

"There are worse reasons for a people to be troubled," she said, "than being made in the image of their own disputes."

Eirik looked at her.

"That sounds unhelpful."

"It is." She picked the knife up again and trimmed a thread end cleanly. "Truth often is."

He let out a breath and sat back.

The house around them was quiet. Leif and Sigrid slept in the corner under the blankets, turned toward one another without knowing it. The roof held. The walls held. Outside, the village lay under frost and dark and the ordinary threat of another winter night.

Inside that small, human stillness, the fracture among the gods seemed somehow more threatening than if they had shouted and struck.

Because stillness lasted.

Because disagreement spoken quietly by great powers did not vanish when men stopped hearing it.

Eirik looked toward the roof hole where no raven showed, only darkness.

"The matter is not ended," he said.

Astrid followed his gaze briefly, then lowered her eyes to the seam in her hand.

"No," she said. "It rarely is, once the true words have been spoken."

He sat with that.

Across from him, Astrid's knife moved through wool, neat and exact. The sound was small. Mortal. Comfortingly so.

Yet even there, in the warmth of the hearth's last coals, Eirik could not shake the sense that the gods had not only spoken in some distant realm and turned away.

They had left the fracture open.

And somewhere beyond the dark roof, beyond the sleeping village, beyond the frost and fjord and all the little mortal things that still needed doing by morning, the stillness waiting between them felt more dangerous than war.

Chapter Ten

The Cost of Seeing

Morning came clear and cold, with frost silvering the fence rails and the yard hard beneath Eirik's boots.

He stood by the woodpile with an axe in his hands and a split log at his feet, though he had not swung for several breaths. The village was waking around him. Smoke lifted from low roofs into pale air. Somewhere farther down the slope, a dog barked twice and fell silent. A woman called for a child. A cart wheel creaked over frozen ground.

All of it was ordinary.

That was what unsettled him.

The world had not changed its face to match what he had seen. The sky still brightened the same way. Wood still needed splitting. Goats still tested fences for weakness. Bread still baked or burned according to the same small laws of fire and patience. Yet beneath it, or behind it, or perhaps simply woven through it more openly than before, he felt the strain of something larger.

The gods were not one in will.

He knew that now.

Not from tale. Not from priestly certainty spoken over a feast horn. He had seen enough to understand that power did not mean agreement, and wisdom did not mean mercy, and love did not mean peace. Odin's silence had held one kind of judgment. Freyja's anger another. Frigg's calm had unsettled him most of all, because it carried not comfort but scale. She had looked at him as though he were both a man and a thread.

He set the axe head lightly against the block and stared out across the yard.

A raven landed on the fence post near the goat pen.

Eirik watched it.

The bird turned its head once, black eye bright in the morning light, then drove its beak into its wing and began preening with complete indifference.

Eirik let out a breath through his nose and took up the axe.

The kitchen door opened behind him.

Astrid stepped out with a basket on one arm and a wool shawl drawn over her shoulders against the cold. Pale strands had slipped loose from her braid, and the morning light caught them so that for a moment she seemed outlined in frost. She paused beneath the roof edge, looking over the yard in that quiet way of hers, taking in more than she said.

"You are arguing with a bird," she observed.

"It began it."

Astrid glanced at the raven. "Then you are losing."

The bird hopped once along the fence as if in agreement.

Eirik snorted and brought the axe down cleanly through the waiting log. The halves fell apart with a crack that carried through the morning.

Astrid came closer and set the basket on the chopping block. "You missed breakfast."

"I was thinking."

"That rarely improves hunger."

He rested both hands on the axe handle and looked at her. She had that same stillness about her she often wore after storms, whether those storms had been weather, blood, or words from places men were not meant to stand. She did not ask him what he was thinking. She knew enough not to waste time on questions that would only make a burden speak before it was ready.

Instead she drew a cloth back from the basket and revealed bread, hard cheese, and dried apple slices.

"This is what remains between you and foolishness," she said. "Eat before the balance worsens."

"That is a cruel amount of responsibility to give bread."

"It has broad shoulders."

He took the bread and ate because she was right and because not eating would only make the mind louder. The raven watched with patient insult.

Astrid stood beside him without speaking. It was one of the things he loved most in her, though he did not always say it aloud. She knew how to share silence without making it feel empty.

After a while she said, "You are farther away this morning."

Eirik chewed, swallowed, and looked toward the far edge of the yard where frost lay white on the grass. "Not far. Only divided."

"Between what?"

He took a breath.

There had been a time when he could have answered with simpler things. Between duty and desire. Between anger and sense. Between the need to protect and the cost of doing it. Those were heavy enough. Human enough.

Now the answer felt larger and less clean.

"Between the life I know," he said at last, "and the knowledge that it is not as self-contained as I once believed."

Astrid let that sit in the cold air between them.

"The walls are thinner," she said.

He looked at her.

She met his eyes only briefly, then turned her gaze to the frost on the fence. "You keep walking into places where the world forgets to end where it should."

"That sounds like blame."

"It is observation." Her mouth shifted slightly. "Blame uses warmer words."

He laughed once, softly.

The sound surprised him.

Astrid reached into the basket again and handed him the cheese. "You are not meant to carry all understanding at once."

"That would be kind advice if the understanding asked permission before arriving."

"It never does."

There it was again—that unsettling ease she had with truths other people fought. Not because she knew everything. He had long since learned she did not. But because she did not panic when certainty cracked. She simply made room for the crack and watched what came through.

The back door opened again and Leif burst out of it as though the morning had personally insulted him by arriving before he was ready. He had a stick in one hand and one boot only half-laced.

“Father, Sigrid says I tied the gate badly, but it held until the goat pushed it, which means it mostly held, which should count.”

Sigrid emerged more quietly behind him, cloak fastened properly, boots tied, expression already carrying the patient burden of being right near her brother.

“It did not hold,” she said. “It failed after meeting the goat.”

Leif spun toward her. “Everything fails after meeting that goat. That is the goat’s character, not my knot.”

Astrid picked up the basket again. “A comforting defense. Perhaps use it when the roof collapses.”

Leif frowned. “The roof is not a goat.”

“Yet.”

Sigrid looked at Eirik. “The gate sagged on the lower hinge. The knot was poor, but that was not the first problem.”

Leif folded his arms. “You always add extra rightness.”

“It saves time.”

Eirik looked between them and felt something in his chest loosen.

This too was ordinary. Not simple. But ordinary in the best way: Leif all forward motion and untested confidence, Sigrid steady as winter ground, already seeing the second cause where most people stopped at the first. Even now, after everything, they still carried the day on their own terms.

He crouched and held out his hand.

Leif handed him the stick at once, though his face suggested he believed this would become instruction. Eirik used it to scrape a quick shape in the frost-dusted dirt: a post, a hinge, a line of strain.

"If the hinge gives first," he said, "the knot works harder than it should. Then even a decent knot fails, and a poor knot fails faster."

Leif looked down, following the shape with sudden seriousness.

Sigrid said, "That is what I told him."

"You said it with less artistry," Leif replied.

Eirik handed back the stick. "Fix both. Then we will see if the goat remains more clever than the two of you together."

Leif brightened immediately. "It will not."

Sigrid considered this. "That depends whether he helps."

Astrid moved past them toward the door. "If blood is shed, make sure it belongs to the gate."

Leif looked scandalized. "Mother."

"It was a joke," she said.

"It sounded like a warning."

Astrid opened the door. "That is why it was successful."

She disappeared inside.

For a moment Eirik watched the children cross the yard toward the gate, Leif already speaking too fast, Sigrid already preparing to correct him when needed and let him think some of the better ideas had been his. He loved them with an ache that had sharpened since the visions, not because love was new, but because it now seemed exposed to a scale he had not wished to measure.

The gods argued over things men bled for.

That knowledge did not make his family smaller. It made them more precious and more vulnerable at once.

The raven lifted from the fence with a beat of wings and was gone.

Eirik split three more logs before the feeling returned.

Not sight. Not sound. Only the old sense of being observed from just beyond the edge of ordinary attention.

He lowered the axe slowly.

Nothing moved in the yard beyond his children at the gate. Smoke rose. Frost melted where the sun reached. A neighbor's cow bellowed from farther uphill.

Still, he felt it.

Not threat.

Measure.

He set the axe aside and wiped his hands on his tunic, annoyed at himself for even noticing. But annoyance changed nothing. Some knowing could not be untaught once gained.

By midday he went down toward the lower fields where several men were repairing a boundary ditch damaged by rain and hoof churn. The ground there had softened under the surface frost, making the work heavier than it first appeared. Shovels bit, lifted, and thudded. Mud clung to boots. Curses drifted now and then, mostly directed at the earth, which rarely listened.

Jarl Sten Hakonsson stood near the ditch with a shovel in hand, speaking to two men about where to cut the waterline so the next thaw would not flood the lower pasture again. He looked much as he always had—large through the shoulders, red hair braided back from a scarred face, ringed beard moving when he spoke—but age and command had settled on him without softening him. He did not stand apart from labor unless necessity forced it. Eirik had always respected that.

Sten noticed him and straightened. "You are late enough to seem important."

"I was hoping to seem useful instead."

"That would be a rarer achievement."

They clasped forearms.

Sten's grip was hard as old oak. His pale eyes studied Eirik more closely than his words had. That was another thing rank had taught him well: how to look without making it obvious to everyone else.

"You look tired," Sten said.

"I have children."

"You had those yesterday."

"They have not improved."

That earned a rough laugh from the jarl.

They worked a while before speaking further. Earth first, talk after. Eirik was grateful for it. There was sanity in labor that asked the body honest questions and required honest answers.

At last Sten thrust his shovel into the soil and leaned on the handle. "Arn says you have the face of a man listening to distant thunder."

"That sounds like Arn."

"He also says the thunder may be standing still, which I did not enjoy."

Eirik almost smiled. "He seldom aims for comfort."

"No." Sten wiped dirt from his hands. "But he notices rot before other men smell it. That is useful, though unpleasant."

He let the silence stretch one moment longer.

"Whatever you saw in the hills," Sten said quietly, "it has not finished with you."

Eirik did not ask how much Arn had said. With Arn, one never knew whether a thing had been told plainly, hinted sideways, or disguised as mockery until it was too late to stop listening.

"I do not know what has finished with me," Eirik said.

Sten absorbed that without visible surprise.

"We ask much of our gods," the jarl said. "Victory. Harvest. Sons. Fair weather when it suits us and harsh weather when it harms our enemies. We speak of them as though they are a council that merely waits to be petitioned."

He looked over the fields where women were turning cut strips of winter fodder, where two boys chased each other with reed stalks until an elder cuffed one lightly and sent both back to work.

"But if they are not of one mind," Sten said, "then a man must choose more carefully what kind of life he offers the world."

Eirik studied him. "You say that too easily."

Sten's scar tugged when he frowned. "No. I say it as a man who has led enough burials to distrust simple certainties."

There was no priest's comfort in the words. Only leadership stripped down to its hard bones.

"I cannot explain what I saw," Eirik said.

"I did not ask you to."

"It changes things anyway."

"Yes." Sten's gaze rested on him. "Seeing always does."

Eirik looked toward the village roofs, dark against the pale afternoon light. "I keep thinking understanding should make the road clearer."

"And?"

"And it has not."

Sten huffed a breath through his nose. "Then perhaps you are finally understanding something worth having."

That might have sounded harsh from another man. From Sten it came as simple weight.

He left the shovel where it stood and looked at Eirik a moment longer. "Do not make the mistake of thinking that because the gods are divided, men are freed from choosing well."

Eirik met his gaze. "I had not."

"Good." Sten nodded once. "Because confusion can dress itself as depth if a man lets it."

That struck harder than Eirik expected.

The jarl saw that and did not soften it. "A hard road does not excuse a weak foot."

Then he took up the shovel again and drove it into the earth.

Eirik worked beside him in silence for several more minutes, the ditch deepening, the cold water finding the new cut and slipping through it with a faint rush. Around them life moved in its familiar patterns, yet Sten's words settled beside the others he had been carrying. Understanding worth having. Confusion dressed as depth. A hard road asking a firm step anyway.

Later, as the light lowered toward afternoon, Arn appeared the way he often did—without warning, as if he had stepped out of some private argument with the air itself.

He came down the path with both axes hanging at his hips and a bundle of rabbit snares over one shoulder. He paused at the edge of the ditch, looking at the men sunk in mud to the shins.

"You have all chosen ugliness," he declared.

Sten did not look up. "We save the pleasing work for warriors who carry no shield."

Arn dropped the snares by a fence post and crouched at the ditch edge. "Wise. I would only improve this until you felt inadequate."

"You often confuse disturbance with improvement," Sten said.

Arn looked at Eirik. "He grows more poetic with rank. It is a warning sign."

Eirik rested on his shovel. "You smell like wet fur."

"I have been successful."

"That was not the question."

"It should have been."

Arn's grin flashed and vanished. Then his eyes narrowed slightly as he studied Eirik. The shift was small, but Eirik had known him too long to miss it. Arn often wore mockery like a bright cloak. The man beneath it was quicker and sharper than most guessed.

"You still have that look," Arn said.

"What look?"

"The one men get when they have swallowed a truth too large to digest and are hoping work will grind it down."

Sten made a low sound that might have been amusement.

Eirik sighed. "Do you ever arrive like a normal man?"

Arn considered. "Once, in winter. It was poorly received."

Sten leaned on his shovel. “Say what you came to say.”

Arn glanced up at the sky. “Three ravens this morning. Two on your roof beam, one at the goat pen. None of them behaved like proper thieves.”

“That narrows it not at all,” Sten said.

“I know.” Arn’s eyes came back to Eirik. “Also, old Runa says the air near the upper path felt heavy enough to press tears out of her, though she had no reason to cry. And your son asked me whether gods argue like married people, which is a question no child invents without a house already leaning in that direction.”

Eirik felt a brief, tired admiration. Arn gathered patterns the way some men gathered firewood—roughly, without neatness, but enough to keep a long night lit.

“I did not speak of gods to him,” Eirik said.

“You did not need to.” Arn shrugged. “Children smell strain. Dogs too. Goats merely exploit it.”

Sten looked between them. “Is there a point beneath all this?”

“There usually is,” Arn said. “It only dislikes being rushed.”

He crouched lower, picked up a clod of frozen mud, and broke it apart with his fingers.

“You have begun to live like a man standing in two rooms,” he said to Eirik. “One is this one. Mud, fences, kin, sore backs, too little ale. The other”—he flicked the dirt away—“is where the great ones notice and disagree. Most men never see the second room. Lucky for them. But once you have, you keep trying to fit one life inside both. That tears the edges.”

Sten was silent.

So was Eirik.

Arn stood and brushed his hands together. “There. I have said something unpleasant and likely true. You may thank me by not becoming stupid.”

“What would stupidity look like?” Eirik asked.

Arn’s expression sharpened. “Believing that seeing more makes you above ordinary duty. Or believing the opposite—that ordinary duty no longer matters because greater things are moving. Both are vanity, only dressed differently.”

The words hit harder than Eirik expected because they had already been circling in him without shape.

Sten nodded once. “On that, at least, he speaks like a sober man.”

Arn looked offended. “I resent the surprise.”

Eirik leaned on the shovel and studied his friend. “You make madness sound almost useful.”

“It is useful,” Arn said. “So long as it knows where to stop.” He tilted his head. “Mine rarely does, but that keeps the day from becoming dull.”

Sten snorted and returned to the ditch.

When the work ended and the men went their separate ways, Eirik walked home with Arn along the path above the lower pasture. The grass there bent under the wind in long pale strokes. Sheep moved like dirty stones against the hillside. Farther off, the fjord shone under thin afternoon light.

Arn was quiet longer than usual.

That, more than anything, made Eirik wary.

At last Arn said, “Do you know what troubles me most?”

“That you are asking instead of declaring.”

Arn ignored it. "The gods not agreeing. Men always knew it in story, perhaps. One favors this, one favors that. But stories are easy. They remain on the tongue. What troubles me is the thought that their disagreements are not distant. They fall through us."

Eirik looked at him.

Arn kept his eyes ahead. "A storm does not argue with a mountain by words. It argues by breaking trees."

"That is a cheerful thought."

"I am full of them." Arn kicked a stone from the path. "You spare a man. Another kills too quickly. A jarl waits. A mother grieves. A child grows into a different shape because of one hour no god can seem to leave alone. Men call these choices theirs." He shrugged one shoulder. "Perhaps they are. But the wind on them is not always mortal."

Eirik thought of Odin's gaze, of Freyja's sharp refusal, of Frigg speaking not like someone who predicted but like someone who remembered what had not yet happened. He thought too of Thor, blunt and solid, like earth refusing abstraction.

"I do not want my children living as pieces on another being's board," he said.

Arn answered at once. "Then raise them stubborn."

That made Eirik laugh, though not fully.

"It is not enough," he said.

"No," Arn agreed. "Very little is. That is why men build with more than one beam."

They walked on.

By the time Eirik reached home, dusk was leaning over the village. Smoke hung low. Lamps had begun to glow in windows like small captured suns. Inside his own house, warmth met him with the smell of barley stew and onions.

Leif was at the table carving notches into a scrap of wood until Sigrid told him he was carving the table by mistake. He inspected the damage and declared it decorative. Sigrid disagreed with visible fatigue.

Astrid stood over the pot, stirring. She looked back as Eirik entered, and in that glance he felt the day gather itself around the hearth.

"Did the ditch survive your supervision?" she asked.

"Barely."

"Then Sten must be grateful."

"He concealed it well."

Leif looked up eagerly. "Arn says gods may argue through weather."

Sigrid said, "He said storms break trees without asking which side they are on."

Leif lifted his chin. "That is nearly the same."

Astrid set the ladle down. "And why were you discussing divine weather with Arn?"

"Because he was mending a snare and I asked whether Thor likes rabbit better than fish."

Astrid closed her eyes once.

"That," she said, "is how foolishness enters a house. It knocks politely first."

Eirik sat down slowly. "And what answer did Arn give?"

Leif grinned. "He said Thor likes whatever men earn honestly and eat before it goes cold."

Astrid opened one eye. "That is annoyingly reasonable."

Sigrid folded her hands. "Then he said Odin probably prefers questions, which is why one should be careful feeding him."

Astrid's mouth shifted. "There. That sounds more like Arn."

They ate.

The children argued over whether one goat was actually wicked or merely efficient. Astrid judged the distinction unimportant. Leif insisted wickedness required intention. Sigrid replied that repeated behavior became intention whether admitted or not. Eirik listened, spoke when needed, and let the warmth of the room work slowly into his bones.

Yet even here, with the fire low and steady and the bowl warm in his hands, a piece of him remained apart.

It was not distance from them. Not exactly.

It was the knowledge that he could not lay the full weight of what he had seen upon this table between the bread and the stew and expect family life to remain itself. Some things, once spoken too plainly, changed a room. Perhaps they needed to. But he was not yet certain he knew how to do it without stealing something from the ordinary holiness of this life.

After the meal, when the children had gone to their bedding and the house had quieted, Astrid sat near the hearth mending a torn sleeve by firelight. Eirik was on the bench beside the wall, elbows on knees, hands loosely clasped.

The silence between them was deep and familiar.

At length Astrid said, without looking up, "You are trying to decide whether silence is protection or cowardice."

Eirik exhaled slowly. "You make irritating guesses."

"They improve with age."

He watched the fire settle around a collapsing piece of wood. “I do not know how much to say.”

“To whom?”

“Anyone.”

Astrid drew the thread through and turned the sleeve in her hands. “Truth is not one thing. Some truths are doors. Some are knives. Some are weather. A wise man does not hand them all to a child, a friend, and a jarl in the same shape.”

“That sounds suspiciously like comfort.”

“It is not comfort.” She bit the thread and set the sleeve aside. “It is craft.”

He looked at her then.

Firelight moved over the planes of her face and the loose strands by her temple. She seemed, as she so often did, both fully of this room and slightly beyond it, not distant but difficult to corner with plain meaning.

“I am afraid,” he said quietly.

Astrid’s gaze lifted to him.

It was not a confession he made often, and not because pride forbade it. He had long ago learned pride was a poor shield inside a home. But fear, once named, always sharpened.

“Of what?” she asked.

He considered lying. Not fully, perhaps, but enough to soften the answer. There was no use in that. Not with her.

“That what I have seen will change how I choose,” he said. “That every decision will now carry more than the moment itself. That I will look at a quarrel, a judgment, a raid, even a child’s mistake and wonder what larger hand leans over it.” He rubbed his thumb against one knuckle. "And that in trying to see rightly, I may fail to live rightly."

Astrid was quiet.

Then she stood, came to him, and sat beside him on the bench.

Not touching at first. Simply there.

"The burden is real," she said. "But it flatters itself."

He turned slightly toward her.

She continued, voice calm. "It would like you to believe that because the world is larger than you knew, your ordinary choices have become less clear. Some may. But not all. A hungry child still needs feeding. A frightened man still needs steadying. A cruel thing is still cruel, even if a god watches it happen with interest."

A small, tired laugh escaped him. "You speak like someone scolding fate."

"I would, if it were present and worth the effort." Now she laid her hand over his. "Seeing more does not free you from being a man. It binds you more tightly to doing that work well."

He let those words settle.

The fire cracked softly. Outside, wind moved against the walls in a long low brush.

"Astrid."

"Yes?"

"I do not know whether that eases anything."

"It was not meant to." Her fingers tightened once over his. "Only to keep you from becoming abstract."

He smiled despite himself. "You have a cruel tenderness."

"I have an efficient one."

He turned his hand and clasped hers properly.

For a while they sat in quiet. He could hear the children breathing from the back of the house. He could smell ash, wool, the faint lingering broth of supper. These things mattered. Not because they canceled what he had seen, but because they did not.

At last he rose and stepped outside.

Night had settled fully over the village. Stars stood clear above the roofline, cold and innumerable. Frost was returning to the yard. The fence rails gleamed faintly. Somewhere in the dark a horse stamped once, then went still.

Eirik stood with his hands at his sides and looked up.

He did not ask for a sign.

He was no longer sure signs were gifts.

The night felt wide enough to contain every god's silence.

After a long moment he lowered his gaze to the yard, to the gate Leif and Sigrid had repaired, to the stacked wood, to the tracks already freezing hard in the dirt. Mortal things. Daily things. Fragile things that had to be tended whether watched by heaven or not.

He understood then, not as revelation but as a hardening truth, that seeing more had not made life clearer.

It had made it heavier.

Not because ordinary life had lost meaning, but because it had gained weight under a sky no longer simple. Every kindness, every judgment, every restraint, every act of protection now seemed to stand in more than one world at once.

He had wanted understanding to sharpen certainty.

Instead it had sharpened responsibility.

The stars gave nothing back.

Still, Eirik stood a while longer beneath them, breathing the cold, feeling both smaller and more bound to what was his to guard.

When he finally went inside, the warmth met him again, and he closed the door carefully behind him.

Nothing had become easier.

That, perhaps, was the true cost of seeing.

Chapter Eleven
Embers and Old Tales

By night the longhouse had gone soft around the edges.

The day's work still clung to it—the smell of wool damp from melted frost, a hint of fish oil near the door, the sharper scent of fresh-cut birch by the wall—but the fire had gentled everything. The flames were mostly down now, burned into a bed of red-orange embers that breathed quietly beneath a drift of ash. Smoke wandered upward in a thin blue thread toward the roof hole, and the shadows around the rafters seemed less like darkness than like old company.

Outside, the wind moved along the village path and around the turf walls, but inside it was warm enough for boots to be loosened and shoulders to ease.

Eirik Halvardsson sat on the bench nearest the hearth with one arm draped along the back of it and a horn of watered ale resting untouched near his knee. His sword belt hung on a peg by the door. His boots were still on, but unlaced. Across from him, Astrid was mending a tear at the hem of Leif's tunic with the calm patience of someone who knew cloth, children, and men all shared the habit of coming apart at useful moments.

Leif sprawled on the floor furs with a carved horse in one hand and a stick in the other, using the stick as a spear, sword, mast, and king's staff in turn depending on what the story in his head demanded. Sigrid sat nearer the fire with her legs folded beneath her, sorting a handful of polished bones and pebbles into neat little rows for no reason Leif could understand and therefore disliked.

Arn was there too, because Arn had arrived at dusk claiming he had only come to return a borrowed knife and then somehow stayed through stew, bread, and half the firewood. He sat cross-legged near the end of the bench, sharpening one of his bearded axes with slow strokes and the expression of a man listening harder than he wished to appear.

"It is too quiet," Leif said.

"It is evening," Sigrid replied.

"That is not the same thing."

"No," she said, "but it usually comes with it."

Leif flopped onto his back and stared up at the rafters. "Someone should tell a story."

Arn looked up from the axe edge. "That sounds like work. I came here to avoid work."

"You sharpen axes for pleasure," Sigrid said.

"That is different. Axes improve when spoken to kindly."

Astrid did not look up from her sewing. "Then yours must be very lonely."

Arn pressed a hand to his chest as if struck. "Cruel."

Eirik watched the fire settle in on itself and felt, for the first time in some days, the deep plain comfort of a house that held no argument sharper than this.

Leif rolled over at once and fixed on him. “Father.”

That one word carried enough demand that even Arn grinned.

“There,” Arn said. “The boy has chosen his victim.”

“I’m not a victim,” Eirik replied.

“No?” Arn’s grin widened. “Then you may tell the story willingly.”

Leif had already pushed himself upright. “Tell one of the gods.”

“Which god?” Eirik asked.

“The strongest one,” Leif said at once.

Sigrid looked at him. “That depends who is being asked.”

Leif frowned. “No, it doesn’t.”

“It always does,” Astrid said.

Leif turned in exasperation from one to the other and then back to his father, as though Eirik alone might preserve order in a world determined to ruin clear thinking. “Tell one with fighting.”

“Of course,” Eirik said. “You would wilt if there were sheep in it.”

“I would not.”

“You would ask when the sheep became men with axes.”

“That is because it would be a better story.”

Arn nodded solemnly. “The boy has instinct.”

Sigrid stacked her stones into two equal lines. “That is not always praise.”

Eirik let them run a few breaths longer, then leaned back against the bench and looked into the embers. The room quieted in the natural way a family room quiets when one voice begins to gather the others without asking for silence.

"All right," he said. "Then I'll tell you about Thor and the fishing line."

Leif brightened at once. Even Sigrid looked up with interest. Arn made a pleased sound in his throat and settled the axe across his knees. Astrid kept sewing, but the corner of her mouth changed, just slightly. She had heard the story before, of course. That had never stopped her from listening.

Eirik began.

"There was a day when Thor decided he wanted a fish larger than sense."

Leif grinned immediately.

"That sounds right," Arn muttered.

Astrid passed the needle through cloth and said, "Most strong men eventually mistake appetite for wisdom."

Arn looked wounded again. "You say such things as if I should learn from them."

"I have given up that hope."

Leif laughed. Sigrid hid hers more carefully.

Eirik went on. "Thor went out in a boat with the giant Hymir, who had the sort of face that looked carved from old driftwood and improved by no season. Hymir meant to fish close to shore, where sensible men fish and return before their wives complain."

Astrid glanced up. "That is also where men return alive."

"There is always a price to cowardice," Arn said.

Astrid met his eyes across the fire. "Yes. It is called old age."

That won a real laugh from Eirik.

Leif leaned forward. "What did Thor do?"

"He rowed farther," Eirik said. "And then farther still. Far enough that Hymir began to worry and say things like, 'This is where decent men stop,' which is always a poor thing to say to Thor."

Leif snorted.

Sigrid asked, "Did Thor know where he was going?"

Eirik considered. "Thor often knows where he is going in the way a storm does."

"That is not an answer," Sigrid said.

"It is the best one available."

Arn pointed the whetstone toward her. "That is how truth escapes when pinned."

She gave him a flat look and returned her attention to Eirik.

"So Thor baited a line," Eirik said, "not with herring, not with eel, but with an ox head."

Leif's eyes widened with delight. "An ox head?"

"A whole one."

"That's wasteful," Sigrid said.

"It was Thor," Eirik replied.

"That explains the waste, not the wisdom."

Astrid bowed her head a little over the tunic, hiding what was very nearly a smile.

"Down went the line," Eirik said, "deep enough to bother things that had no wish to be bothered. Hymir caught smaller fish and muttered complaints while Thor sat there like a mountain pretending to be a man. Then the line went tight."

Leif had gone utterly still now, his stick forgotten in one hand.

"Tight enough," Eirik said, "that the boat lurched. Tight enough that Thor braced both feet through the boards and pulled with all the strength in him. The sea rose. Foam churned black. And up through the water came Jormungandr himself, the Midgard Serpent, great enough to girdle the world and mean it."

Leif let out a low sound of astonishment.

Arn grinned.

Sigrid's brows lifted slightly.

"His eyes were like green fire under storm water," Eirik continued. "His coils were thick as tree trunks and longer than any man could count without forgetting his own name. Thor looked at him and, being Thor, smiled."

"That part sounds true," Arn said.

Astrid murmured, "It sounds stupid."

"Those are cousins," Arn replied.

Eirik stretched his hand toward the fire as if weighing the serpent there in his palm. "Thor took up Mjolnir with one hand while the line strained in the other, and for a moment it seemed the whole world had drawn breath to watch whether god or serpent would strike first."

Leif nearly bounced where he sat. "Did he hit it?"

"Not then," Eirik said. "Because Hymir, who had reached the end of his courage and found the place empty beyond it, cut the line."

Leif groaned in outrage.

Arn spat a curse under his breath.

Sigrid only said, "That was sensible."

Leif turned on her. "No, it wasn't."

"It was if you wished not to be drowned."

"He ruined it."

"He lived."

"That isn't the same thing."

Sigrid looked back at the stones and nudged one into place with a fingertip. "It often is."

Eirik watched that exchange and felt, not for the first time, how clearly each child already leaned toward a different shape of the world. Leif toward greatness, danger, boldness. Sigrid toward consequence, aftermath, what came after the shout. Neither wrong. Neither complete.

He went on before the argument could grow legs.

"Thor was angry, of course."

"Good," Leif said.

"Because his fish was gone," Sigrid said.

Arn laughed softly. "You'd have made an excellent skald if you had any mercy at all."

"I have mercy," she said. "For people worth the effort."

Astrid's needle flashed in the firelight. "A daughter after my own peace."

Eirik smiled and leaned his head back against the bench.

"But here is the part men often miss," he said. "They tell the tale as if it were only about Thor wanting a fight with the serpent, and that is certainly part of it, because Thor has never been known for avoiding a blow if one might be thrown instead. But the serpent circles the world. If it stirs, all things stir. Storm, sea, field, house, ship, child asleep in bed—none are left outside it."

The room quieted a little.

Leif was still watching him, though now with more thought in his face.

Sigrid had stopped sorting the bones.

Astrid sewed on, but more slowly.

"So Thor goes after it not only because he is strong," Eirik said, "but because strong things that threaten the world are his business whether he enjoys them or not."

Arn tilted his head. "That sounds almost noble."

"It pains me to hear it," Eirik said.

Astrid's mouth curved. "Careful. If you make Thor sound too thoughtful, Leif will stop admiring him."

"I won't," Leif protested at once. "I can admire thinking."

Sigrid looked at him. "When it happens near you."

He ignored her by force.

Eirik let the warmth of their voices rest in him a moment before he continued. "Now, if Odin had been in that boat, he would likely have spent half the voyage wondering what the serpent's rising meant for all the years yet to come, and whether losing the boat might teach him something useful."

Arn barked a laugh.

Leif looked fascinated.

Sigrid nodded as if that sounded exactly right.

"And Freyja," Eirik said, "might have asked whether the men on shore had enough sense to know what the serpent's stirring would cost the women waiting on them."

Astrid lifted one brow. "She would ask that first."

"Yes."

"And likely with better words."

"Also yes."

Leif frowned in concentration. "What would Tyr say?"

Arn looked suddenly pleased with the boy.

Eirik took a breath before answering. "Tyr would likely ask whether raising the serpent then and there served justice, or only courage."

Leif's face tightened as he thought that through.

"That sounds difficult," he said.

"It usually is."

Sigrid spoke quietly. "And Frigg?"

The fire shifted. A soft red flare ran through the embers and sank again.

Eirik looked into it a moment before he said, "Frigg might ask what happened to the people waiting at home while gods and giants pulled at monsters in the deep."

No one answered at once.

The room had not grown dark. Only thoughtful.

Astrid broke the hush first, her tone dry enough to keep the weight from settling too hard on the children. "So, by this telling, Thor wanted the serpent, Odin wanted the meaning, Tyr wanted the measure, Freyja wanted the cost, and Frigg wanted everyone to remember there was a world besides the boat."

Arn laughed under his breath. “That may be the truest tale told in this house yet.”

Leif looked from one face to the next. “Then how does anything ever get done if the gods all want different things?”

Eirik smiled faintly.

“There,” Astrid said. “The right question at last.”

Sigrid looked toward the hearth. “Maybe that is why things so often become a mess.”

“A comforting thought,” Arn said.

Eirik rested his forearms on his knees and leaned slightly closer to the fire. The embers painted his hands in red and gold. He thought of the things he had seen—not in songs, but in the strange harder truth beneath them. He thought of Odin’s severity, Thor’s blunt strength, Freyja’s sharp feeling, Frigg’s wider knowing, Tyr’s clean measure. He thought of how once he had believed the gods stood above such differences as men argued in halls.

Now he knew better.

But he also knew this was not the hour to hand his children the whole weight of that knowledge.

“Things get done,” he said, “because the world does not wait for agreement. A roof still needs mending in rain. A child still needs feeding. A field still needs sowing. A wolf still has to be driven off whether one god wants wisdom, another justice, and a third a larger net.”

Leif grinned at that. “Thor would want the larger net.”

“Thor would want a hammer,” Sigrid said.

“For a fish?”

“For anything.”

That sent even Astrid into a quiet laugh.

Eirik looked around at them—the children in the firelight, Arn pretending at laziness while listening like a man storing each word, Astrid with the half-mended tunic in her lap and that look in her eyes that always told him she had seen more in his meaning than he'd intended to show.

He went on, more softly now.

"The gods are not simple. That does not mean men must despair of them."

Leif frowned a little. "Then what do they need?"

The question came more nakedly than the others had.

Eirik sat with it a moment.

Astrid did not rescue him. Neither did Arn. Even Sigrid waited.

At last he said, "Not blind praise."

That sharpened the room.

He looked into the fire as he found the rest of it.

"They do not need your worship as if they were hungry for flattery. They need your attention. Your honesty. They need you not to sleep through the world they've put you in."

No one spoke at once.

Sigrid nodded first, small and thoughtful. "That sounds harder."

"It is," Eirik said.

Leif lay back on the floor furs and folded his hands behind his head. "If I ever meet Thor, I'll ask him if he truly smiled at the serpent."

"If you ever meet Thor," Sigrid said, "I hope you first ask whether you are standing somewhere safe."

"That is not the first question."

"It should be."

Eirik chuckled under his breath.

The story should have ended there, perhaps. Yet Leif was not done.

"What happened after Hymir cut the line?" he asked.

Eirik looked at him. "Thor was angry."

"I know that part."

"He may have knocked Hymir into the sea."

"Good."

"That is not certain."

"It should be."

Sigrid shook her head. "You only approve of endings if someone falls off something."

"Not always."

"Usually."

Arn held up one hand. "In fairness, good endings improve with splashing."

Astrid folded the mended tunic and laid it aside. "That explains much about your life."

Eirik took a sip of the now-cool ale.

"He did not catch the serpent," he said. "And that stayed with him." He looked into the embers. "The sea went dark again. The boat rose and settled. Hymir rowed like a man trying to outdistance his own terror, and Thor sat there with the hammer still in his hand and the water on his beard."

The room was quiet now.

"He came back angry," Eirik said. "Not because he had failed, but because he had come close enough to know the thing would have to be faced again."

Arn's grin faded into something more thoughtful.

Sigrid's fingers rested still on the pouch in her lap.

Leif looked at his father with the bright seriousness children sometimes reach by instinct when a story changes shape beneath them.

"And that," Eirik said, "is often worse."

No one answered at once.

Eirik let the silence hold.

Then he looked around at them—the children in the firelight, Arn pretending at laziness while listening like a man storing each word, Astrid with the half-mended tunic in her lap and that look in her eyes that always told him she had seen more in his meaning than he'd intended to show.

He felt the lesson beneath the evening settle into him in the gentlest way yet.

The gods were complicated.

The world was complicated.

But a family gathered close around a low fire was not made lesser by that knowledge.

If anything, it made this warmth dearer.

Leif's voice slowed first. "Tell another one tomorrow."

"That depends," Eirik said.

"On what?"

"On whether you split more wood than words."

Leif made a tired sound of protest and curled onto one side.

Sigrid gathered her bones and pebbles into a little pouch and tied it shut. Arn finally sheathed the sharpened axe and leaned back against the bench leg with a low groan, as if comfort itself had ambushed him.

Astrid rose and came to stand near Eirik, one hand resting lightly on the back of the bench. She looked down at him with that unreadable, knowing expression he had come to trust more than any clear answer.

"You told it kindly," she said.

He looked up at her. "Was that wrong?"

"No." Her mouth curved faintly. "Only unusual."

"That is cruel."

"That is marriage."

He took her hand and pressed his thumb once over her knuckles.

The room had nearly fallen to embers now. Leif was half asleep. Sigrid leaned against the wall with her eyes heavy but still open. Arn looked as though he intended to leave and already knew he would not for another quarter hour.

At last Astrid said, "If you are done teaching them the nature of heaven, help me put them to bed."

Arn opened one eye. "I notice you said them."

"I did."

He sighed. "A cold thing to hear from kin."

"You are not kin."

"No," Arn said, sitting up with a grin. "Only better company."

Leif, not fully awake, muttered, "Stay. Tell the part where Hymir falls in."

Eirik looked at him. "He did not fall in."

Leif's eyes stayed shut. "He should have."

That finally broke the room into easy laughter.

Sigrid, already standing, said, "If you stay, you snore."

"That is a song of sleep."

"It is a punishment."

Even that made Eirik laugh.

And as the night drew close around the longhouse, with smoke above, warm furs below, and the last of the fire glowing like a held memory in the dark, the house seemed for a little while to stand outside all harsher things.

Not beyond the gods.

Not beyond fate.

But beyond fear.

Only home.

Only family.

Only laughter carrying a little wisdom in it, like sparks lifted softly from dying fire and carried upward into the night.

Chapter Twelve

Tyr's Measure

Morning came hard and clear.

The night wind had swept the smoke from the village and left the sky pale as bone above the fjord. Frost lay thick in the shadows of the fences and silvered the path between the longhouses. Down near the shore, the boats knocked softly at their moorings, and the sound carried farther than it should have in the cold.

Eirik Halvardsson stood in the yard with a splitting maul in his hands and brought it down through a knot of birch that had resisted him twice already. The log cracked at last and fell apart in two uneven halves.

"You're taking offense from firewood again," Astrid said from the doorway.

Eirik rested both hands on the maul haft and looked over his shoulder. "The wood started it."

Astrid had a basket against one hip and a strip of dried fish in one hand, which she was dividing with a knife for the morning meal. Her braid had come slightly loose near the temple, though she had not yet bothered to fix it. That usually meant her mind was already ahead of the hour.

"The wood cannot defend itself," she said.

"That is why I choose it carefully."

"That sounds less honorable than you think."

A breath of laughter left him.

That was one of the things he loved in her. Even now, with all that had passed between gods and men, between blood and conscience and sleep, Astrid could still bring him back to the shape of a morning by speaking to him as if nothing in the world was too great to survive a dry answer.

Behind her, Leif was pulling on one boot while trying to eat at the same time. He managed to do neither well.

Sigrid sat on the bench by the hearth, already dressed, already awake in the sharper way she always was, watching her brother with the patient disapproval of someone older than her winters.

"You'll fall before the threshold," she said.

"I won't."

"You are putting the wrong foot in the wrong boot."

Leif froze, looked down, and scowled. "No, I'm not."

He was.

Sigrid did not smile. She only held his gaze until he pulled the boot off and changed it.

Astrid handed Eirik the fish strip as he came in. "Eat while you still remember where your mouth is."

"That is a harsh beginning to the day."

"It is a merciful one."

Leif looked up at once. "Father, when can I train with the real shield again?"

"When you stop treating the practice one as if it has offended your family."

"It never does what I tell it."

"That may be because it is wood," Sigrid said.

Leif ignored her with effort. "I held better yesterday."

"You did," Eirik said.

That pleased the boy enough to light his whole face, though he tried to stand straighter and hide it.

Then there came the sound of quick feet on the frozen path, and a man's voice calling from the gate.

"Eirik! Astrid!"

The tone was wrong for ordinary greeting.

Eirik went to the yard at once. Astrid followed more slowly, setting the basket down just inside the threshold.

It was Hrolf Ketilsson's cousin Asgeir from the lower sheds, red-faced from cold and hurry.

"There's trouble by Runa's store hut," he said. "Sten's already there."

That was enough.

Eirik took his cloak from the peg without another question. Astrid met his eyes once in passing. No words were needed between them. The children saw the look and quieted of their own accord.

"I'm coming," Leif said at once.

"No," both parents said together.

Leif's jaw tightened. "I can at least stand back and watch."

"That is how boys get kicked by mules and shouted at by jarls," Astrid said.

"I wouldn't stand that close."

Sigrid rose and fastened her cloak at the throat. "You would."

Leif turned on her. "Not if I was told not to."

"You would only call it obeying from a better angle."

Even Eirik might have smiled at that if the messenger had not still been shifting hard from foot to foot in the yard.

"Stay with your mother until I see what this is," Eirik said.

Leif looked mutinous but nodded. That, more than his expression, showed he was learning.

By the time Eirik reached Runa's store hut, half the lane had already gathered.

No one was shouting. That made the tension worse.

Jarl Sten Hakonsson stood in the center of it all with his red braided hair caught back over one shoulder and his ringed beard bright where frost had touched it. The jagged scar across his face looked almost white in the morning light. He did not need to raise his voice to hold the space. Men made room for him because his presence carried command as naturally as smoke carried scent.

Runa stood beside the open store hut, narrow and hard as winter root, her old hands clenched in her apron wool. Opposite her stood Einar, a broad young farmer from the western plots, with his wife pale behind him and two sacks of barley at their feet.

One of the sacks had split near the mouth. Grain lay scattered across the frozen ground.

Arn leaned against the fence post nearby as though he had arrived merely to enjoy someone else's inconvenience. His twin axes hung at his hips, and his grin was too slight to be called cheerful.

When Eirik came up, Sten glanced at him once. "Good."

That meant more than greeting. It meant listen.

Eirik did.

Runa spoke first. "He took it."

Einar's face reddened. "I borrowed it."

"You borrowed in the night?"

"My wife was sick. The child too. We had no meal left."

Runa's mouth thinned. "Then you knock on a door. You do not lift a bar and creep like a thief."

"It was before dawn."

"That makes you quieter, not cleaner."

A few men shifted at that.

Sten looked at the torn sack, then at Einar. "Did you mean to return it?"

"Yes."

"When?"

"After the next fish trade. Or when the milling was done."

Sten's gaze did not change. "You had no right to take what was not yours without word."

"No."

Runa's anger did not soften. "If I had not woken, he'd have taken both sacks."

"I would not."

Arn spoke then, not loudly. "Men say many good things when caught in poor work."

Einar shot him a furious glance and then thought better of speaking back.

Eirik looked at the scattered barley on the frost, then at Einar's wife. She had one hand pressed hard over her own wrist as though trying not to show how frightened she was. She looked more ashamed than her husband did. There was hollowness around her eyes. The child beside her coughed once, a deep little sound, then buried his face in her skirt.

A theft, yes.

Need, yes.

Wrong done, yes.

He felt at once how the morning had sharpened into something larger than grain.

Sten turned slightly toward him. "What do you see?"

Eirik knew Sten was not asking merely for facts.

"A man who stole," he said.

Runa nodded sharply.

"A man who feared his child going hungry," Eirik added.

Runa made an irritated sound, but Sten lifted a hand and she held her tongue.

"And?" the jarl asked.

Eirik looked at Einar again. The young man did not look hardened in guilt. He looked trapped between shame and need, and perhaps also between the foolish pride of a man who would rather steal than admit helplessness before neighbors.

"And I see that hunger makes weak men stupid," Eirik said.

Arn snorted softly. "At least the gods preserve honesty in you."

Einar bristled, but Sten stepped in before anger could turn the lane into a worse sort of lesson.

"You wronged Runa," Sten said. "And you wronged the village. A bar lifted in the dark does not stay one man's business once done." His voice stayed level. "You'll repay the grain double by spring measure. You'll mend the store door you lifted, and until that debt is settled, you work one day in every six for Runa's household."

Einar's face darkened. "Double?"

"You stole from winter stores."

"I took one sack."

"You broke trust as well as wood," Sten said. "Both cost."

Runa's mouth did not soften, but some of the hurt left her shoulders.

Eirik watched Einar's wife more than Einar himself. Relief and fear crossed through her at once. The sentence was hard enough to sting, not hard enough to break them. Order preserved. Wrong marked. Need acknowledged without cleansing the act.

It was just.

Or near enough to justice that men could live under it.

Einar bowed his head stiffly. "I'll do it."

Sten looked at him for another long beat. "See that you do."

The crowd began to loosen then, not because the matter felt pleasant, but because it had been measured and named. That was often all people needed before turning back to their own burdens.

Arn pushed off the fence post and fell in beside Eirik as the others drifted away.

"Well," he said. "There it is. Grain, hunger, shame, and a jarl's face long enough to scare honesty out of a fox."

"That is one of Sten's better skills," Eirik said.

Arn glanced sideways at him. "You watched the wife more than the husband."

"Yes."

"Good. Wives usually tell the truth with their shoulders before husbands admit it with their mouths."

Eirik looked at him. "That sounds like experience."

"It is pain," Arn replied. "A nobler teacher."

That drew a short laugh from Eirik.

They walked a little farther down the lane together before Arn said, too casually, "You know what this smells like."

"Poor grain?"

"Justice." Arn adjusted one axe at his hip. "Ugly little thing. Never enters through the front door."

Eirik said nothing.

Arn gave him a brief look. "You're thinking of Hrolf again."

"Yes."

"I would be worried if you weren't." Arn scraped frost from his beard with one thumb. "Leave a wolf breathing, sometimes he takes a child. Kill him too quick, sometimes you become the wolf yourself. There's your pretty choice."

"That is not a better answer."

"No. But it is truer." Arn's grin thinned. "Tyr likes such mornings."

Eirik turned his head slightly. "You speak of him as if he walks the lanes."

"He does, when men start pretending justice is only revenge with nicer boots."

Arn said it half in jest, half in something else.

That stayed with Eirik longer than the line ought to have.

By midday the sky had gone white again. The sun showed as a pale coin over the fjord and gave little warmth. Eirik spent the next hours in ordinary tasks—hauling split birch to the shed, resetting a loose hinge on the goat pen, helping Hakon's grandson drag a broken fish rack upright after the night wind. Yet the judgment in the lane lingered in him.

Runa had been wronged.

Einar had been desperate.

Sten had punished the theft and preserved the family.

No blood had been spilled.

No one had called it mercy.

No one had called it vengeance.

Justice, Eirik thought, often looked less glorious than men preferred.

When he returned to his yard, Leif was waiting with a practice axe in hand and impatience written all through him.

"What happened?"

"A man stole grain," Eirik said.

Leif blinked. "That's all?"

"That was enough."

"Did Sten beat him?"

"No."

Leif frowned. "Then what?"

Eirik told him, briefly.

Leif listened hard, brow pulling in as he tried to understand a punishment not made of blood or bruises. Beside him, Sigrid was sorting dried onions into smaller bundles with the kind of care that made the whole task look more intelligent than it was.

At last Leif asked, “If a man does something bad, why not just punish him hard and be done?”

Sigrid answered first. “Because after he’s punished, he still has to live somewhere.”

Leif looked at her. “That doesn’t make him less wrong.”

“No,” she said. “But it means other people still have to eat beside him.”

The simplicity of it landed harder than if an elder had spoken.

Leif frowned down at the axe handle. “If Hrolf had lived in the village, Sten wouldn’t have just doubled his grain.”

“No,” Eirik said.

Leif looked up quickly. “Then bad men should die.”

Eirik held his son’s gaze a moment before answering. “Some should.”

Leif waited.

“Some should not,” Eirik said.

“That sounds useless.”

“Most true things do at first.”

Sigrid’s hands never stopped moving over the onions. “You want everything to sort itself the way wood does.”

Leif scowled. “Wood makes sense.”

“Only because Father uses an axe.”

Eirik almost smiled, but the question beneath Leif’s bluntness cut too close to ease.

When does a bad man become a dead man?

When is sparing him weakness?

When is killing him justice?

When is either only the easier road dressed in better words?

The afternoon thinned around those questions.

Toward evening, Sten sent for him.

This time the summons was not urgent, only direct. Eirik found the jarl not in the great hall, but near the boundary stones above the village where old disputes were sometimes settled when men wished to stand outside their own thresholds while doing it.

The place overlooked the fjord and the clustered roofs below. The stones themselves were broad and weathered, carved with marks half-lost to wind and rain. Men had stood there for generations and named what was theirs, what was owed, and what must not be crossed.

Sten stood with his cloak thrown back from one shoulder, red braid hanging over his chest. He was alone.

"You handled the lane well," he said when Eirik came up.

"You handled it."

"I asked what you saw."

Eirik inclined his head a little. That was fair.

Sten looked out over the village. "Men think strength makes judgment simple."

"It often makes it louder."

Sten grunted. "Aye."

For a while they stood in silence.

Then the jarl said, "You're still carrying Hrolf."

Eirik did not answer at once. "Yes."

"Good." Sten looked at him now. "Only fools drop a lesson before it has finished cutting them."

"That is a cheerful thought."

"I am known for cheer."

Eirik snorted softly.

Sten went on. "You were wrong to leave him if leaving him meant danger returned to the innocent." He let that stand only a moment. "You would have been wrong also if you had cut him down only to satisfy anger after the fight had ended."

Eirik studied him. "That sounds like a narrow bridge."

"It is." Sten folded his arms. "That is why so many men miss it."

The wind moved between the stones and off over the water.

Eirik looked out across the fjord, then down toward the village roofs. "And what do you call the bridge?"

Sten thought a moment. "Right measure."

The words hit him with a force out of all proportion to their calm.

Not mercy.

Not vengeance.

Not softness.

Not hunger.

Measure.

He had heard similar truths from Thor, from Frigg, even from the crack between Odin and Freyja, but always through the larger and stranger language of gods. In Sten's mouth it came down to earth and stood on mortal legs.

Eirik drew breath to answer.

Instead, the world changed.

Not dramatically. Not with thunder or hall fire or ravens darkening the sky.

It sharpened.

The wind seemed to clean itself.

The edges of the stones grew harder.

Every sound below in the village thinned away until only the scrape of Eirik's own boot on frost and the quiet settling of Sten's cloak remained.

Sten went still.

Not frozen. Aware.

Both men turned.

A third figure stood between the boundary stones where no one had stood a heartbeat before.

He was not larger than Thor had been, nor more unsettlingly vast than Frigg, nor as weight-heavy as Odin. Yet something in him made the whole place feel exact. Measured. As if every line of stone and path and oath had suddenly been drawn straighter by his presence.

Tyr.

He wore no excess. No flowing splendor. No hidden mystery. A dark cloak lay over broad shoulders built for battle and endurance both. His face was spare, hard in the way of a blade well-forged and often used. Nothing in him invited comfort, but neither did anything in him seek to wound. His gaze was clean enough to feel almost merciless. Not because it lacked understanding. Because it admitted no fog where truth required cutting.

Sten bowed his head first.

Eirik followed.

When they lifted their eyes again, Tyr had not moved.

"Jarl," he said to Sten.

The voice was plain, low, and utterly without ornament. No hall could have held it falsely.

"Lord," Sten answered.

Tyr looked to Eirik.

There was no mystery in the gaze. No layered seeing as with Frigg. No strategic weight as with Odin. He looked at Eirik as a man might look at a line carved into oak and ask only whether it had been cut true.

"You spared a guilty man," Tyr said.

It was not accusation. It was fact.

"Yes."

"He returned and innocent blood followed."

"Yes."

The words stood between them in the cold.

Tyr came one step nearer. "Was your mercy just?"

Eirik felt the question land like an axe edge set against green wood.

He did not answer quickly.

Tyr did not fill the silence for him.

At last Eirik said, "No."

Sten's head shifted slightly, though he remained silent.

Tyr's face did not change. "Why?"

"I spared him because I would not kill a beaten man for anger's sake after the fight was done."

"That answers why you withheld death," Tyr said. "It does not answer whether justice was served."

The distinction opened in Eirik like cold water.

He stood under it.

"I thought," he said slowly, "that ending him there would have made me lesser."

"Would it?"

"I do not know."

That was the hardest truth available. He gave it.

Tyr's gaze did not soften. It deepened, just enough to show that honesty mattered there even when certainty did not.

"A man may preserve his own soul by sparing the guilty," Tyr said. "And in doing so, fail the innocent who must live with what he spared." His voice remained level. "What do you call that?"

Eirik swallowed once. "Failure."

"Yes."

The word cut cleanly.

Not condemnation. Recognition.

Sten kept his place and said nothing. Yet Eirik felt, strangely, no humiliation in the moment. Only the stark relief of a wound finally named correctly.

Tyr went on. "And if you had killed him in anger, after battle, with no thought beyond satisfaction—what then?"

Eirik answered more quickly this time. "That would not have been justice either."

"No."

Again the word fell like a measured stone.

Tyr turned slightly, one hand resting briefly against the nearest boundary marker. "Men confuse vengeance with justice because vengeance burns hotter. It feels cleaner in the blood. It promises an end." His eyes came back to Eirik. "Justice is colder."

The wind moved through the stones.

Below them, the village remained half-visible in the dimming light. Smoke. Roofs. Pens. Path. People who knew nothing of the god standing above their roofs and deciding nothing for them, only sharpening what they themselves must carry.

"What is justice, then?" Eirik asked.

Tyr answered without pause. "Right measure."

Sten let out a slow breath through his nose, and Eirik knew at once the jarl had walked near this truth all his life without ever naming it beyond mortal words.

Tyr continued. "Mercy is not justice by itself. Vengeance is not justice by itself. Honor is not justice by itself. Each may serve it. Each may also corrupt it."

Eirik thought of the shore.

Of Hrolf kneeling.

Of Leif's blooded hands.

Of the raiders in the lane.

Of the theft that morning and the doubled grain debt.

Of every moment when action had seemed simple until the living had to go on afterward.

"What does a warrior owe?" he asked, almost to himself.

Tyr heard it all the same.

"To the dead: truth," he said.
"To the innocent: protection."
"To the guilty: rightful judgment."
"To the living: order that can be endured."

The words entered Eirik one by one, leaving no room for easy comfort.

"And to himself?" Eirik said.

Tyr held his gaze.

"To himself, he owes no lie."

That struck hardest of all.

Because the lie would have been easy. He could have called his mercy pure. He could have called Hrolf's death later proof that mercy was always weakness. He could have hidden in either extreme and spared himself the harder road between them.

Instead Tyr left him standing where the truth was narrower.

Restraint was not righteousness unless it also guarded the community.

Killing was not justice unless it was rightly measured.

A warrior's soul was not preserved by refusing hard acts, but by refusing false ones.

Tyr looked toward the village below. "You are husband, father, warrior, and man of your jarl's peace. You do not get to choose only one of those and call the rest unfair."

A dry breath of something like humor touched Sten's mouth. "He learns slowly, but he learns."

Eirik cast him a brief glance. "You might have told me the gods were waiting behind every hard thought."

"I suspected you were already burdened enough."

"That is kindness from a jarl."

"It is economy," Sten said.

Even Tyr's expression shifted by the smallest degree, though whether it was approval or amusement Eirik could not say.

The god looked back to Eirik. "There will be lives you must end."

Eirik said nothing.

Tyr stepped closer still. The air around him did not grow colder or heavier. It grew cleaner.

"When that time comes, do it without hatred if you can. Without pleasure if you are worthy. Without false mercy if justice forbids it." His voice stayed flat and exact. "A man who kills rightly is not made holy by it. He is made responsible."

The line settled deeper than anything said before.

Eirik thought then of Leif asking bluntly whether bad men should always die. Of Sigrid seeing consequence where others saw only punishment. Of Astrid saying truth bruised more cleanly than wood. Of the kind of people his children would become by watching what he called right.

Tyr followed that thought as if it had spoken aloud.

"The justice you live by will teach them what kind of world they inhabit."

No godly thunder marked the statement.

None was needed.

Eirik looked down toward the clustered roofs below. Somewhere under those roofs Leif was likely arguing with a bucket or a knife sheath. Sigrid was likely correcting him without thanks. Astrid would see both before either child realized it. They were ordinary things. Mortal things. Yet the order that held such life together rested on judgments no less serious for being made in lanes, doorways, and cold yards.

He said quietly, "Then a father has less right to be wrong."

Tyr answered, "He has less excuse."

That was harsher.

And truer.

For a while no one spoke.

The last light thinned over the fjord. Frost crept back across the edges of the stone. Down in the village, a dog barked, then was called into silence.

At last Eirik said, "What should I have done with Hrolf?"

Tyr did not answer at once. When he did, the plainness of it hurt.

"You should have judged him."

Eirik felt his jaw tighten. "And if judgment required death?"

"Then death."

"And if it did not?"

"Then not."

The clean edge of the answer left no room to hide in feeling.

Not anger.

Not pity.

Judgment.

Rightful measure.

That was what he had failed to do on the shore. He had chosen between mercy and hardness as if those were the only roads. He had not judged. Not fully. Not coldly enough. Not rightly enough for the innocent who would later pay for his hesitation.

Tyr stepped back then, not because the matter was lightened, but because the cut had been made.

"Do not mistake this for command to become ruthless," he said. "Ruthlessness is often only cowardice that found steel." His gaze held Eirik fast. "Justice asks more."

Then, for the first time, Tyr looked directly to Sten.

"You know this."

Sten bowed his head once. "I try to."

"That is all men can do."

The words, spoken from that mouth, were not leniency. They were burden.

Eirik felt them as such.

The air shifted.

Tyr's presence did not vanish dramatically. It lessened with the same severe clarity it had brought. One moment the boundary stones held three men and a god. The next they held only Eirik and Sten in the cold evening, with the fjord below and the village beginning to light its hearths.

Eirik breathed out slowly, as if he had not trusted his lungs while Tyr stood there.

Sten rubbed one hand over his beard. “Well.”

“That seems to be the word men use after gods leave,” Eirik said.

“It saves time.”

They stood together a little longer.

At last Sten said, “You understand?”

“More.”

“Not enough?”

“Not comfortably.”

Sten nodded. “That is usually how you know a thing is worth keeping.”

They walked back toward the village in growing dark.

Smoke had begun to rise thicker from the roofs. Firelight showed at the cracks of shutters and doorframes. The world below them was unchanged and yet, to Eirik, more exact than before.

When he entered his yard, Leif looked up at once from the chopping block where he had been trying to split kindling into pieces too small to matter.

“You were gone long.”

“Yes.”

“Did Sten need you?”

“Yes.”

Leif frowned. “For what?”

Sigrid answered from the step before Eirik could. “If he wanted us to know already, he would say it first.”

Leif gave her a look. "You always speak as if you're already old."

"And you always speak as if questions are arrows."

"They are."

"No," she said. "They only feel like it when you throw them badly."

Astrid came from the doorway then, wiping her hands on a cloth. One glance at Eirik's face was enough.

"You found a hard answer," she said.

He looked at her.

She met his gaze calmly, waiting.

"Yes."

"Did it improve your mood?"

"No."

"Good," she said. "Easy truths usually belong to fools."

That might almost have made him laugh.

Instead he crossed the yard and stood near the hearth-door warmth with the smell of woodsmoke and evening meal wrapping around him. Leif was still watching him too hard. Sigrid too, though more quietly. Astrid, of course, saw all three of them.

Leif said, with the bluntness only a child can carry without shame, "If a bad man hurts people, should he always die?"

The yard went still.

Astrid did not stop him. Neither did Eirik.

At last Eirik said, "Not always."

Leif frowned. "Then how do you know?"

Eirik looked at his son, then toward the open door where firelight moved over the floor. He did not reach for too much.

"You judge what is owed," he said.

Leif made a face. "That still sounds like work."

"It is," Eirik said.

Sigrid's voice came quieter. "Owed to who?"

Eirik turned toward her.

There it was—the sharper question, as always.

"To the dead, truth," he said.
"To the innocent, protection."
He let the next words settle before speaking them.
"To the guilty, rightful judgment."

Leif frowned. "That doesn't tell me when."

"No," Eirik said. "It tells you what must be remembered before you decide."

That quieted him more than a sharper answer might have done.

Astrid shifted the door wider with one hand. "Then come inside before your justice freezes in the yard."

That, finally, drew a low laugh from him.

He followed them in.

Later, when the children slept and the fire had burned to a low steady glow, Eirik sat near the hearth with his hands clasped loosely between his knees. Astrid was across from him mending a torn hem. The room was quiet except for the crackle of coals and the faint wind outside.

He thought of Tyr's face. Of the clean hard shape of the truth he had been given. Of how little comfort there was in it and how much order.

"Some lives must be ended rightly," he said at last.

Astrid did not look up from the hem. "Yes."

"Not angrily."

"No."

"Not to satisfy the wound in yourself."

"Never that."

He looked at her. "You say it as if it were easy."

Astrid's mouth curved faintly. "No. I say it as if it were necessary."

He sat with that.

The fire shifted, throwing a brief red flare against the beam above them. In the next room-space, Leif turned in sleep and muttered something about shields. Sigrid, half awake perhaps, made a small sound of annoyance and went quiet again.

Eirik listened.

The house held.

The children breathed.

The world beyond the walls remained full of need, danger, labor, and men who would fail one another in ways great and small.

Justice, he thought, was not glory.

It was not softness either.

It was a weight that had to be carried cleanly, or it dirtied everything beneath it.

He looked toward his children's bedding in the dimness and understood with a heaviness that was almost tenderness that the justice he lived by would teach them more than any words he ever chose.

That was the burden Tyr had left him.

Not peace.

Not permission.

Measure.

And in the low red light of the hearth, with Astrid's quiet presence across from him and the sleeping shape of his family near at hand, Eirik knew he would never again be allowed the comfort of calling mercy good enough simply because it spared his own hand.

Some mercies failed the living.

Some deaths were owed.

And the hardest right acts were often the ones that left no pride behind at all.

13
The Measure of Men

Morning came pale and brittle over the village.

The frost had taken the ground hard in the night and left every path edged in white. Smoke rose slow from the roof vents and drifted low toward the fjord. Somewhere near the lower sheds, a dog barked twice and then fell silent, as if remembering the cold was not worth arguing with.

Eirik Halvardsson stood in the yard with a practice shield on one arm and a stick in his hand.

Leif faced him with a wooden axe, feet planted too wide and jaw set with more determination than balance. His breath smoked in quick bursts. A lock of hair kept falling over his brow, and he kept trying to shake it aside without taking his eyes off his father.

"Again," Eirik said.

Leif came in fast.

Too fast.

Eirik turned the blow with the shield rim and tapped the boy's shoulder with the stick before the second swing had even begun.

"You're dead."

"I'm not."

"You are if the man across from you owns a shield and two eyes."

Leif lowered the axe and scowled. "I nearly had you."

Sigrid, seated on the step with a basket of split willow switches in her lap, said, "That is your favorite place to live."

Leif turned toward her. "I was not talking to you."

"No," she said. "You were arguing with failure."

Eirik hid the edge of a smile and reset the shield on his arm. "Your sister is cruel because the gods were careless with her."

Sigrid looked up. "Or efficient."

Astrid stood in the doorway behind them, one hand braced against the frame, her braid thrown over one shoulder. She had flour on the back of one wrist and the look of a woman already halfway through three tasks before the house had properly warmed.

"Leif," she said, "if you die before the porridge is cooked, I'll still expect you to carry water."

That drew a short laugh from Eirik.

Leif groaned. "Why is no one on my side?"

"I am," Eirik said. "That is why I keep killing you before worse men try."

The boy's expression changed at once. Not softer. Sharper. He nodded and set his feet again.

This time he came in slower, more honestly. Eirik checked the first strike, let the second glance wide, and caught the third on the shield boss.

"Better," he said.

Leif's whole face brightened, though he tried to hide it.

Before Eirik could say more, the bark came again—closer now, rougher, with the strained edge dogs used when they had cornered something uncertain.

All four of them turned.

It was Hakon's dog, old Skalli, running hard from the shore path with his tail stiff and his fur up along the neck. Behind him came Hakon's grandson Tori, breathless and red-faced from cold and haste.

"There's a man in the boat shed!" the boy shouted. "Skalli found him. Arn says come armed."

The yard went still.

Eirik did not waste a word. He handed the practice shield to Leif, crossed to the peg by the door, and took down his real one and sword belt. Astrid had already gone back inside and returned with his cloak.

“Was he armed?” Eirik asked Tori.

“I saw a knife. Maybe more.”

“Did he run?”

“No. He hid.”

Arn hiding no excitement had already told Eirik enough. A man hiding in the boat shed after the weeks they had lived through was no hungry fisher with a lost path.

Astrid fastened Eirik’s shoulder clasp with quick capable fingers. Her face was calm, but he knew the stillness in it.

“I’m coming,” Leif said at once.

“No,” Eirik and Astrid said together.

Leif’s jaw tightened.

Sigrid stood, setting the basket aside. “He’ll follow if you don’t tell him why.”

Leif shot her a look. “I wasn’t going to follow.”

She said nothing.

Eirik settled the shield on his arm and looked at his son. “You stay here because I need one person in this yard to obey before being told twice.”

Leif drew in a breath, held it, then nodded. It cost him. That mattered more than if it had come easily.

Sigrid was watching him, ready to catch the first sign of foolishness.

Astrid said, “If he forgets himself, trip him.”

Leif stared at her in outrage.

“It would save time,” she said.

Then Eirik was already moving down the path.

The village had not fully woken to alarm yet, but tension was spreading faster than smoke. Two men stepped out of a doorway as he passed, saw the shield and sword, and turned toward the shore without being told. A woman at the well clutched her bucket handle tighter and called her youngest inside. The memory of Hrolf's return had not faded enough for anyone to mistake urgency for harmlessness.

By the time Eirik reached the boat sheds, half a dozen men had gathered in a loose half-circle around the open doorway. Arn stood nearest the entrance, one axe in hand, the other still at his belt. He looked entirely too pleased for the hour.

"You took your time," Arn said.

"I stopped to die three times in the yard."

"That explains your mood."

Sten was there too, broad and steady as a standing stone, red braid over one shoulder, the old scar pale in the morning light. He gave Eirik one glance and nodded toward the doorway.

"Inside," he said quietly. "Young. Wounded. Frightened enough to lie badly."

Eirik stepped closer and looked into the dimness.

A young man crouched between stacked oars and a coil of tarred rope, one shoulder against the wall. He had a knife in his hand, though the grip on it was weak. His beard was patchy. He could not have seen more than eighteen winters. Dried blood had stiffened one sleeve, and his left cheek was swollen yellow and blue from some older blow. Hunger had hollowed him around the eyes, but there was still enough life in them to show fear clearly.

Eirik knew him after a moment.

"Eyvind."

The young man flinched at the name.

He was from a smaller holding south of the village, kin by marriage to one of the families here. Eirik had seen him in summers past at boat launches and autumn slaughter days. Not close kin. Not close enough to matter in law. Close enough to make the thing uglier.

Arn spat to one side. “I told them I knew his face.”

Eyvind’s knife rose a little, though his hand shook. “I only wanted food.”

“And a boat?” Arn asked. “You’re ambitious for a hungry man.”

Sten said, “Drop the knife.”

Eyvind’s eyes moved between them—Sten, Eirik, Arn, the men outside the shed, the bright morning beyond the doorway. Cornered things always measured exits even when there were none.

“I didn’t kill anyone,” he said.

No one answered at once.

That told Eirik enough.

Sten took one slow step forward. “Drop the knife.”

Eyvind swallowed. “If I do, you’ll kill me.”

Arn gave a short laugh without humor. “If you don’t, you’ll make it quicker.”

Eirik said, “Do it.”

Something in his voice reached the young man where Arn’s threat and Sten’s authority had not. The knife lowered. Then, after one long uncertain heartbeat, Eyvind let it fall to the floorboards.

Arn kicked it away and dragged him out by the arm before the men outside could lose patience and become a mob.

The lane filled quickly after that.

Word moved faster than kindness in a village, and fear fastest of all. By the time Sten had Eyvind bound to the outer post beside the sheds, old Runa had come to spit at his feet, Bjorn was loudly proposing three different deaths, and two women from the southern path were staring with the pale, stunned faces of people who had recognized the boy after all.

"He was with them," one man said.

"He signaled from the far rise," said another.

"My brother saw someone wave from the rocks before the raiders came," a third put in.

"He was no more than a stripling," someone muttered.

"A stripling with a knife."

Eyvind stood bound and said nothing.

The shame in him was harder to look at than if he had been defiant.

Leif had disobeyed, of course.

Eirik saw him near the back of the crowd with Sigrid beside him, one hand twisted in his sleeve as though she had allowed him this far only so she could drag him back if needed. Astrid stood a little apart from them, not intruding, not retreating either. Her eyes met Eirik's briefly. Not approval. Not censure. Only attention.

Sten raised one hand, and the crowd quieted by degrees.

"Who saw him strike?" the jarl asked.

No one answered.

"Who saw him with Hrolf's men?"

Two hands rose. One of them belonged to Tori's father, who looked ill at having to say it aloud.

“He was on the ridge the night of the attack,” the man said. “Not in the first rush. Watching.”

Another spoke. “I saw him later by the lower wall when the fires took. He ran when he saw me.”

Eyvind shut his eyes.

Sten turned to him. “Speak.”

The boy’s lips parted and closed once before sound came. “I didn’t think…” He stopped, swallowed, and tried again. “Hrolf said there’d be silver. That we’d scare you, take goods, and go. He said no one would be touched if they yielded.”

The silence that followed was colder than shouting.

Runa’s voice cut through it. “And did you believe a wolf promising to guard lambs?”

Eyvind’s head dropped lower. “No.”

There it was.

Not innocence. Not foolishness alone. Chosen wrong, with enough understanding to make the choosing matter.

Leif’s face in the crowd had gone hard and bright with the blunt certainty of youth. Sigrid’s had gone stiller, as if she were already looking past this moment to what it would leave behind.

Sten looked to Eirik.

No words. Only that look again.

What do you see?

Eirik stood for a long heartbeat without speaking.

He heard the fjord below, the knocking of boats, the creak of leather as one man shifted his weight, the wind combing once through the roof straw of the nearest shed. He thought of Hrolf. Of the spared life. Of innocent blood later spilled. Of Tyr's clean voice: *Mercy without justice may endanger the innocent.* He thought of the theft in Runa's lane and how grain and trust had been weighed together. He thought of what a warrior owed the dead, the guilty, the innocent, the living.

Eyvind lifted his head just enough to look at him.

Not pleading exactly. But hoping still. That made it worse.

At last Eirik said, "He came with raiders against homes."

Bjorn nodded sharply, as if that settled everything.

Eirik did not look at him. "He watched. He signaled. He helped bring armed men to sleeping families." He let the words stand as what they were. "Whether or not he struck with his own hand, he stood with those who did."

Eyvind's breath shook. "I never wanted—"

Eirik cut across him, not harshly. "No. You only wanted what came before and not what followed."

The boy went silent.

That, Eirik thought, was what youth often mistook for freedom: the right to choose a thing and not bear its whole shape once it ripened.

Arn said, "He's guilty, then."

"Yes," Eirik said.

The crowd leaned inward.

Leif did too.

Sten asked, very level, "And what is owed?"

The old easier answer would have been swift now. The crowd wanted blood. Fear had left them hungry for clean endings. Arn would not have opposed it. Bjorn would have celebrated it. Even

Sten, if pushed by order alone, might have accepted it without protest.

But the question was not what would satisfy them.

It was what was right.

Eirik looked at Eyvind, then at the men and women around him, then briefly toward his children.

Leif's eyes burned for a blunt answer.
Sigrid's held something sadder, harder.
Astrid only watched.

"To the dead," Eirik said slowly, "truth."

No one spoke.

"To the innocent, protection."

Sten's face did not move, but Eirik felt the jarl's attention sharpen.

"To the guilty," Eirik went on, "right judgment. Not anger."

Arn's mouth twitched at that. Not mockery. Recognition.

Eirik looked at Eyvind again. "If we beat him in the lane, we feed fear and call it justice. If we free him because he is young and sorry, we teach every fool with weak pride that regret is enough once blood is spilled."

A murmur moved through the crowd.

Astrid said, from where she stood, "Peace tears most easily where men mistake softness for mercy."

Several heads turned toward her. She ignored them all.

Eyvind's face had gone white.

Sten said, "Finish it."

Eirik nodded once.

"He came armed with raiders against the village. He helped bring them to our doors. Men and women died because of what he chose to stand with." He drew a breath that felt cold all the way down. "For that, his life is forfeit."

The words fell into the morning like stones into deep water.

Leif stood utterly still.

Bjorn gave a hard approving grunt.

One of the women by the path crossed herself in the old way against ill-luck and looked away.

Eyvind swayed against the post and almost lost his legs. "Please—"

The word cut off when Sten stepped closer.

But Eirik was not finished.

"He will not be beaten." Eirik's voice carried more sharply now. "He will not be cut apart by anger in a lane like a thief under dogs. He will confess before witnesses. He will name what he did and who stood with him. Then he will be given a clean death at the boundary stones."

Arn let out a slow breath. Sten's gaze flicked to him and back.

That was the bridge, Eirik thought. Narrow and hard. No satisfaction in it. No mercy that left danger roaming. No vengeance dressed up as honor. Only measure.

Sten asked, "You would do it?"

The question mattered. More than if the jarl had simply ordered it.

Eirik felt the weight of every eye. Of Eyvind's breath coming too fast. Of Leif somewhere behind the crowd seeing what sort of man his father would be.

"Yes," he said.

The word cost him more than he had expected, and he let it cost him.

Sten studied him a moment longer, then nodded. "So be it."

The crowd broke and reshaped itself around that decision. Some were relieved. Some disappointed there would be no blood in the lane. Some simply wanted the thing ended before it could infect the rest of the day.

Eirik went first to his children before the men took Eyvind up the path.

Leif spoke before he reached them. "He should have died at once."

Sigrid said, "That would have been easier."

Leif turned on her. "Because it's true."

"Because it's hot," she replied. "Those aren't the same."

Eirik stopped before them both.

Leif looked up at him, jaw hard, eyes too young for the certainty in them. "He helped them come here."

"Yes."

"And now you'll kill him anyway."

"Yes."

Leif frowned, trying to find the shape of the difference and hating that it would not sit still for him.

"Then why not do it now?"

Eirik looked at his son for a long moment. "Because justice is not hunger."

Leif said nothing.

Sigrid did.

"It has to leave something people can still live under," she said quietly.

Eirik turned his head toward her. The words were close enough to Tyr that they struck him almost bodily.

"Yes," he said.

Astrid came nearer then and laid one hand briefly on Leif's shoulder. "Go home with your sister."

"I'm not a child."

"No," she said. "You're a boy standing too near a hard lesson. That is close enough."

Leif's mouth tightened, but he obeyed. Sigrid took his sleeve, not dragging this time, only making sure he truly turned toward home.

Astrid remained.

Her eyes met Eirik's, and he saw there not comfort exactly, but the deep steady knowing she carried when pain and necessity had begun walking side by side.

"You found the harder road," she said.

"It does not feel better."

"It rarely does."

He almost smiled. "You are poor at soothing."

"I am excellent at accuracy."

That, too, was a kind of mercy.

At the boundary stones the village gathered again, though fewer this time and quieter. The place always felt colder than the rest of the path, perhaps because men brought their hardest truths there and left them in the wind.

Eyvind confessed what he had done. Not bravely. Not with dignity worth song. Simply because there was nowhere left to hide in words. He named the ridge. The signal cloth. Hrolf's promise of silver. His own belief that the raid would frighten, not slaughter. His own shame in knowing even then that he lied to himself.

Sten heard it all.
Hakon heard it.
Runa heard it.
Eirik heard it.

So did Arn, leaning on one axe with none of his usual grin left.

When the confession was done, Sten asked Eyvind if he had anything else to say.

The boy's eyes found Eirik.

"I was afraid," he said.

"I know," Eirik answered.

It was not absolution. Only truth.

Then Eirik drew his sword.

He did not hate the boy.
He did not pity him enough to lie.
He did not rush.

That, perhaps, was the hardest part. To do a thing rightly without letting anger carry it for him.

Eyvind knelt.
Sten placed one hand on his shoulder and removed it.
The wind moved once between the stones.

Eirik ended it cleanly.

Afterward, no one cheered.

Bjorn kept his mouth shut.
Arn looked away toward the fjord.
Sten said only, "It is done."

Yes, Eirik thought. Done. Not mended. Not made good. Done.

By evening he sat once more by his own hearth, the fire low and steady, Astrid across from him with Leif and Sigrid close enough to warmth that their shadows touched on the wall behind them.

No one spoke much at first.

Leif finally said, "Was it just?"

The room stayed very still.

Eirik looked at the boy, then at the girl beside him, who was watching him with that quiet sharpness that made lying to her feel like spitting into clean water.

"It was what was owed," he said.

Leif frowned. "That is not the same as yes."

"No," Eirik said. "It isn't."

Sigrid spoke softly. "Then maybe justice is what still hurts after you know it was right."

Astrid's eyes lifted from the fire to her daughter and stayed there a moment.

Eirik felt the words settle into him like cold iron finding its shape.

"Yes," he said at last. "Perhaps it is."

Leif leaned back against the bench, unsatisfied but thinking. That would have to be enough for now.

The house held its warmth around them. Outside, the village settled under frost and dark, roof by roof, door by door. Inside, Eirik listened to the breathing of those he loved and understood with a new heaviness that all he had learned from gods and men alike had not made life cleaner.

Only stricter.

A man could not keep his soul by avoiding hard acts.
He could only try not to stain it by doing them falsely.

And as the fire sank lower and the children drifted nearer sleep, Eirik knew he had crossed into a sterner part of his life.

Not because the gods had spoken.

Because he had acted, and could not unknow what that required.

Chapter Thirteen

The Measure of Men

Morning came pale and brittle over the village.

The frost had taken the ground hard in the night and left every path edged in white. Smoke rose slowly from the roof vents and drifted low toward the fjord. Somewhere near the lower sheds, a dog barked twice and then fell silent, as if remembering the cold was not worth arguing with.

Eirik Halvardsson stood in the yard with a practice shield on one arm and a stick in his hand.

Leif faced him with a wooden axe, feet planted too wide and jaw set with more determination than balance. His breath smoked in quick bursts. A lock of hair kept falling over his brow, and he kept trying to shake it aside without taking his eyes off his father.

"Again," Eirik said.

Leif came in fast.

Too fast.

Eirik turned the blow with the shield rim and tapped the boy's shoulder with the stick before the second swing had even begun.

"You're dead."

"I'm not."

"You are if the man across from you owns a shield and two eyes."

Leif lowered the axe and scowled. "I nearly had you."

Sigrid, seated on the step with a basket of split willow switches in her lap, said, "That is your favorite place to live."

Leif turned toward her. "I was not talking to you."

"No," she said. "You were arguing with failure."

Eirik hid the edge of a smile and reset the shield on his arm. "Your sister is cruel because the gods were careless with her."

Sigrid looked up. "Or efficient."

Astrid stood in the doorway behind them, one hand braced against the frame, her braid thrown over one shoulder. She had flour on the back of one wrist and the look of a woman already halfway through three tasks before the house had properly warmed.

"Leif," she said, "if you die before the porridge is cooked, I'll still expect you to carry water."

That drew a short laugh from Eirik.

Leif groaned. "Why is no one on my side?"

"I am," Eirik said. "That is why I keep killing you before worse men try."

The boy's expression changed at once. Not softer. Sharper. He nodded and set his feet again.

This time he came in slower, more honestly. Eirik checked the first strike, let the second glance wide, and caught the third on the shield boss.

"Better," he said.

Leif's whole face brightened, though he tried to hide it.

Before Eirik could say more, the bark came again—closer now, rougher, with the strained edge dogs used when they had cornered something uncertain.

All four of them turned.

It was Hakon's dog, old Skalli, running hard from the shore path with his tail stiff and his fur up along the neck. Behind him came Hakon's grandson Tori, breathless and red-faced from cold and haste.

"There's a man in the boat shed!" the boy shouted. "Skalli found him. Arn says come armed."

The yard went still.

Eirik did not waste a word. He handed the practice shield to Leif, crossed to the peg by the door, and took down his real one and sword belt. Astrid had already gone back inside and returned with his cloak.

"Was he armed?" Eirik asked Tori.

"I saw a knife. Maybe more."

"Did he run?"

"No. He hid."

Arn hiding no excitement had already told Eirik enough. A man hiding in the boat shed after the weeks they had lived through was no hungry fisher with a lost path.

Astrid fastened Eirik's shoulder clasp with quick capable fingers. Her face was calm, but he knew the stillness in it.

"I'm coming," Leif said at once.

"No," Eirik and Astrid said together.

Leif's jaw tightened.

Sigrid stood, setting the basket aside. "He'll follow if you don't tell him why."

Leif shot her a look. "I wasn't going to follow."

She said nothing.

Eirik settled the shield on his arm and looked at his son. "You stay here because I need one person in this yard to obey before being told twice."

Leif drew in a breath, held it, then nodded. It cost him. That mattered more than if it had come easily.

Sigrid was watching him, ready to catch the first sign of foolishness.

Astrid said, "If he forgets himself, trip him."

Leif stared at her in outrage.

"It would save time," she said.

Then Eirik was already moving down the path.

The village had not fully woken to alarm yet, but tension was spreading faster than smoke. Two men stepped out of a doorway as he passed, saw the shield and sword, and turned toward the shore without being told. A woman at the well clutched her bucket handle tighter and called her youngest inside. The memory of Hrolf's return had not faded enough for anyone to mistake urgency for harmlessness.

By the time Eirik reached the boat sheds, half a dozen men had gathered in a loose half-circle around the open doorway. Arn stood nearest the entrance, one axe in hand, the other still at his belt. He looked entirely too pleased for the hour.

"You took your time," Arn said.

"I stopped to die three times in the yard."

"That explains your mood."

Sten was there too, broad and steady as a standing stone, red braid over one shoulder, the old scar pale in the morning light. He gave Eirik one glance and nodded toward the doorway.

"Inside," he said quietly. "Young. Wounded. Frightened enough to lie badly."

Eirik stepped closer and looked into the dimness.

A young man crouched between stacked oars and a coil of tarred rope, one shoulder against the wall. He had a knife in his hand, though the grip on it was weak. He could not have seen more than eighteen winters. Dried blood had stiffened one sleeve, and his left cheek was swollen yellow and blue from some older blow. Hunger had hollowed him around the eyes, but there was still enough life in them to show fear clearly.

Eirik knew him after a moment.

"Eyvind."

The young man flinched at the name.

He was from a smaller holding south of the village, kin by marriage to one of the families here. Eirik had seen him in summers past at boat launches and autumn slaughter days. Not close kin. Not close enough to matter in law. Close enough to make the thing uglier.

Arn spat to one side. “I told them I knew his face.”

Eyvind’s knife rose a little, though his hand shook. “I only wanted food.”

“And a boat?” Arn asked. “You’re ambitious for a hungry man.”

Sten said, “Drop the knife.”

Eyvind’s eyes moved between them—Sten, Eirik, Arn, the men outside the shed, the bright morning beyond the doorway. Cornered things always measured exits even when there were none.

“I didn’t kill anyone,” he said.

No one answered at once.

That told Eirik enough.

Sten took one slow step forward. “Drop the knife.”

Eyvind swallowed. “If I do, you’ll kill me.”

Arn gave a short laugh without humor. “If you don’t, you’ll make it quicker.”

Eirik said, “Do it.”

Something in his voice reached the young man where Arn’s threat and Sten’s authority had not. The knife lowered. Then, after one long uncertain heartbeat, Eyvind let it fall to the floorboards.

Arn kicked it away and dragged him out by the arm before the men outside could lose patience and become a mob.

The lane filled quickly after that.

Word moved faster than kindness in a village, and fear fastest of all. By the time Sten had Eyvind bound to the outer post beside the sheds, old Runa had come to spit at his feet, Bjorn was loudly proposing three different deaths, and two women from the southern path were staring with the pale, stunned faces of people who had recognized the boy after all.

"He was with them," one man said.

"He signaled from the far rise," said another.

"My brother saw someone wave from the rocks before the raiders came," a third put in.

"He was no more than a stripling," someone muttered.

"A stripling with a knife."

Eyvind stood bound and said nothing.

The shame in him was harder to look at than if he had been defiant.

Leif had disobeyed, of course.

Eirik saw him near the back of the crowd with Sigrid beside him, one hand twisted in his sleeve as though she had allowed him this far only so she could drag him back if needed. Astrid stood a little apart from them, not intruding, not retreating either. Her eyes met Eirik's briefly. Not approval. Not censure. Only attention.

Sten raised one hand, and the crowd quieted by degrees.

"Who saw him strike?" the jarl asked.

No one answered.

"Who saw him with Hrolf's men?"

Two hands rose. One of them belonged to Tori's father, who looked ill at having to say it aloud.

"He was on the ridge the night of the attack," the man said. "Not in the first rush. Watching."

Another spoke. "I saw him later by the lower wall when the fires took. He ran when he saw me."

Eyvind shut his eyes.

Sten turned to him. “Speak.”

The boy’s lips parted and closed once before sound came. “I didn’t think…” He stopped, swallowed, and tried again. “Hrolf said there’d be silver. That we’d scare you, take goods, and go. He said no one would be touched if they yielded.”

The silence that followed was colder than shouting.

Runa’s voice cut through it. “And did you believe a wolf promising to guard lambs?”

Eyvind’s head dropped lower. “No.”

There it was.

Not innocence. Not foolishness alone. Chosen wrong, with enough understanding to make the choosing matter.

Leif’s face in the crowd had gone hard and bright with the blunt certainty of youth. Sigrid’s had gone stiller, as if she were already looking past this moment to what it would leave behind.

Sten looked to Eirik.

No words. Only that look again.

What do you see?

Eirik stood for a long heartbeat without speaking.

The lane pressed close around him. Frost. Breath. Tar. Wool. A man coughed into his fist and then fell silent. Someone farther back shifted his boots on the hard ground. Eyvind stood bound to the post, pale and shaking, and for one fleeting instant Eirik saw not the raider’s accomplice, but the awkward boy he had once known by sight at summer launches—eager, foolish, still close enough to youth that a better road might once have held him.

Then the memory broke.

He saw Leif's blooded hands.

Sigrid white-faced and steady.

Astrid standing over the threshold darkened by violence.

Hrolf spared once and returned with steel.

And beneath all of it, Tyr's voice, clean as frost: *Mercy without justice may endanger the innocent.*

The lane came back sharp around him.

Eyvind lifted his head just enough to look at him.

Not pleading exactly. But hoping still. That made it worse.

At last Eirik said, "He came with raiders against homes."

Bjorn nodded sharply, as if that settled everything.

Eirik did not look at him. "He watched. He signaled. He helped bring armed men to sleeping families." He let the words stand as what they were. "Whether or not he struck with his own hand, he stood with those who did."

Eyvind's breath shook. "I never wanted—"

Eirik cut across him, not harshly. "No. You only wanted what came before and not what followed."

The boy went silent.

That, Eirik thought, was what youth often mistook for freedom: the right to choose a thing and not bear its whole shape once it ripened.

Arn said, "He's guilty, then."

"Yes," Eirik said.

The crowd leaned inward.

Leif did too.

Sten asked, very level, “And what is owed?”

The old easier answer would have been swift now. The crowd wanted blood. Fear had left them hungry for clean endings. Arn would not have opposed it. Bjorn would have celebrated it. Even Sten, if pushed by order alone, might have accepted it without protest.

But the question was not what would satisfy them.

It was what was right.

Eirik looked at Eyvind, then at the men and women around him, then briefly toward his children.

Leif’s eyes burned for a blunt answer.

Sigrid’s held something sadder, harder.

Astrid’s gaze stayed steady, reading him the way she always did—for what he would not say as much as what he would.

“To the dead,” Eirik said slowly, “truth.”

No one spoke.

“To the innocent, protection.”

Sten’s face did not move, but Eirik felt the jarl’s attention sharpen.

“To the guilty,” Eirik went on, “right judgment. Not anger.”

Arn’s mouth twitched at that. Not mockery. Recognition.

Eirik looked at Eyvind again. “If we beat him in the lane, we feed fear and call it justice. If we free him because he is young and sorry, we teach every fool with weak pride that regret is enough once blood is spilled.”

A murmur moved through the crowd.

Astrid said, from where she stood, "Peace tears most easily where men mistake softness for mercy."

Several heads turned toward her. She ignored them all.

Eyvind's face had gone white.

Sten said, "Finish it."

Eirik nodded once.

"He came armed with raiders against the village. He helped bring them to our doors. Men and women died because of what he chose to stand with." He drew a breath that felt cold all the way down. "For that, his life is forfeit."

The words fell into the morning like stones into deep water.

Leif stood utterly still.

Bjorn gave a hard approving grunt.

One of the women by the path crossed herself in the old way against ill luck and looked away.

Eyvind swayed against the post and almost lost his legs. "Please—"

The word cut off when Sten stepped closer.

But Eirik was not finished.

"He will not be beaten," Eirik said. His voice carried more sharply now. "He will not be cut apart by anger in a lane like a thief under dogs. He will confess before witnesses. He will name what he did and who stood with him. Then he will be given a clean death at the boundary stones."

Arn let out a slow breath. Sten's gaze flicked to him and back.

That was the bridge, Eirik thought. Narrow and hard. No satisfaction in it. No mercy that left danger roaming. No vengeance dressed up as honor. Only measure.

Sten asked, "You would do it?"

The question mattered. More than if the jarl had simply ordered it.

Eirik felt the weight of every eye. Of Eyvind's breath coming too fast. Of Leif somewhere behind the crowd seeing what sort of man his father would be.

"Yes," he said.

The word cost him more than he had expected, and he let it cost him.

Sten studied him a moment longer, then nodded. "So be it."

For a breath, no one moved.

Then the lane loosened. Some faces showed relief. Some disappointment that there would be no blood in the open road. Others only the dull hunger of people wanting the thing settled so the day could go on. The crowd did not break cleanly; it shifted, muttered, re-formed itself around the sentence the way water folds around a stone and keeps moving.

Eirik went first to his children before the men took Eyvind up the path.

Leif spoke before he reached them. "He should have died at once."

Sigrid said, "That would have been easier."

Leif turned on her. "Because it's true."

"Because it's hot," she replied. "Those aren't the same."

Eirik stopped before them both.

Leif looked up at him, jaw hard, eyes too young for the certainty in them. "He helped them come here."

"Yes."

"And now you'll kill him anyway."

"Yes."

Leif frowned, trying to find the shape of the difference and hating that it would not sit still for him.

"Then why not do it now?"

Eirik looked at his son for a long moment. "Because justice is not hunger."

Leif said nothing.

Sigrid did.

"It has to leave something people can still live under," she said quietly.

Eirik turned his head toward her. The words were close enough to Tyr that they struck him almost bodily.

"Yes," he said.

Astrid came nearer then and laid one hand briefly on Leif's shoulder. "Go home with your sister. You're not a child, but you are a boy standing too near a hard lesson. That is close enough."

Leif's mouth tightened, but he obeyed. Sigrid took his sleeve, not dragging this time, only making sure he truly turned toward home.

Astrid remained.

Her eyes met Eirik's, and he saw there not comfort exactly, but the deep steady knowing she carried when pain and necessity had begun walking side by side.

"You found the harder road," she said.

"It does not feel better."

"It rarely does."

He almost smiled. "You are poor at soothing."

"I am excellent at accuracy."

That, too, was a kind of mercy.

At the boundary stones the village gathered again, though fewer this time and quieter. The place always felt colder than the rest of the path, perhaps because men brought their hardest truths there and left them in the wind.

Eyvind confessed what he had done. Not bravely. Not with dignity worth song. Simply because there was nowhere left to hide in words. He named the ridge. The signal cloth. Hrolf's promise of silver. His own belief that the raid would frighten, not slaughter. His own shame in knowing even then that he lied to himself.

Sten heard it all.

Hakon heard it.

Runa heard it.

Eirik heard it.

So did Arn, leaning on one axe with none of his usual grin left.

When the confession was done, Sten asked Eyvind if he had anything else to say.

The boy's eyes found Eirik.

"I was afraid," he said.

"I know," Eirik answered.

It was not absolution. Only truth.

Then Eirik drew his sword.

He did not hate the boy.

He did not pity him enough to lie.

He did not rush.

That, perhaps, was the hardest part. To do a thing rightly without letting anger carry it for him.

Eyvind knelt.

Sten placed one hand on his shoulder and removed it.

The wind moved once between the stones.

Eirik ended it cleanly.

Afterward, no one cheered.

Bjorn kept his mouth shut.

Arn looked away toward the fjord.

Sten said only, “It is done.”

Yes, Eirik thought. Done. Not mended. Not made good. Done.

By evening he sat once more by his own hearth, the fire low and steady, Astrid across from him with Leif and Sigrid close enough to warmth that their shadows touched on the wall behind them.

No one spoke much at first.

Leif finally said, “Was it just?”

The room stayed very still.

Eirik looked at the boy, then at the girl beside him, who was watching him with that quiet sharpness that made lying to her feel like spitting into clean water.

“It was what was owed,” he said.

Leif frowned. “That is not the same as yes.”

“No,” Eirik said. “It isn’t.”

Sigrid spoke softly. “Then maybe justice is what still hurts after you know it was right.”

Astrid's eyes lifted from the fire to her daughter and stayed there a moment.

Eirik felt the words settle into him like cold iron finding its shape.

"Yes," he said at last. "Perhaps it is."

Leif leaned back against the bench, unsatisfied but thinking. That would have to be enough for now.

The house held its warmth around them. Outside, the village settled under frost and dark, roof by roof, door by door. Inside, Eirik listened to the breathing of those he loved and understood with a new heaviness that all he had learned from gods and men alike had not made life cleaner.

Only stricter.

A man could not keep his soul by avoiding hard acts.

He could only try not to stain it by doing them falsely.

And as the fire sank lower and the children drifted nearer sleep, Eirik knew he had crossed into a sterner part of his life.

Not because the gods had spoken.

Because he had acted, and could not unknow what that required.

Chapter Fourteeen

The Boy Who Asked Too Much

Leif felt it as he stepped out into the night—the low hearth heat still caught in his tunic, the smell of birch smoke in his hair, the last of the laughter from the fire still bright somewhere in his chest.

Behind the turf wall, Astrid's voice had gone softer. Sigrid would still be awake, likely putting away something Leif had left half-done. Eirik's deeper murmur would come now and then between them. Home was there, close enough that if he changed his mind he could be back inside in three long strides.

He did not change his mind.

The cold was clean and sharp. Frost had silvered the fence rails and laid a white edge along the woodpile. The fjord below was black and still beneath a strip of pale sky where the last of the day had not fully died. The village had gone mostly quiet. A dog barked once, then stopped as if the night itself had told it to be sensible.

Leif crossed the yard to fetch the splitting wedge his father had forgotten by the chopping block.

That was all.

A simple task.

Out.

Grab it.

Back in before Astrid noticed he had lingered.

He bent and took hold of the iron.

And the world changed.

Not with thunder.

Not with light.

Not with any sound at all.

That was what frightened him.

The night did not grow louder. It grew stiller. Too still. The wind stopped as if someone had caught it in a shut hand. The fjord ceased its dark whisper at the shore. Even the cold seemed to hold itself differently, no longer moving around his face but pressing against him from all sides.

Leif straightened too fast, and the wedge slipped from his hands at once.

It struck the frozen ground with a sharp iron crack that seemed far too loud in the wrong silence.

He jumped back from it as if it had betrayed him personally.

For one foolish heartbeat he stared at the wedge lying there between him and the open yard, then snatched up the nearest thing at hand—a short stick of kindling no thicker than his wrist—and held it out in both hands like a spear.

The effect was not impressive.

He knew it was not impressive.

That did not stop him.

Two figures stood at the far edge of the yard where no one had been a moment before.

One was taller and held himself with such stillness that even in fear Leif knew this was not an ordinary man. He wore no bright finery, no boast of gold or fur. The lines of him were plain, severe in a quiet way. His cloak fell straight. His face was calm, not empty calm, but the kind that made a man feel his own breathing was too loud. He looked as if he had weighed ten arguments already and found nine of them wasteful.

The other stood easier, though no less dangerous for it. He seemed made for cold air and open ground. There was something of winter about him—not only in the pale light that caught the edges of him, but in the feeling that he belonged to snow, distance, the drawn bow, and the track found before dawn. He looked younger than the first, or perhaps only less burdened by stillness. One corner of his mouth sat half a breath from a smirk.

Leif, still gripping the kindling as if it were a noble weapon and not half of tomorrow's fire, took one cautious step toward the fallen wedge.

Then another.

He crouched without taking his eyes off them, stretched the stick out, and tried to drag the wedge toward himself from a safe distance.

The wedge did not move.

He hooked it again, harder this time.

The stick slipped off with a dry scrape and nearly pitched him onto one knee.

The second figure laughed first.

It was not a cruel sound. It was brief, startled, and so genuinely amused that the whole impossible moment tilted sideways.

The taller figure looked at the kindling rod in Leif's hands, then at the wedge, then back at Leif.

"That could be a weapon," he said calmly. "If you chose it so."

Leif froze in a half crouch, still holding the kindling out before him.

His face burned hot.

"I did choose it."

"No," said the taller one. "You panicked and grabbed it."

The words were plain. Not mocking. Worse than mocking for the moment, because they were true.

The second figure folded his arms. "If a man chooses a thing for a weapon, he must hold it as one. You're still treating it like frightened firewood."

Leif straightened slowly, still clutching the stick because abandoning it now felt worse than keeping it.

The second figure added, "Leave it. If we meant you harm, the wedge would not help you, and neither would the stick in the way you're using it."

That was sensible, which made it worse.

Leif swallowed.

"Who are you?" he asked, and hated at once that the last word lifted a little in his throat.

The taller one answered.

"Put the kindling down."

Leif obeyed before deciding to.

The stick fell beside the wedge with a sound far less noble than he had hoped.

The second figure's smile deepened. "Good. You've survived your first battle with timber."

Leif stared at him.

Fear was still in him, yes, but it had been joined by something else now—something sharper, stranger. Recognition, though it came not from certainty but from all the old stories stacked behind his eyes since he was old enough to beg for them.

The stillness of the first.

The winter-edge of the second.

The impossible fact of them being there at all.

His mouth opened before his mind caught up.

"Oh."

The second figure glanced sideways at the first. "That may be the best answer anyone has given us in years."

Leif blinked. "You're not men."

"No," said the taller one.

"No," said the second.

Leif looked from one to the other, and fear went out of him like water from a kicked bucket.

It left awe in its place so suddenly he almost lost his balance.

"Oh," he said again, stronger this time. Then, "Oh!"

The second figure laughed under his breath.

Leif pointed, then thought better of it and snatched his hand back. "You're gods."

"Yes," the taller one said.

"Yes," said the second. "Though I begin to regret how quickly you reached it. The guessing would have been entertaining."

Leif forgot entirely to be cautious.

"Which ones?" he asked at once. "No, wait—don't tell me. You look like someone who would be angry if people argued badly in front of you. And you look like winter if winter could shoot a bird through the eye at two hills' distance."

The second figure's mouth twitched. "That is not the worst description I've heard."

The first said, "I am Forseti."

Leif's eyes widened.

The second added, "And I am Ullr, since you are already thinking the question faster than your tongue can climb to it."

That almost stopped Leif's breath.

Forseti.

Ullr.

Not Odin with ravens.

Not Thor with storm.

Not even Tyr with the hard clean weight his father had carried afterward in silence.

Forseti, whose name came in law-talk and old judgments.

Ullr, whose name men said on winter hunts, in bow-work, and sometimes quietly when snow grew strange.

Leif stared so hard his eyes watered.

Ullr looked at him and said, "You can blink. We'll remain."

That finally broke the spell enough that Leif inhaled properly again.

Then the questions came.

"Why are you here? Is this because of Father? Does he know? Does Mother know? She always knows things. Does Sigrid know? No, she'd hate that if she didn't. Are you here to warn me? Or test me?

Am I dead? No, that's stupid, I'd know if I were dead. Probably. Have you seen Thor recently? Is he really as large as—"

"Leif," Forseti said.

That one word stopped him harder than shouting would have.

Leif snapped his mouth shut so quickly his teeth clicked.

Ullr nodded. "Useful skill. Keep it."

Leif looked at them both, heat rising in his face again. "I ask quickly."

"So we noticed," Ullr said.

Forseti's expression had not changed, though Leif had the strong feeling he was not angry. Only exact.

"You were frightened," Forseti said. "Then curious. Now excited. None of those improve your speech."

Leif swallowed. "No."

"Good. Then you can still learn."

That should not have sounded kind. Somehow it did.

Ullr stepped a little to one side, the frost not seeming to mark under his boots. "He learns fast enough. He only learns in every direction at once."

Leif brightened despite himself. "That's not the worst thing."

"It is," Ullr said, "when one of the directions is a cliff."

Leif laughed before he could stop himself.

Forseti watched him a moment. "You want to be a warrior."

"Yes."

No reason to lie there.

"You want to be strong like your father."

"Yes."

"You want men to know your name."

That one caught him.

Leif hesitated, then nodded slower. "Yes."

Ullr answered first. "Because names are often loudest in the mouths of fools and the dead."

Leif frowned at once. "That's not true."

Ullr lifted one brow. "No?"

"No." Leif leaned forward a little, the answer coming faster now because he had found ground he believed in. "Braggi sings the names of heroes. Men remember them. That's not foolish."

Forseti watched him a moment. "No. It is not."

Leif brightened, almost triumphant. "Then it matters."

"It does," Forseti said. "But not in the way boys first think."

That slowed him.

Ullr looked out toward the dark yard as if seeing farther than the fence. "A name remembered in song is no small thing. But songs are easiest for the dead. The living are harder to keep."

Leif frowned. "What does that mean?"

Forseti answered with the same calm precision as before. "A hero's name may be sung in a hall for many winters. But the wife he leaves behind still wakes cold. The children still grow without his hand on their shoulders. The old father still carries wood alone. The field still needs cutting. The roof still leaks if no one climbs it."

The words settled into the silence between them.

Leif's face changed. Not into full understanding. Into the beginning of it.

Ullr said, more quietly now, "Braggi may remember the dead. But the living must remember how to go on."

Leif looked down.

He thought suddenly of evenings when his father was away and his mother moved through the house carrying the work without complaint. Of Sigrid bundling kindling or righting some small thing Leif had knocked loose. Of how Eirik, when home, seemed always to notice what still needed doing before he sat by the fire.

The thought made him feel both smaller and older at once.

Forseti said, "A name worth remembering is not only a name sung. It is a name the living can still bless when they speak it."

Leif took that in slowly.

He did not dislike it. He simply wished it had been less heavy.

Forseti said, "You saw justice done."

Leif's smile left him.

He knew which justice the god meant. Eyvind at the stones. Blood in the frost. His father's face when he came home and sat too quietly by the fire.

"Yes."

"And you wanted it swifter."

Leif looked aside. "Yes."

"Why?"

That was harder.

Because it seemed obvious.

Because bad men should die.

Because waiting made fear grow teeth.

Because if someone helped bring raiders to your door, he had already chosen wrong enough.

But none of those answers felt complete standing there beneath the eyes of gods.

At last he said, “Because he helped them come here. Because people died. Because if someone does something bad enough, it seems…” He frowned and searched for it. “It seems like waiting only makes it worse.”

Forseti listened without interruption.

“At times,” he said, “waiting does make it worse.”

Leif looked up quickly.

“But not because justice should be hungry,” Forseti went on. “Because justice must be clear.”

Leif thought of his father at the stones—not rushed, not angry, not merciful in the weak easy way either. Just steady. That had unsettled him more than shouting would have.

Ullr glanced toward the boundary of the yard where the fence met dark air. “A man can strike in anger and still hit the guilty. That only proves the guilty were near.”

“It does not prove justice,” Forseti said.

Leif let that sit.

He did not like how much it made sense.

“Then how do you know?” he asked. “How do you know when it’s justice and not just wanting someone hurt because they deserve it?”

Ullr’s mouth shifted as if he liked the question more than the others.

Forseti answered plainly. "You learn what is owed."

Leif almost groaned. "Father says that."

"Then he has learned something worth keeping," Forseti said.

Leif straightened a little at once.

Ullr saw it and gave him a sideways look. "You brighten every time someone praises your father."

Leif folded his arms, then unfolded them because Forseti's presence made sulking feel childish in a way he resented.

"Well," he said, "he is worth praising."

"That," Ullr said, "is the best thing you've said yet."

Leif did not know whether that was insult or approval.

Probably both.

Forseti said, "To the dead, truth. To the innocent, protection. To the guilty, rightful judgment. To the living, order they can still endure."

The words were simple. Leif knew they mattered because they sounded like stones laid one by one into place.

Ullr added, "And to yourself, enough discipline not to make every strong feeling into law."

That stung a little more.

Leif looked down at his hands. They were empty now, but he remembered too well how they had looked the night at the door, slick and red after the raider fell on his practice blade. He had not meant to remember that here. He had not meant to remember it at all.

Forseti saw the thought in him as if it had spoken aloud.

"You want to protect," he said.

Leif nodded once.

"You also want to prove."

Leif hesitated. Then nodded again.

Forseti took one slow step nearer, and when he spoke again his voice was no louder, but it seemed to settle into the frost and wood around them.

"Hear this clearly, Leif Eiriksson. Strength is not only what you can break. It is also how well you notice what is in front of you before you rush past it."

Leif listened without moving.

"A boy runs at the largest thing first and calls that courage," Forseti said. "A man sees the loose strap, the weak hinge, the stone that turns underfoot, the fear in another's face, the opening half a breath before it vanishes. He gives each thing its due attention. That is how work is done rightly. That is how judgment is made cleanly. That is how warriors stay alive."

Leif thought of the dropped wedge.

The kindling in his hands.

The wrong boot.

The way he so often lunged before seeing.

The way Sigrid noticed the small things and Eirik never seemed surprised by them.

He looked up then, and the question came from him more quietly than any before it.

"Why did you come to me?"

The yard seemed to sharpen again around those words.

Leif swallowed and pressed on, because once spoken they would not go back.

“My father has spoken to gods. But he is a warrior and a leader of men.” He looked from Forseti to Ullr and back. “I’m only a boy. What would gods want from a boy like me?”

For the first time since they had appeared, neither god answered at once.

Ullr’s expression lost some of its teasing.

Forseti’s gaze deepened.

At last Ullr said, “Boys become men whether guided or not. We prefer fewer bad surprises.”

Leif almost laughed, but the question in him was too real now.

Forseti answered next.

“You are not only a boy,” he said. “You are a son, a brother, and the beginning of a man. What grows badly in the young becomes burden in the grown.”

Leif stood very still.

Forseti went on. “Your father is being weighed for what he carries. You are being seen for what you may yet become. That is not a lesser matter.”

The words struck somewhere deep and strange in Leif’s chest.

Not praise.

Not warning alone.

Something weightier than either.

Ullr said, with that dry half-humor returned, “Also, you are loud enough to be difficult to ignore.”

That finally made Leif laugh.

But it did not loosen the truth of what Forseti had said.

Not a lesser matter.

He did not know whether that made him proud or afraid.

Probably both.

Forseti looked at him and seemed to know that too. “A boy who listens can save years of foolishness.”

Ullr glanced aside. “Not all the years. Let us stay honest.”

Forseti did not quite smile. “No. Not all.”

Leif breathed out slowly.

He had wanted to be noticed. By his father. By warriors. By the gods, if he was honest enough to name the wish.

Now that it had happened, it felt less like triumph and more like standing straighter beneath a load he had not expected to be handed so soon.

He asked, “What if I fail at it?”

Forseti answered without pause. “Then learn before failing becomes habit.”

Ullr nodded once. “And don’t fail in the same stupid way twice. That offends everyone.”

That sounded so much like something Arn might say that Leif barked a surprised laugh.

The two gods looked at one another then, and for a heartbeat both seemed amused by something he could not quite follow.

He frowned. “What?”

Ullr said, “Only that men always think the grand failings are the dangerous ones.”

Forseti added, “And not the small repeated ones that shape them.”

Leif looked from one to the other and then down at the frost.

He understood enough of that to feel it.

The wrong boot.

The dropped wedge.

The hurry.

The lunge.

The talking before thought.

The wanting to prove before noticing what was actually needed.

The gods were not asking him to become someone else.

They were warning him that what was already in him could sharpen into worth or foolishness depending on how he held it.

That was worse.

And better.

He looked up again.

"How do I start?"

Ullr answered first. "By listening before you leap."

Leif made a face. "That sounds like Sigrid."

"That should concern you," Ullr said.

Forseti said, "You start by seeing that your life is joined to others. A man who thinks only of his own courage will fail the people standing behind it."

The yard had grown so quiet that Leif could hear frost settling from the fence rail in tiny dry clicks.

He said, "Will I see you again?"

Ullr's eyes brightened with mischief. "If you improve, perhaps. If not, Forseti may come alone and you'll enjoy the visit much less."

Leif looked quickly at Forseti, trying to decide if that was a joke.

Forseti said, "That depends on your conduct."

It was impossible to tell if he was adding to Ullr's tease or not. That somehow made it funnier.

Leif grinned before he could stop himself.

Then the stillness changed.

Not broken. Loosened.

The pressure holding the yard apart from the rest of the world thinned. Wind crept back under his sleeves. The fjord below gave a dark whisper against the shore. From inside the house came the small crack of a settling coal and the murmur of voices.

Ullr looked toward the house, then back to Leif. "You should go in before they decide you're wolf food."

"That is not likely," Forseti said.

"No," Ullr agreed. "But it would improve his pace."

Leif opened his mouth with one last question already climbing up.

Forseti said, "Enough."

Leif shut it again.

He nodded.

This time without being forced to.

Forseti looked at him one final moment. "Be lively, if that is how you were made. But be worth relying on."

Ullr added, "And learn the ground before you charge across it."

Then the yard exhaled.

The two gods did not vanish in a blaze or thunderclap. They were simply there one breath, and gone the next, as if the world had decided it could not possibly continue containing them and ordinary frost at the same time.

Leif stood alone by the woodpile.

The wind moved.

The fjord whispered.

The doorway glowed again with hearthlight.

He looked wildly around the yard.

For one sick heartbeat he thought perhaps he had dreamed it standing up like a fool with a stick of kindling in his hands.

Then he saw the fence post.

An arrow stood buried in it to the fletching.

Neat. Deep. Perfectly placed.

Leif stared.

He crossed the yard in three quick steps, stopped, then forced himself to take the next two slowly. He touched the shaft with two fingertips.

Cold.

Real.

Straight as a thought.

Behind him the door opened.

"Leif," Astrid said. "If you've gone outside only to freeze in admiration of darkness, come back in."

He turned too fast.

Astrid stood in the doorway with firelight behind her, one hand on the frame. The warm light ran over her hair and down one side of her face. She looked first at him, then at the arrow, then back to him.

Something in her eyes sharpened.

“What happened?” she asked.

Leif opened his mouth, and for once no flood came.

Everything in him wanted to tell it all at once—the fear, the gods, the questions, the way Ullr had laughed, the way Forseti made the whole yard feel judged without ever seeming cruel. Yet some new quieter instinct held him just long enough to keep the words from tumbling over each other and dying stupidly.

“I…” He glanced once at the arrow. “I think I was told to stop being foolish.”

Astrid looked at the shaft again. The corner of her mouth moved. “Then the gods have joined this household usefully.”

That broke something loose in him, and he grinned.

She stepped aside. “Come in before they decide you require more instruction.”

Leif bent, picked up the wedge, and looked once more at the arrow before he went inside.

The warmth met him at once—smoke, embers, wool, family.

Sigrid sat near the fire with bone pieces spread in rows before her. She looked up immediately and narrowed her eyes.

“You look strange.”

“I always look strange.”

“No,” she said. “Worse than usual.”

From the bench near the wall, Eirik looked up too.

Something passed over his father's face then—some quiet recognition that did not ask more than Leif could yet say. It was not surprise. Not exactly. More like the look of a man who had learned the world sometimes reached for children too.

That steadied him more than he expected.

He set the wedge carefully by the wall instead of dropping it.

Sigrid noticed that first. Of course she did.

"What happened?" she asked.

Leif looked at her, then at Eirik, then at the fire. For once the words in him arranged themselves before leaping.

"I'll tell you," he said, "but if you interrupt too much, I'm starting over."

Sigrid stared.

Then, very carefully, she said, "Now you truly are strange."

Leif laughed.

Not loudly.

Not wildly.

Just enough to feel that something in him had shifted and not broken.

And as the family gathered close again around the low red fire, with the arrow still waiting outside in the frost-dark post and the warmth of the house closing gently around him, Leif understood only this much for certain:

He had been seen.

He had been tested.

And whatever kind of man he became from here would no longer be only a thing he imagined in stories.

Chapter Fourteen

Water Between Words

The docks creaked under them with each slow push of the tide.

It was one of those gray mornings when the world seemed made of wind, weathered wood, and dull silver light. The fjord stretched wide beneath a low sky, its surface broken here and there by fish rising sharp and quick before vanishing again. Gulls wheeled overhead, crying at one another like quarrelsome old women. Ropes rubbed against wet posts. The boats rocked gently in their places, hulls knocking with soft hollow sounds that seemed older than any man listening to them.

Eirik Halvardsson sat on the outer edge of the dock with his boots planted wide and his forearms resting on his knees. Beside him, Leif sat in almost the same posture, though with less ease in it, as if he had carefully chosen to look like his father and then forgotten what to do with the rest of himself.

A cormorant broke the surface farther out, shook dark water from its neck, and dove again.

For a while neither of them spoke.

That was not unusual for Eirik. It was unusual enough for Leif that Eirik noticed the effort of it and respected him for trying.

Men worked farther down the shoreline. Someone shouted for a rope coil. Another shouted back something unfriendly about blind hands and poor knots. A hammer rang twice against a bent nail and then stopped. The smell of tar, salt, wet wood, and old fish drifted together in the cold air.

Leif picked at a splintered place in the dock plank beside his knee and then stopped when he realized what he was doing.

Eirik watched the water.

He had chosen the docks because a man could speak more honestly beside open water than he often could inside walls. Houses kept warmth. They also kept people too close to their own pride.

Leif cleared his throat once. Then again.

"You don't have to start well," Eirik said.

Leif looked at him sharply. "I wasn't trying to."

"You were failing at it with great care."

That won the smallest breath of laughter from the boy, quick and embarrassed.

Leif looked back over the water. "It sounds foolish once I try saying it."

"Most true things do."

Leif glanced sidelong at him. "That sounds like Mother."

"That is because your mother improves many things simply by being right before others arrive."

Leif snorted.

The gulls swept low over the water and rose again on the wind. One dropped hard toward the surface, missed whatever silver flash had tempted it, and wheeled upward with a scream of outrage.

Leif watched it go. "I was afraid at first."

Eirik said nothing. He only waited.

Leif drew a breath and let it out slowly. "Not like when you hear shouting and know men are coming. Not like that. It was worse because everything went still." His fingers rubbed once along the worn edge of the dock. "It felt wrong. Like I had stepped where I wasn't supposed to."

Eirik turned that over and found it true enough to keep.

Leif went on, words coming a little quicker now that he had started. "The wind stopped. The water stopped sounding like water. Even the cold felt different. I thought…" He hesitated, his mouth tightening. "I thought maybe I'd done something so stupid the world had finally noticed."

"That would be a long list to sort through," Eirik said.

Leif barked a laugh despite himself, then shook his head. "You're not helping."

"I am. You only prefer grand fear to ordinary mockery."

"That isn't true."

"It is exactly true."

Leif looked out at the harbor again, and his face changed. The quickness remained in him, but quieter now. More thoughtful.

"When I saw them," he said, "I knew they weren't men before I knew who they were." He frowned a little, as if the memory still sat strangely in him. "That sounds foolish."

"No," Eirik said. "It sounds like seeing."

Leif was quiet a moment after that.

Then, more slowly than usual, as if trying to make the words stand straight before letting them leave him: "I talked too much."

"Yes."

Leif whipped his head around. "You weren't there."

"No." Eirik looked at him at last, one brow lifting. "But you are my son. The odds were poor."

Leif groaned and dropped his forehead briefly against one fist.

Eirik let him suffer for half a breath and then added, "You also listened enough to remember it with shame. That means you did not talk too much for nothing."

Leif sat up again and stared at the water.

A fish broke the surface near one of the moored boats, flashed white once, and was gone.

"They were not angry," he said. "That was the strangest part. I thought if gods came close, I'd either be dead or too frightened to breathe. But they…" He frowned, searching. "They found me amusing."

"That seems accurate too."

Leif gave him a dark look. "I'm trying to be serious."

"You can be serious and amusing at once. Arn manages it by accident."

Leif laughed again, this time easier, and the sound carried out over the water before the wind took it.

Then he grew quiet.

"Forseti made me feel…" He stopped, then tried again. "Not small. Straight. Like I couldn't wriggle around my own thoughts while he was looking at me."

Eirik nodded once.

"And Ullr—" Leif's face shifted toward something like wonder. "He was easier to speak to. Not softer. Just… sharper in a way I almost understood already."

That, Eirik thought, was well seen.

Leif glanced sideways at him, suddenly wary. "You know what I mean."

"Yes."

Leif's eyes narrowed. "Because you've seen them too."

It was not fully a question.

Eirik looked back over the fjord. A small rowing boat was crossing the harbor mouth, its oars moving slow and even. Beyond it, the outer water looked darker where the cloud shadow lay.

"Yes," he said.

Leif sat up straighter. "All of them?"

"No."

"Which ones?"

"Enough."

"That is not an answer."

"It is the one you're getting first."

Leif made a face, but he did not press at once. That in itself told Eirik the boy had listened better than he often did.

After a few moments Leif said, "Did they frighten you?"

Eirik thought before answering.

"Yes."

Leif blinked. "You?"

"Yes."

"That helps."

"It should not."

"It does."

Eirik almost smiled.

Leif drew one knee up and rested an arm over it. He looked younger in that posture and older in the eyes.

"They told me to be a warrior," he said. "A man. A brother. A son." He frowned. "That sounds simple when I say it now, but it didn't feel simple there."

"It isn't."

Leif turned his head. "Then what does it mean?"

Eirik rested his hands together between his knees and looked down at the tide washing slowly beneath the dock timbers.

"It means glory is the smallest part of it," he said.

Leif made a dissatisfied sound at once.

"There," Eirik said. "That noise tells me they came at the right time."

Leif scowled. "I didn't say glory was all of it."

"No. Only most of what boys notice first."

"That isn't fair."

"It rarely is."

Leif's mouth tightened, but he did not argue further.

Eirik went on, voice low and even with the water sounds beneath them.

"To be a warrior means men behind you are safer because you are standing there. That part matters." He paused. "The rest is harder to say cleanly."

Leif waited.

Eirik looked out over the fjord before continuing. "A son is not another weight hung on his father's neck. A brother knows when to stand near and when to stop crowding the air out of a room. And a man…" He let out a breath through his nose. "A man learns how to carry what is his without flinging it into everyone else's hands and calling that honesty."

Leif frowned, thinking it through.

"That still sounds like work."

"It is work."

"And the part about glory being small sounds like something old men say after their knees go bad."

That won a low laugh from Eirik.

"There," he said. "That is at least a living answer."

Leif looked faintly pleased with himself despite the subject.

Eirik added, “You want the truth? Most boys think being a man means being seen. Most men learn too late it means being relied on.”

That quieted him better than the longer answer might have done.

The wind shifted and brought with it the smell of wet nets and tar. Farther down the dock, two men were hauling a basket of line-caught cod into a boat. One of them lost his footing, swore loudly enough to insult three generations of his own blood, and nearly went to one knee. The other laughed at him without mercy.

Leif watched them and then said, more quietly, “They told me names remembered in song aren’t enough.”

Eirik glanced at him again and saw the line had gone deeper into the boy than he had first shown.

“What did they say?” he asked.

Leif swallowed once. “Not like a lesson. Not neatly. Ullr said songs are easiest for the dead. And Forseti…” He hesitated. “Forseti said the living still wake cold. The wife. The children. The father. The roof. The field.” He looked down at his hands. “That a name worth remembering is one the living can still bless.”

Eirik let that settle between them.

A gull landed on a piling three arm-lengths away and stared at them with bright foolish malice before hopping sideways twice and flapping off again.

“That is true,” he said.

Leif rubbed his thumb along the edge of the plank. “It made me think of you. When you’re gone.”

Eirik said nothing.

"And Mother," Leif went on. "And Sigrid." He grimaced faintly, as if admitting the thought cost him something. "I used to think being sung after was enough if the death was good enough."

"And now?"

Leif stared over the water. "Now it sounds like a thing men say because they're not the ones left cold."

The honesty in it hit Eirik harder than he had expected.

He looked at his son and saw not wisdom yet, not fully, but the first honest bruise left by deeper thought. That mattered.

"It is easier," Eirik said, "to dream of death than to imagine those who keep living after it."

Leif nodded once.

For a little while they sat in the wind and let the harbor speak instead. A rope strained. A post groaned. Somewhere out over the gray water a flock of birds rose all at once, turned, and settled again.

At length Leif said, "I asked them why they came to me."

Eirik waited.

"I told them you had spoken to gods and it made sense because you're…" He looked uncomfortable now. "You're you. A warrior. A leader. A man people listen to. But I'm only—" He stopped.

"A boy?" Eirik said.

Leif's face tightened. "Yes."

"And what did they tell you?"

Leif looked out across the fjord, but Eirik could tell he was not seeing it.

"Not exactly in the same words I keep thinking," he said. "Ullr said boys become men whether anyone bothers to guide them or not. And

Forseti…" He hesitated. "Forseti said what begins crooked early is harder to straighten later."

Eirik drew in a long breath and let it out.

No boast stirred in him. No pride of the loud sort. Only the quiet ache of hearing the world reach for his son before he had quite learned how to stand steady under it.

"That sounds like gods," he said at last.

Leif shot him a look. "You could say more than that."

"I could. But much of it you'll understand better later."

"That is a terrible answer."

"Yes." Eirik's mouth moved faintly. "That is another way you know it's true."

Leif wanted to be annoyed. Eirik saw the effort of it. But the mood would not hold there, and at last the boy let out a breath that became half a laugh.

Then his expression changed.

"What if I fail at it?"

The question was quieter than any he had asked so far.

Eirik turned toward him more fully.

"You will," he said.

Leif stared. "That was quick."

"You asked for honesty."

"That isn't encouraging."

"No." Eirik kept his voice even. "But it is survivable. You'll fail. Then you'll learn whether you are the kind of man who learns cleanly or the kind who keeps making a shrine of his own foolishness."

Leif frowned, thinking hard.

"I don't want to be the second one."

"Then don't."

"That sounds simple."

"It isn't. Most important things are simple and difficult at the same time."

Leif let that lie there and looked down the length of the dock.

A boat was coming in from farther out now, low in the water and rowing without any of the loose talk or lazy pace of men returning from ordinary fishing. Two rowers bent and rose in an even rhythm. A third figure sat in the stern, wrapped in a dark cloak, unmoving.

Eirik noticed it and said nothing at first.

Leif was still inside his own thoughts.

"They also told me to notice the small things," he said. "That rushing past them weakens the whole act."

"Yes."

"That sounded like you."

"It should."

"It also sounded like Sigrid."

"That should trouble you."

Leif snorted softly.

Then he looked up and followed Eirik's gaze.

The boat was close enough now that the men at the nearer moorings had begun to notice it too. One straightened from his rope work.

Another shaded his eyes with one hand, though the light was too flat to trouble them.

Leif frowned. “Who’s that?”

Eirik did not answer at once.

The boat was wrong for the hour.

Not a trader. Too few men.

Not a local fisherman. Wrong hull shape.

Not a storm-lost drifter. Too purposeful in its coming.

The stern figure had not moved.

One of the dock men called out, but no answer came back across the water.

That changed the whole harbor at once.

Not into panic. Into readiness.

The gulls still cried.

The ropes still creaked.

The boats still knocked gently against their moorings.

But men began looking up rather than down. Hands stopped what they were doing and remained near tools that could become weapons if needed.

Leif sat straighter. The last of the private softness went out of him.

“What is it?” he asked.

“I don’t know yet.”

The boat slid nearer, cutting a dark line through the gray water. One rower shipped his oars without a word. The other followed. The stern swung, corrected once, and came softly against the lower dock posts.

Eirik rose.

Leif rose with him.

"Stay behind me," Eirik said.

Leif opened his mouth to object and then, perhaps remembering gods and small things and the cost of rushing, shut it again.

That alone made Eirik glance at him once with brief approval.

The cloaked figure in the stern moved at last.

Not a man.

A woman stepped up first, travel-worn and salt-streaked, her cloak dark with spray to the knees. Her hair had been braided once and was half loose now, whipped by weather and hard rowing. Her face was pale with fatigue, but her posture was wrong for weakness. She held herself like someone who had come too far to spend the last of her strength on drama.

Behind her, one of the rowers climbed out and tied off the boat. Eirik recognized him only after a breath.

"Halvard?"

The man looked up sharply.

It was Halvard Sigtryggsson, a trader and sometime messenger from farther up the coast, one who had shared fire and ale here in better seasons. He looked ten years older than he had in summer.

"Eirik," he said. Relief ran through the word, but strain thinned it almost to breaking. "Good. Good."

The woman stepped fully onto the dock and pulled back her hood.

Leif felt Eirik go still beside him.

Not in fear.

In recognition.

The woman's face was older than Eirik's, and there was something in the eyes that made the blood between them visible even before the name came.

"Yrsa," Eirik said.

His sister.

Leif turned hard toward him in surprise.

He had heard of her. She lived north, married into another holding near the headland, too far for easy visits, close enough for names to remain alive in winter talk. He had not seen her in years.

Yrsa looked from Eirik to Leif and back again, and whatever she had held together through rowing and weather nearly broke in her face before she mastered it.

"Brother," she said.

The word carried too much.

Eirik stepped forward at once and caught her by the shoulders. "What happened?"

Yrsa's breath shook once. She swallowed it down.

"Not here," she said.

That was answer enough to chill the dock.

Halvard climbed up behind her. The years of strain on his face spoke before he did. "There was smoke on the headland three nights running. Men missing. Nets slashed. Then two boats gone before dawn." He looked toward the harbor, toward the village beyond. "And others are seeing lights offshore where there should be none."

Leif felt the world narrow again, though not with divine stillness this time.

With danger.

Real.

Human.

Coming.

Eirik's hand tightened once on Yrsa's shoulder and released.

"Come," he said. "You'll tell it in Sten's hall."

Yrsa nodded, though her eyes had already gone once to Leif, measuring him not as a child now but as someone standing close to the edge of harder things.

Leif looked from his father to the dark boat to the harbor suddenly sharpened into watchfulness.

The docks still smelled of tar and fish and rope.

The gulls still cried.

The water still broke in little black folds against the posts.

Yet nothing of the peace from moments earlier remained untouched.

Eirik looked once at his son.

Not long.

Just enough.

Leif understood.

Whatever the gods had told him in the frost-dark yard, whatever he had half grasped beside his father on the dock, it was no longer a lesson living safely in words. The world was already moving to test it.

He fell in behind Eirik and Yrsa as they crossed the boards toward shore.

And though the harbor looked as it always had—boats rocking, men calling, birds wheeling over the gray water—Leif knew with a certainty that sat cold and bright in his chest that he had stepped past something invisible.

He was no longer only a boy who wanted adventure.

He was walking into the place where duty, family, and fate had begun to knot themselves together, and none of them would be separated cleanly again.

Chapter Fifteen

What Enters With the Cold

They left the docks without hurry, but no one mistook that for ease.

The ground between harbor and hall was wet in places where the frost had not yet fully taken and hard in others where boots struck a dull sound against frozen earth. Yrsa walked beside Eirik with the same hard steadiness she had carried from the boat, though now that they were moving inland, Leif could see the wear of the road more clearly in her. Salt had dried in pale streaks along the hem of her cloak. One glove was mended badly across the palm. Her face was drawn not by panic, but by the sort of tiredness that came from choosing to keep going after comfort had ceased to matter.

Halvard followed a few steps behind them, head lowered against the cold. Leif came next, not because anyone had ordered him there, but because no one had told him to go back either. That alone felt like a thing to notice.

He noticed many things now.

The way men at the harbor had gone quiet without being told.

The way Eirik did not grip Yrsa's arm again once they left the dock, though he kept his pace matched to hers.

The way no one spoke openly on the path, as if words were being saved for a place with walls.

The village itself seemed to feel it too. A woman outside the smokehouse lifted her head as they passed and then went very still. Two boys carrying split wood stopped their muttering and pressed themselves aside. A dog trotted out from beneath a cart, looked at Yrsa once, then slipped back under as if wiser than most men.

The air smelled of wet wool, hearth smoke, tar from the harbor, and the faint bitter edge of fish guts cooling in bins. Somewhere down the lane a hammer struck wood three times and then stopped.

Leif wanted badly to ask a dozen questions.

He wanted to ask why Yrsa had not answered at the docks.

He wanted to ask whether the missing men mattered more than the boats.

He wanted to ask whether the lights offshore were raiders or something worse.

He wanted to ask whether Eirik already knew the answer and was simply carrying it in silence because that was what grown men did when boys were near.

He asked none of them.

That alone made him feel strange enough that Sigrid would have noticed at once if she had been there.

Jarl Sten's longhouse stood above the rest of the village with the same plain certainty it always had. Not grand in the foolish way some men built halls, but broad, well-kept, and weathered by years of smoke and winter. The carved heads on the roof beam had long since gone black from soot. The door stood half open, and warm air breathed in and out with each passing gust, carrying the scents of peat, cooked broth, leather, damp wool, and old timber that had held too many winters to smell young.

A man at the doorway stepped aside the moment he saw Eirik and Yrsa together.

Inside, the hall was warm enough to sting after the dock wind.

Firelight turned the rafters dark red and gold. Smoke drifted under the roof and found its slow path upward through the vent. Men sat on benches along the walls, some with cups in hand, others bent over quiet work, but conversation had thinned by the time Eirik crossed the threshold. Heads lifted. Eyes moved. No one called out. The room seemed to gather itself inward around what had entered.

Leif stepped in last and stood just inside the warmth, blinking once as his sight adjusted.

Sten was already there.

He sat not at the highest end of the hall, though that seat waited for him, but halfway between hearth and door where he could see both without turning. His long red braided hair fell over one shoulder, the ringed beard beneath it catching firelight in copper flashes. The scar across his face made one side of his expression seem harsher than the other, though Leif had learned by now that this was often misleading. Sten did not waste force. That was why men obeyed him before he asked twice.

He looked at Yrsa first.

Then at Halvard.

Then at Eirik.

His eyes narrowed almost invisibly.

"Sit," he said.

The word was not loud, but it moved the room.

A place was cleared near the hearth. One of the women from the cook side set down another bowl without comment and vanished back into the smoke. Halvard lowered himself onto the end of a bench like a man who had remembered too late that his body was made of flesh. Yrsa sat straighter, not leaning into the warmth though she had every right.

Leif remained standing for a heartbeat until Eirik glanced once toward the lower bench. That was enough. He moved there and sat where he could still see the center of the hall.

Arn was there too, of course.

Leif had not noticed him at first because Arn had a way of looking like part of a room until he chose otherwise. He sat with one boot braced against a bench leg and one arm draped over his knee, one axe set beside him rather than worn. His face gave little away, but there was a brightness in his eyes that meant he had already smelled trouble and found it worth staying for.

Sten did not ask what had happened at once. He looked instead toward the fire, then back to Yrsa, and said, "You rowed hard."

Yrsa accepted the bowl handed to her and wrapped both hands around it before answering. "Hard enough."

"No pursuit?"

"Not close."

That was the first true discomfort in the room. Not the words themselves. The shape of them.

Sten rested both forearms on his knees. “Then something held them.”

Yrsa’s eyes lifted to his and held there. “Or something delayed them.”

No one in the hall moved.

Leif felt the sentence go through the room like cold water finding cracks.

Sten said, “Begin where the ground still felt ordinary.”

That, Leif thought, was how grown men with real power spoke when they knew fear was listening.

Yrsa drew breath once and set the bowl down untouched.

“There were signs before the boats vanished,” she said. “Small ones first. Two nets cut at the inlet south of our headland. We thought boys or jealous hands. Then a steer found dead near the upper pasture—not butchered, only spoiled, as if someone had taken offense and not profit.” Her voice remained level. That made what she described worse. “Then smoke on the outer ridge three nights running. Not hearth smoke. Signal smoke.”

Halvard nodded once, weary and grim.

Sten listened without interruption.

Leif watched Eirik instead.

His father did not look startled. Only stiller. That was somehow more serious.

Yrsa went on. “My husband sent two men to watch the shore road. Neither returned. On the fourth morning, two boats were gone from the lower beach. Not stolen cleanly. Taken in haste.” She paused. “And after that we began seeing lights offshore after moonrise. Too low for stars. Too steady for lanterns on fishing boats.”

A man farther down the hall muttered something to his cup.

Sten did not look at him. “And you came because?”

This time Halvard answered. “Because if they’re testing the coves up the coast, they’ll test the harbor next. And because Yrsa said waiting would be a finer way to die than row.”

A few men gave brief humorless breaths at that.

Yrsa did not.

“My husband stayed,” she said. “Someone had to.”

The line sat there harder than the rest.

Leif felt something in Eirik tighten though his father did not move.

Sten folded one hand over the other. “How many?”

Yrsa shook her head. “Enough to vanish what they do not want seen. Not enough yet to strike openly.”

“Raiders?”

“Perhaps.”

The answer was wrong in the room the moment it left her mouth.

Not false.

Insufficient.

Arn spoke for the first time.

“That’s not raider work.”

Every head in the hall shifted a little toward him.

Arn did not seem to notice or care. He picked at a crack in the bench with one thumb, eyes on the fire rather than the others.

"Raiders come for noise, silver, fear, and women," he said. "These ones are trimming edges. Testing knots. Taking what matters to movement before touching what matters to pride."

His voice was quiet, but it dropped into the hall exactly as his presence always did—small and impossible to ignore.

Yrsa turned toward him slowly.

Arn looked back at her then, and whatever he saw in her face made the brightness in his own eyes sharpen.

"This isn't about one cove," he said. "It's about the roads between them."

The room changed.

Not with shouting.

Not with panic.

With recognition half-born and unwelcome.

Sten's scar caught the firelight as he lifted his head. "Say it plainly."

Arn did.

"Someone is teaching the coast to feel cut apart before the blade truly falls."

No one answered at once.

Leif did not fully understand why the line chilled the room more than missing men and vanished boats had done. Yet he felt the reason all the same. Missing things could still be accidents, raids, separate griefs. This suggested intention. Pattern. A hand behind the small wounds.

Eirik spoke then, his voice steady and low. "You think someone wants the outlying holds frightened into silence before they strike anywhere worth naming."

Arn shrugged one shoulder. "I think whoever did this knows men row slower toward neighbors once they start guarding only their own doors."

Yrsa looked at him long enough to make Leif uneasy.

Then she said, "Yes."

That was all.

But it was enough.

Sten leaned back only slightly. "And your husband?"

The question carried more than family concern. Leif heard that much now.

Yrsa heard it too.

"He sent me because he trusts Eirik," she said, and then, after the smallest pause, "and because he thought you would listen before deciding which fear to feed."

A murmur moved at the edges of the hall and died quickly.

Sten's face did not change. Leif had begun to learn that this meant more than calm.

"I feed none of them willingly," the jarl said.

"No," Yrsa replied. "Only carefully."

That might have sounded insolent in another mouth. Here it landed like truth already paid for.

Eirik finally sat forward and rested his forearms on his knees. "Who else knows?"

Yrsa answered at once. "Enough to gossip. Not enough to prepare."

Sten exhaled through his nose once. "Then we keep it that way until dawn."

Halvard looked up sharply. "You think they'll move that soon?"

Sten's gaze shifted to him. "I think men row hard in winter either because they are already too late or because the lateness is close behind them."

That sent a quieter kind of tension through the room than open alarm would have. Men straightened. One set his cup down and forgot it there. Another rubbed his beard as if feeling for what had suddenly aged in it.

Leif noticed all of it.

He noticed too the way Eirik did not look at him. Not from disregard. From trust, perhaps. Or because children in halls heard more when not directly managed.

That thought made him sit straighter.

Sten spoke again, but now more as a man laying order over fear than merely questioning it.

"No horn. No shouting through the village. We watch the shore road, the inlet, and the harbor mouth. Boats stay drawn and ready but not openly armed. If this is a net, we do not teach it our full shape before we cut through it." His eyes moved to Eirik. "You'll take the harbor."

Eirik nodded once.

To Arn: "You'll take the ridge path with two men who know how to stay quiet."

Arn gave the faintest grin. "At last. Work fit for decent boots."

Sten ignored that and turned to Yrsa. "You'll sleep here tonight."

Yrsa's mouth tightened. "I didn't row to sleep."

"No," Sten said. "You rowed to be believed. That work is done. The rest begins at first light."

For the first time since entering, Yrsa seemed on the edge of open disagreement.

Then Eirik said quietly, "Stay."

She looked at him.

Not as sister to brother only.

As one burdened person to another.

At length she nodded.

Leif felt then, without understanding all of it, that Yrsa's coming had not only brought news. It had shifted old loyalties and older roads beneath the hall. She was no messenger passing through. She was now part of what would happen next.

The men near the farther wall began moving in quieter ways—one slipping outside on Sten's signal, another crossing to speak low to a third, someone at the cook side adding more wood to the hearth as if warmth itself were now part of strategy.

Leif watched the room work.

Not loudly.

Not grandly.

But with the same truth the gods had pressed into him: that what mattered most often happened in the small things men either noticed or missed.

He had the strange sudden wish for Sigrid beside him. Not because he needed explaining. Because she would already have seen what mattered most and would say it without asking permission.

As if thought might bring her, he turned his head.

And there she was, half-hidden in the darker edge of the hall near the rear post, where she must have slipped in after the others. Astrid stood nearby, speaking low to one of the women, but Sigrid's attention was fixed on Leif.

When she saw him look, she tipped her chin very slightly toward the side passage.

Not now.

Soon.

Leif nodded once.

The hall carried on around him. Sten asked Halvard three more questions about currents and inlets. Eirik and Yrsa bent over a rough map scratched into soot-dark wood with a charred stick. Arn said something too low for most to catch, and whatever it was made Sten go still for a breath before answering.

Leif wanted to hear all of it.

He also knew, in the new uncomfortable way gods had sharpened into him, that wanting was not the same as being needed in the center of a thing.

So he waited.

When at last the hall loosened just enough and no one's eyes were on him directly, he slipped from the bench and crossed toward the side passage where storage jars and hanging herbs shadowed the wall. Sigrid met him there, arms folded, expression unreadable in the half-light.

For a moment neither spoke.

Leif rubbed one thumb against the heel of his other hand, suddenly aware that whatever she was about to say mattered more because she almost never began such moments herself.

At last Sigrid said, "You listened."

Leif blinked. "What?"

"In there." She jerked her chin toward the main hall. "You listened."

He frowned faintly. "I know how."

"Usually after speaking first."

"That is unfair."

"It is accurate."

He opened his mouth to defend himself and then shut it again, because the old answer would only prove her point.

Sigrid watched that happen. Something softened in her face, though it was so small another person might have missed it.

"I have a small pride in it," she said.

Leif stared.

She looked almost annoyed with herself for having said it aloud.

"In what?" he asked, because for once he truly did not know.

"In you," she said, and then, as if the words needed reducing before they grew too large, "and in whatever road you've started stepping onto since your talk with the gods. You're still exhausting. But not in quite the same way."

Leif felt heat rise in his face so fast it was almost pain.

That was worse than praise shouted before a crowd.

Worse than Eirik's approval.

Worse than any song.

Because Sigrid gave such things rarely, and never to waste them.

He looked away first, toward the hall light at the edge of the passage. "That sounded almost kind."

"It was a mistake."

"No, it wasn't."

Sigrid's mouth twitched. "You're becoming unbearable."

"I was already unbearable."

"Yes," she said. "Now you may become difficult on purpose."

That finally made him laugh.

Not loudly. Just enough.

He looked back at her. "I have some pride in you too."

She narrowed her eyes at once. "That sounded dangerous."

"It was honest."

"That is often worse."

They stood there in the dim side passage, herb scent and smoke around them, the murmur of the hall just beyond, and Leif felt the moment settle into him in a place the gods themselves had not reached.

Not because their words mattered less.

Because this did.

To be seen by a sister who knew every foolish thing in him and still offer that small careful pride—there was blessing in it, though she would never have used the word.

A voice from the hall called Eirik's name.

The room shifted again toward work, toward danger, toward whatever waited out beyond the shore lights and cut nets and missing men.

Sigrid glanced once toward the sound and then back to Leif.

"Don't ruin it," she said.

"I'll try."

"That is not the same as succeeding."

"No." He smiled despite himself. "But it's a better beginning than before."

This time she did smile. Briefly. Barely. Enough.

Then they went back into the firelight together.

And as Leif stepped once more into the warmth and watchfulness of Sten's hall—with Yrsa now part of its center, with Eirik carrying the harbor in his silence, with Arn's one sharp remark still widening through the room like a crack in ice—he understood that something had indeed ended.

Not the danger.

Not the story.

Only the smaller way he had once stood inside it.

What came next belonged to roads opened by others: by gods, by kin, by warning carried over black water, by a sister's rare honest pride.

And outside the longhouse walls, where the harbor waited in darkness and the coast held its secrets close, Eirik knew the next move was already made against them.

Author's Note

Thank you for reading this story.

Like many books, this one did not stay in the shape I first imagined for it. It began as one idea and slowly became something else, and I think that is one of the most honest parts of writing. A story can start with a plan, but it rarely stays there if you are truly listening to it. A single scene, a single conversation, even one unexpected choice by a character can change the direction of everything. That happened here more than once, and in the end I am grateful for it.

When I first began this book, I imagined a story more centered on Frigg as the All-Mother, or simply "the Mother" in a more spiritual sense. In ordinary language, some might even think of that presence as something close to Mother Earth. I know that does not fit neatly inside the most familiar or traditional framework of Norse mythology, but one of the questions that kept drawing me forward was this: are our ideas about the old gods sometimes too narrow? Must they only be understood one way? Or can they appear differently depending on who is seeking them, what is being asked of them, and what kind of truth the seeker is ready to receive?

As the story unfolded, it led me somewhere deeper and more difficult than I had expected. It became less about one divine figure and more about the moral weight of choice. One question kept returning again and again: when is it right to spare a life, and when is it right to take one? At first that may sound like a simple question, but once you allow duty, mercy, grief, honor, consequence, and the voices of gods into the same space, it becomes anything but simple.

Real people have to live with the results of those choices, and that is where the story found its center.

I will admit there were times when I worried the book might begin to sound too preachy, and that was never what I wanted. I did not want to write a sermon. I wanted to write something alive. I wanted to ask difficult questions honestly, not pretend I had neat answers ready for them. I wanted these characters to struggle, to misunderstand, to resist, and to grow in ways that felt human. If the story ever leans too hard in one direction, I hope its heart still comes through in the people living inside it.

More than anything, I loved watching the characters become themselves. Eirik, Leif, Yrsa, Arn, Astrid, Sigrid, and the others all grew beyond the outlines I first had in mind. They surprised me. They pushed back. They revealed things I had not planned to find. That always feels like a good sign to me. In the end, the story became richer because the characters refused to remain simple.

I also want to say clearly that the gods in this book are my own imaginative and artistic interpretation. They are not meant to replace, correct, or speak for any living belief, practice, or tradition. They are inspired by Norse mythology and shaped through creative license, with the hope of honoring the feeling and weight of those old stories while exploring something personal, moral, and human through them. If they feel different here, that is because this is a work of fiction shaped by inspiration rather than strict retelling.

This story ends in a place that feels to me like both a closing and a beginning. Eirik's sister has arrived, and with her comes the warning of something larger moving along the coast. Battle is coming. So is reckoning. Leif may yet be drawn into it. Astrid may stand where the line grows hardest. But the next story will not be told from the center of the room.

It will be told through Arn's eyes.

Arn is the funny man, the wild card, the one who seems to make every moment worse simply by arriving in it—and yet somehow he is also one of the steadiest and most reliable men in the story. He sees from the side instead of straight on. He understands more than he says. He has his own relationship to the gods, and his own way of carrying fear, humor, loyalty, and truth. He became one of the most enjoyable characters for me to write, and I am excited to follow the world through his eyes next.

So I leave this story here, with a cliffhanger and a promise.

The road is not finished.
The world is still moving.
And I hope you will come with me into the next book.

Thank you for reading.

M. A. Kirkeby

www.ingramcontent.com/pod-product-compliance
Lightning Source LLC
LaVergne TN
LVHW040216110826
845146LV00005B/1304

9798995848004